A CORNISH GUILT

THE LOVEDAY MYSTERIES BOOK 10

RENA GEORGE

ROSMORNA

GET FREE BOXSET OF 3 LOVEDAY MYSTERIES

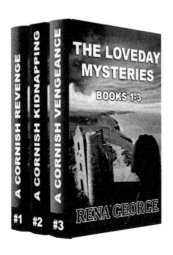

High above a wild Cornish beach a body slowly emerges
from the waves.
It has been staked hand and foot to the shingle. Whoever did
this had only one intention…
MURDER!
Get a free boxset of first three Loveday Mysteries here:
renageorge.net

INTRODUCTION

Maya Brookes is a young single mum.

The man she loved was murdered and she's still recovering from the horror.

She has a job she loves, a comfortable home and friends who support her.

Life is beginning to return to normal, or so she thinks. Everything changes when she finds a body in the heritage centre where she works. It's the strange young woman she saw earlier in the village church.

Horrified, she flees the scene and calls the police.

But when officers arrive the body has vanished. Fear grips Maya. Has she imagined that body? Could it be another of those strange things that have been happening to her lately?

Is she losing her grip on reality?

Her friend, Loveday, doesn't think so. She believes there's a killer at large – and Maya could be the next victim.

CHAPTER 1

The woman sat alone at the back of the church; her eyes travelling over the congregation as people bent their heads in prayer. She drew the hood of her cloak closer and allowed her gaze to stray to the carved figure on the wall of the little chapel.

In her mind's eye she was moving back through the centuries, watching by the ocean as white crested waves carried the holy man to the Cornish shore. She saw him reach the beach at Perran, where he would build his oratory amongst the sand dunes. This oratory would become the oracle of Christianity, drawing people from miles around to hear the holy man preach.

A secret smile twitched at the corners of the woman's mouth. The wooden image of St Piran, the patron saint of Cornish mining, would not be here for long. She wondered how many of the worshippers around her would miss him when he'd gone. The smile became a sneer. These people did not revere the ancient image, not the way she did. They deserved what was going to happen.

The stirring of the congregation brought her back to the

present. Heads were rising as the diminutive figure of the vicar ended the prayer with a murmured '*Amen.*'

The cloaked woman slipped silently away, unaware of the curious green eyes that followed her.

* * *

MAYA WAS FROWNING as she watched the figure go. Who was she? People were getting to their feet as the service came to a close and she picked her way through the throng to hurry after the woman.

Tom's smile of welcome was hesitant when he saw Maya's distracted expression as she emerged from the church. He'd come with baby April Rose in her buggy to meet her.

'Did you see her?' Maya called to him.

His brow furrowed, rain dripping from the hood of his jacket. 'See who?'

'That woman in the green cloak.' Maya was peering behind him into the mist. 'You must have seen her. She must have passed you.'

'I wasn't paying much attention to who passed. I was looking out for you.'

'So you didn't see her?' She sent an irritated glance back to where the congregation was still spilling out of the church.

'Well no, who is she?'

'No one. It doesn't matter.' Maya tried to wipe the annoyance from her voice as she bent over the buggy, smiling as April Rose's chubby face dimpled and she chuckled at the sight of her mother. The woman had unnerved Maya and she didn't know why. She'd seen her leave, so where had she gone? Her gaze went back to where the mist was curling around the moss-covered headstones. She gave herself a shake.

The woman was not her business. April Rose and Tom

were the ones she cared about. Tom was her child's grandfather after all. She linked her arm into his. 'What are you two doing out in this weather anyway? I wasn't expecting a reception committee to be waiting for me outside the church.' She smiled, bending again to kiss the baby's cheek.

'Our plan was to have a stroll around the village,' Tom said. 'But the rain came on so April Rose and I ditched that idea and decided to come along and meet you instead.'

'I'm very glad you did,' Maya said, taking charge of the stroller. 'Thanks for looking after April Rose, Tom. It's not often I get to church these days. I've been missing Sara's inspiring sermons.'

Tom shook his head, his eyes on the child in the buggy. 'I need no persuasion to spend time with my beautiful granddaughter,' he said. 'And don't worry about lunch. Everything is under control. I put the roast you left out into the oven and we've set the table.'

'You're amazing,' Maya said, aware of the slight Cornish lilt that always crept into his voice when he was with them. She was glad he'd kept on the cottage in Karrek. It meant he could keep an eye on the narrowboat anchored down on the creek. The boat was important. It was her last physical connection with Jamie and somewhere she could take their daughter when she needed to feel close to him.

The rain had settled into a steady drizzle, obscuring the far end of the fields and the cliff path beyond. If the mysterious woman in the hooded green cloak was still around then Maya couldn't see her. More important things were occupying her thoughts.

She turned to Tom. 'You didn't say how long you're down for this time.'

'I have to drive back tonight. I have meetings in the morning.'

'Important meetings?'

He sighed. 'Well, yes.'

'I suppose all meetings are important when you're a high-flying city financier,' Maya teased, stealing a glance at him as they walked.

Tom tugged up the collar of his wax jacket and blinked into the rain. 'I'm thinking of giving it up and moving back to Cornwall,' he said.

Maya stopped in her tracks. 'You're not serious?'

'Why not?' Tom said, smiling again at April Rose, who was wrinkling her nose and holding her chubby hand out to feel the rain. 'I've had enough of this double life. I want to be Tom Scobey, who lives in Cornwall and tinkers about on old boats.'

'What about William Bentley? Won't he miss dabbling in the city money markets?'

'I'm done with being him. That life holds no pleasure for me anymore. I changed my name and came to Cornwall to find my son.' He fell silent. Even in the rain Maya could see his eyes clouding over. She choked back a sudden lump in her own throat. Sometimes the sadness of the past caught up with you when you least expected it.

She looked away. 'You'd sell the London company?'

Tom nodded. 'The company, the Mayfair apartment, the lot. I never really wanted to pick up the reins of that life again.' He paused. 'Not after Jamie.'

Maya touched his sleeve. 'Then sell it. Move back here.' She hesitated, nodding down to the child in the buggy. 'Come back to your family, Tom.'

They had arrived at Maya's tiny cottage and Tom bent to lift the child from the buggy. April Rose had begun to grumble. She was impatient for her lunch and was making sure everyone knew it.

Mention of Jamie had sent Maya's thoughts slipping back to the times they'd spent living on the narrowboat together.

Back then Tom Scobey was just an acquaintance who lived in the village and helped them refurbish the old vessel. At least that's what they'd thought.

They didn't know then that Tom was Jamie's father, or that he was a wealthy merchant banker who headed up a successful company in the city.

They weren't aware either that Jamie was soon to die at the hands of a brutal killer.

Maya glanced away, angry for allowing these emotions to rise to the surface again. There was a time for grief and as long as she was in control of when that happened, she could cope with losing Jamie. But it wasn't easy. She needed to concentrate on what he left behind – their beautiful daughter, April Rose.

The delicious aroma of roasting meat filled the cottage as they walked in. Maya reached up and took the crying baby from Tom. 'You want your lunch too, don't you, little one?'

April Rose made angry little fists and yelled louder.

'OK...OK, I get the message.' She smiled up at Tom. 'Maybe Granddad can look after our lunch while we get you changed.'

'No problem,' Tom said. 'Take your time.'

Tom had mashed up April Rose's plate of vegetables and tiny pieces of meat when they returned. He watched with amusement as she tried to feed herself.

Half an hour later, fed and drowsily happy, April Rose settled quickly for her nap. When Maya joined Tom in the kitchen he was pouring wine. He handed her a glass.

'Lovely,' Maya said, taking it and sinking into a chair. She closed her eyes, savouring each delicious sip of the wine.

'I've taken the beef out to rest it and put the potatoes in the oven,' Tom said. 'They should be ready in twenty minutes.'

'You're becoming quite domesticated, Tom. I'm impressed.'

He lifted his glass but didn't sit down.

Maya wrinkled her brow, watching him. 'Everything all right?'

'I've got something to tell you,' he said.

She waited.

'It's about moving back to Cornwall.' He paused. 'The thing is, I won't be coming back alone. I've met someone.'

Maya blinked. 'You've met someone?'

'Her name's Candice.' His eyes were shining. 'And she's beautiful.'

She should have been out of her chair, throwing her arms around Tom's neck and telling him how happy she was for him. So why wasn't she? Tom deserved his happiness. She forced a smile, trying to disguise her hesitation. But Tom was frowning.

'I thought you'd be pleased for me.'

Maya swallowed. What was she thinking? Of course she was pleased for him. It was simply a shock.

She put out her arms and went to hug him. 'That's wonderful, Tom. I couldn't be more delighted.'

It had been a year since Jamie died and Tom had been right there for her every step of the way. No one could have understood her grief better than Tom. She had lost the man she loved. Tom had lost his son. It felt right that they should support each other.

She put down her glass. 'So, tell me about this Candice of yours. I want to know everything.'

He laughed. 'Everything?'

She nodded. 'The lot.'

Tom rolled his eyes to the ceiling. 'Well, she's beautiful.'

'Yes, I got that bit,' she said, moving to the oven and sliding out the sizzling roasties. Tom had put plates in to warm and she removed these too, glad of the distraction. She still hadn't got her head around his news.

'How did you two meet?' she asked, keeping her voice steady as Tom carved the joint and she dished out the vegetables. They sat down and began to eat.

'At the marina,' Tom said between mouthfuls of food. 'Candice was looking to buy a boat and I offered to show her over the *Sea Witch*.'

Maya sat up, staring at him. 'You're selling the *Sea Witch*?'

He shrugged. 'I'm not sure. Maybe.'

'But you love that boat, Tom.'

'Like I said. New beginnings. Candice says the proceeds would be better spent buying property down here.'

'You've got property down here,' Maya said, trying not to snap. She loved Tom's little cottage in Karrek. It might not be as grand and fashionable as his London place but as far as character went, it couldn't be faulted.

'I'm not sure Candice would be as charmed by the cottage as we are. She's quite sophisticated.'

Visions of a glamorous, model-like creature were beginning to form in Maya's mind. Already she was hating Candice.

She should have been feeling contentedly mellow after their meal, but she wasn't. She felt distinctly unsettled, but she didn't know if that was due to Tom's unexpected news about his new friend, or if she was still dwelling on the mysterious woman in the church.

Tom had poured himself a tot of brandy and invited Maya to join him, but she refused, preferring to sip her coffee.

'These important meetings back in London,' she said slowly. 'They wouldn't be with Candice, would they?'

'No.' He laughed. 'I really do have meetings. I have to tell my colleagues that I'm winding up the company.'

Maya's brow wrinkled as she nursed her coffee. She was imagining how difficult it was bound to be to sever the connections that had been his life. Even when Tom came to Cornwall and changed his name to Scobey he still had his finger on the pulse of his life in London. 'Are you sure you're ready to cut loose right now?' she said.

Tom nodded up towards the room where baby April Rose slept. 'My future is here in Cornwall.'

'What about Candice? I take it she knows what you're planning?'

'Not yet. I've hinted about a surprise. I'm sure she'll be as happy as me when I tell her.'

Maya hoped he was right. She got up and went to the window. It was still raining. 'I should check the centre. Are you OK to stay here with April Rose for half an hour or so while I nip over there?'

'Absolutely,' he said as she went to fetch her mac. 'And take the car, don't even think about walking,' he called after her. 'It's like a monsoon out there.'

* * *

As the front door closed quietly behind her, Tom stared into the fire. He felt good now he'd decided to move back permanently to Cornwall, but he wasn't happy about leaving Maya and April Rose here on their own. Maya had seemed so unsettled recently. He knew how much she still missed Jamie. He missed his son too, but life had to go on and there was also her daughter to consider. He wondered if the loss of Jamie had anything to do with Maya's obsession that she was being watched. It was nonsense of course, but how could he convince her of that? She'd been so happy to be appointed conservator of the Carn Hendra Heritage Centre. It was like a dream coming true for her. She had Loveday to thank for that.

Tom remembered how supportive Loveday had been when Jamie disappeared. And when things escalated into the nightmare of Maya discovering the man she loved had been murdered, it was Loveday who had been by her side.

The heritage centre hadn't existed back then. In its place were the ruins of an old cottage that had been bequeathed to Loveday by her great aunt Martha. It had been Maya's idea to gift the site to the archaeological department where she'd been employed as a researcher. Grants were obtained and the old cottage rebuilt as part of a heritage centre telling the story of how people in West Cornwall had lived and worked in days gone by.

A close friendship had developed between Maya and Loveday, whose policeman partner, DI Sam Kitto, had investigated Jamie's murder.

Tom sighed. It was disturbing how Maya imagined someone was playing tricks on her at the centre. According to her, artifacts were being moved around the place and displays had been tampered with. Lights were left on after Maya insisted she had turned them off. Then there was the business earlier when she'd turned up to open the centre and found the place unlocked.

She'd been distraught when she'd reported it back to him, adamant that she had properly secured the place the previous night.

And now Maya's disturbing interest in this woman she'd seen in the church. He was right to be concerned. Maybe it was time to ask Loveday for advice?

CHAPTER 2

*R*ufus North had been staking out the church since the previous weekend. He'd visited the place twice, more often might have raised suspicion. It was enough for him to assess what protection had been provided for the St Piran carving. It hadn't seemed to be cemented to the wall, but it could be wired to a security alarm, although he saw no evidence of this.

The thing didn't look all that special. As far as he was concerned it could have been carved yesterday and made to look old. He'd heard about people who doctored paintings and soaked canvasses in tea to falsely age them. Unless you were an expert it was easy to be fooled. He allowed himself an indulgent smile. Removing the thing would be a piece of cake.

The young woman he'd been watching was concerning him though. Rufus had seen her hanging around the church before. At the Sunday service she'd sat at the back. He'd seen a few curious looks cast in her direction but there had been no connection with anyone. So he guessed she wasn't local. No one bothered about him. This was an old historic church.

People here were used to strangers visiting, but a young woman sitting alone at the back of the church and dressed like she came from another time, was still mysterious enough to attract attention.

She intrigued him and when she slipped out as the rest of the congregation ended their prayers, he followed her.

Pulling down the hood of her long dark cloak she set off against the steady drizzle. The girl hurried along the wet street, turning down behind the pub towards the clifftop. He'd checked out all of this area as part of his previous recce. The only thing in this direction, apart from a thirty-foot drop to the sea, was some kind of exhibition centre. Was this where she was heading?

Still behind her, Rufus kept his distance until the building came into view. He'd been right. The girl had headed straight for it. When she stopped, he saw her take a key from her pocket and open the big double glass doors. She went in, leaving the door ajar. He followed her in, darting out of sight behind one of the display boards. He had no idea what he was doing here. This was none of his business.

He hadn't been prepared for the shock of a man's voice coming from the shadows.

'What kept you?' the stranger said. Rufus had been about to hold up his hands and step out from his hiding place when he realized the man was addressing the girl.

'We've got to stop meeting like this.' The man was grinning as he crossed the floor.

'I thought this was how you liked it.' The girl's voice was low and seductive. She swayed as she slowly untied her cloak and let it fall to the floor, revealing a long red skirt. She unhooked the skirt and stepped out of it, still swaying provocatively as she moved towards the man. She raised her arms as the two drew closer and the man removed her skimpy black top.

Rufus swallowed, unable to take his eyes from the naked girl.

He watched her reach up and stroke the man's cheek.

'You're such a wicked woman, Morwenna Chenoweth,' the man said, taking her in his arms.

Over the next half hour Rufus watched, mesmerized as the couple made slow, lingering love. He hadn't expected this entertainment, nor had he expected the twitches of guilt that shouted he shouldn't be here. He wasn't a voyeur. He should have crept away from his dark, uncomfortable corner and left them to their love-making. But he hadn't. He couldn't drag his eyes away from the couple.

He swallowed, trying to control his emotions. It felt like he was part of it, his own body matching the couple's rising passion until at last, in a great trembling crescendo, it was over.

The couple collapsed, breathless in each other's arms. Rufus closed his eyes, his heart pounding wildly. This shouldn't be happening. He wasn't this vulnerable. He was here in this village for one purpose – to steal the St Piran carving.

He desperately wanted to stand up and stretch, but he couldn't move, not until they did.

'We should go,' he heard the man murmur at last. 'We shouldn't be found here.'

Morwenna's laugh rang out across the space around them. 'But don't you see, Joss? That's the fun of it. Somebody *is* coming. Maya's coming. She checks the centre's security every Sunday about this time. I've followed her.'

Joss scrambled up and frantically began pulling on his clothes. 'Stop fooling about, Morwenna. Get dressed. We have to leave right now.'

'You go,' she said, smiling. 'There's something more I have to do.'

'Don't be ridiculous. I'm not leaving you here. We go together.' He picked up her clothes and threw them at her. 'Get dressed.'

'I will,' she said. 'After you've gone.' She touched his arm. 'You have to trust me, Joss. I have this one last thing to do and after that no one will want to employ sweet little Maya ever again.'

'Leave it,' Joss said. 'You've done enough to cast doubt on the girl's ability to do her job. All those times you've sneaked in here after hours and moved stuff. You've hidden files, changed data on her computer. The girl already believes she's going crazy. Isn't that enough?'

Morwenna had slipped into her clothes and was pulling on the green cloak as she shook her head. 'I have this one final thing to do, but it needn't involve you. We'll meet up later as arranged.' She began to shoo him to the door. 'Go before she comes in and finds you here.'

Joss tilted his head at her. 'What mischief are you up to now, Morwenna?'

'I'll tell you later.' She giggled and pushed him out the door, but left it open.

A single security light lit the car park and Rufus watched the man run and disappear into the shadows before turning his attention back to Morwenna. She was moving through the building, going into the area at the far end. It looked to him as though it had been laid out as an old cottage kitchen. He took in the table and the dresser with its cups and plates and the rocking chair by the black range.

Rufus frowned. What was she up to?

His head snapped up at the sound of a vehicle coming into the car park. He looked back to Morwenna and saw she had moved to sit in the rocking chair. She took a deep breath as she arranged her long cloak around her, pulling up the hood to cover half her face. Rufus frowned. What was going on?

Outside, the sound of a car door closing reached him and he could hear footsteps hurrying through the rain. Suddenly the running feet stopped. Rufus narrowed his eyes and peered out to the car park. He could see the figure standing motionless, rigid, apparently unsure about entering the building. His pulse quickened. Was this the Maya he'd heard Morwenna talk about?

* * *

IT WAS dark and still raining when Maya pulled into the car park. She sat for a moment looking at the new building. Something wasn't right. She couldn't put her finger on it, but there was an uncomfortable feeling in the pit of her stomach.

She got out of the car, tugging up the hood of her plastic mac as she made a dash for the door. She stopped in her tracks, blinking through the rain.

The security lights were on and the big glass doors were open. She blinked. How could that be? She had locked the place herself the previous evening. The cleaner, Jess Tandy, had a key, but she wasn't due to come until the morning. She frowned. Not even Jess was careless enough to leave the centre insecure. Anyway, she'd seen her in church that morning and she hadn't mentioned any change to her cleaning routine.

So how...? Maya needed to ring the police. Her hand shook as she reached into her pocket. No, wait... Her eyes moved over the building. Rain streamed down the glass frontage but there were no broken windows and no sign of any vandalism that she could see. If she phoned the police and there was a perfectly innocent explanation for this she would feel pretty stupid. It would also give Tom another reason to worry about her and she didn't want that.

She needed to check out the place herself.

Her heart pounded as she moved forward, inching the door wider and stepping inside. She took a deep swallow. 'Hello! Is anyone here?'

She could hear the tremble in her voice. No response. Maya reached for the light switch and flicked it on. The building didn't look nearly so threatening when it was lit up.

She looked around her. The heritage centre had been constructed on an open plan system so she could see most of the public area from where she stood. Everything appeared normal. Her eyes slid over the room. The artifacts, the display boards and chairs were all in place. It didn't look like the place had been burgled. She moved forward, still cautious, and turned into the area where Carn Hendra Cottage had been reconstructed in the footprint of the original building. She hit another light switch and froze. Someone was sitting in the rocking chair.

RUFUS HAD WATCHED the young woman step cautiously into the building, looking around, saw her flick on a light and call out, but no one answered. He saw her slowly making her way through the centre. She was heading for the cottage area where Morwenna slumped motionless in the rocking chair. Her one staring eye sent shards of ice shooting through him. She looked dead. Was that the intention?

He heard the scream as Maya fled the building.

Morwenna stirred, a slow smile stealing over her face as she watched the terrified girl flee. Slowly she got out of the chair, raising her arms in a luxurious stretch. Job done!

Rufus couldn't believe what he'd just witnessed. The

woman had staged a death scene so convincing that it sent shivers down his own spine. Poor Maya. No wonder she took off like that. But this was no act of mischief, this was cold, calculated cruelty and it intrigued him. But this was not the time to linger.

At this very minute Maya would be raising the alarm. The place would soon be crawling with coppers. They might already be on their way. Rufus needed to get out of there. Behind him Morwenna was on her phone. She'd put it on speakerphone. Rufus could hear everything.

'You should have stayed, Joss. It was amazing. Our little lady took off like a bat out of hell when she saw me sprawled there. She thinks she's discovered a dead body.'

'What dead body? What are you talking about?'

'It was nothing, only a little joke. I only wanted to frighten her.'

'Sounds like you did that all right.' Joss let out a sigh. *'Get out of there, Morwenna. She will have called the police by now. I doubt if they will find your little trick amusing.'*

'I'm going, I'm going,' Morwenna said, still grinning. *'But don't tell me you didn't find what you've just heard entertaining.'* There was a little laugh in her voice. *'You should have seen her, Joss. She was so spooked. She probably won't want to come back to this place. Her job is as good as mine.'*

Rufus was already on his way out. If the police were coming, and that was a definite possibility, the last thing he wanted was to be discovered here. He'd thought Maya had left the site but he saw the headlights of her car come back round the corner. He ducked into the shadows as the car came to a halt. The headlights stayed on. He looked back to the centre. Had Morwenna already left? He would have to be doubly careful if he was to get away from here without being detected.

Twice he was forced to duck into a dripping hedge as a police car raced past. The girl's staging of that bizarre death scene was likely to see the village crawling with coppers. Stealing the St Piran carving from right under their noses could pose an extra challenge.

He made his way back to the village and the hire car he'd parked by the travellers' hostel. He'd used a false driving licence to get the vehicle. Hopefully he would be far away before that was discovered. In the car he stripped off his wet things and sat back in the dark. It was a refuge of sorts. What he really needed was a hot meal and some dry clothes. He would pick up a takeaway on his way back to the lock-up where there was also a change of clothes. He'd been confident his planning was watertight, but that was before Morwenna Chenoweth appeared on the scene. He couldn't let her spoil it all now.

CHAPTER 3

*L*oveday and Sam were enjoying a leisurely Sunday evening in the cottage at Marazion when his phone buzzed.

'Don't answer it,' she said, wrapping her arms around him and drawing him back down onto the sofa.

He laughed. 'You know I have to answer it.' He kissed the top of her head.

Loveday made a face as he crossed the room and picked up his mobile phone from the table. 'Yes, Will,' he said. 'What's up?'

She saw his expression change. 'What? When was this?' His voice was urgent. 'OK, I'll see you there.'

'What is it?' She was on her feet. 'What's happened, Sam?'

'It's Carn Hendra,' he said. 'Maya's called in. She says she's found a body.'

'I'm coming with you.' Loveday was already scrambling into her trainers.

'That's not necessary,' Sam said. 'You stay here and I'll ring as soon as I get there.'

'You know that's not going to happen,' Loveday said.

'Maya is my friend. And I know every inch of the heritage centre. Of course I'm coming with you.'

She followed him out to the car, snapping on the seatbelt as he fired up the Lexus and they took off up the drive and out onto the seafront. 'What exactly did Maya say?' Loveday asked as they sped along the front.

'Will didn't have much information, only that Maya had been doing her routine check at the centre.' His hands tightened round the wheel. 'All I know is she reported finding a body, a woman's body in the cottage.'

'The cottage?' Loveday's heart sank. She'd been hoping it wasn't the cottage area.

'Poor Maya,' she said quietly. 'She'll be devastated. Did they tell her to hang on there until you arrived?' She looked at Sam's profile as he nodded. The unsettling feeling in the pit of her stomach was getting worse. Carn Hendra had a special place in her heart. Images of the first time she and Sam had wandered on the clifftop searching for the remains of the old cottage her great aunt Martha had bequeathed to her came edging in. She could still remember that surge of emotion when they found it, although it wasn't a cottage any more, only a pile of stones. Standing on the same spot where Martha and her ancestors had scratched a living from the land had made her feel strangely humble.

They were driving into the village where Maya lived. Loveday peered through the rain watching for that first sight of the heritage centre. She caught her breath, as she always did, when the shape of the cottage section appeared through the mist.

'Is that Maya's car?' Sam glanced to a small dark car by the entrance.

Loveday nodded. 'Yes, that's her. You can let me out here, Sam. I'll see if she's all right.'

Sam brought the Lexus to a halt and she could see Will

Tregellis, his detective sergeant, walking towards them. She jumped out, pulling her hood over her hair as she sprinted across to Maya.

'Loveday, you've come. Thank God.' Maya leaned across to open the car door for her. 'This is a nightmare.'

'What on earth's happened? Sam said you found a body.'

Maya pointed. 'She was there, sitting there in the rocking chair staring at me.' She shuddered. 'You can't imagine how awful it was. I just turned and ran.'

Loveday was no stranger to finding bodies. She put a hand on her friend's arm. 'You did right. It's what anyone would have done in the circumstances.'

Maya's face crumpled as she struggled against bursting into tears. 'No, you don't understand. It's worse, much worse than that. I don't even know if I did the right thing in calling the police.' She turned, meeting Loveday's stare. 'The body I saw...it's not there anymore.' Her shoulders rose in a confused shrug. 'She's gone.'

'Gone?' Loveday frowned. 'What do you mean *gone*?'

'Exactly that.' She nodded towards the policeman standing by the entrance. 'The officer over there, he went in and looked around but he couldn't find anything.' Her voice trembled. 'The body had gone! She *had* been there, Loveday. I know she was. I saw her.'

'It's fine, Maya, try to stay calm. I believe you.'

'But there's more.' She swallowed. 'I recognized her. She was in church this morning. I can't have imagined that, not when I recognized her.' She gave Loveday a desperate look. 'Am I going mad, Loveday?'

'Of course you're not.' Loveday spoke gently. 'You don't just imagine something like that. Sam and Will know what they're doing. They will find this body.'

'Will they? I'm not so sure. So many odd things have been

happening lately. Ask Tom. He doesn't exactly call me crazy but he gives me plenty of worried looks.'

Loveday didn't like what she was hearing. 'Let's get you home,' she said quietly. 'We need to be away from here.'

'You're right. I should get back. Tom will be wondering where I've got to. He's driving to London tonight. He'll be wanting to get off.'

'It was you I was thinking of, Maya, not Tom. I'll find Sam and tell him we're leaving. He'll find us at the cottage when he's ready.'

Loveday got out of the car, and made a sprint for the main door, but the uniformed officer stopped her.

'Sorry, miss. No one is allowed inside the building.'

'Can you get a message to DI Kitto?' she said. 'Tell him Loveday and Maya have gone to her cottage. He can meet us there.'

The constable gave her an unsure look.

'Just tell him,' she said, turning and hurrying back to Maya's car.

'OK, WHAT HAVE WE GOT?' Sam said, striding after Will as they walked through the building.

'The cottage is through here, boss,' Will said and then gave Sam an embarrassed look as he remembered how involved his boss and Loveday had been in getting the heritage centre up and running.

Sam said nothing as he followed Will along the short passage linking the centre to the cottage. They moved into the reconstructed kitchen.

Will pointed to the rocking chair. 'That's where the young woman said she saw the body. She said she was sitting right there.'

Sam moved forward. He'd stopped at the entrance to pull covers over his shoes and tug on a pair of protective gloves. He tilted his head, examining the chair.

'What d'you make of it?' Will asked. 'Was there a body?'

Sam pulled a face. 'I know Maya and she's not the fanciful kind. If she said there was a body, then I'm pretty sure that's what she saw.' His face was grim. Or what she believed she saw, he thought. He moved closer to the chair. 'We need forensics down here.'

'OK, boss, but I doubt if they'll find anything. I know the young woman *thought* she saw a body.' Will shook his head. 'But according to uniform there wasn't one. They went round the building and couldn't see anything untoward. If there had been a body here, then either she let herself into the building with a key or the person who killed her did and took the body with them.'

'The forensic team, Will,' Sam repeated. 'Now please.'

Will was already on his phone.

They walked from one room to another. 'So no signs of a break-in,' Sam said. He'd been here many times and as far as he could tell everything looked as it always did. He could see no signs of a struggle either. 'We need to know everyone who holds a key to the premises.'

The policeman on the door appeared at Will's side and whispered something in his ear. Will turned to Sam. 'It appears Loveday has taken the young woman home,' he said.

Sam nodded. 'That's fine. Maya needs to keep a level head. She'll be more relaxed in her own surroundings.' He glanced up at the camera on the wall. 'What about the CCTV? Has anyone organized for us to see that?'

'I was waiting for you to arrive. The young woman who says she found the body.' It was clear Will was still not convinced about that. 'She will know about the CCTV. I thought you'd like to have a word with her yourself.'

Sam nodded. 'Yes it's fine. Come with me, Will. We'll see her now.'

* * *

'ARE you sure you're all right to drive?' Loveday said, sliding Maya a concerned look as she reversed out of the car park.

'I'm still a bit shaky, but yes. I'm so glad you're here.'

Loveday smiled. 'Sam will get this sorted, Maya. Don't worry. He'll know what to do.'

The rain hadn't let up as they drove into the village and parked behind Tom's sporty red Audi. Loveday could see the curtains twitch and knew Tom had been watching for Maya's return.

He came to the door. 'What the hell's happened, Maya?' He glanced at Loveday and she gave what she hoped was a reassuring smile.

'Let's get everybody inside before we all drown out here,' she said.

The women stepped into the cottage and shook off their wet things. 'I'm sorry, Tom,' Maya said. 'I should have called you.'

'Tell me what's happened. Are you OK?' His face was full of concern.

'Of course I am. Where's April Rose?'

'April Rose is fine,' Tom said. 'We've been making castles with her building bricks. I've just put her down again. She's quite happy in her cot, so you don't have to worry about her.' He gave Maya a concerned look. 'It's you we have to look after. You look white as a ghost.'

Maya managed a shaky smile. 'Thanks, Tom. I'm fine.'

Tom slid Loveday a look. 'Is she fine, Loveday? She doesn't look it.'

'You need to talk to Tom, Maya. And Sam will probably want to question you if you think you're up to it.'

'Question her?' Tom repeated. 'About what? Will someone please tell me what's going on?'

Maya drew in a shaky breath. 'There was a dead woman back there at the centre. I can still see her sitting there.' Her hand went to her throat. 'She was staring at me, Tom.'

'You found a body?' Tom's shocked look went from one to the other.

'I did, but then she disappeared.' She blinked, frowning. 'I don't think the police believed me.'

'What do you mean *disappeared*?' Tom said.

'Well I don't know,' Maya snapped. 'Somebody must have moved her. Wait a minute.' She hesitated as the relevance of what she'd said began to sink in. 'That means the killer must still have been there when I went blundering in. He must have been right there in the building. It was him who moved her.' She put her hands on her head. 'Oh, my God. The killer was there all the time. He could have murdered me too.' She stared at them, wide-eyed. 'April Rose! What would have happened to April Rose if I had died?'

'Hey, come on.' Loveday put her arms around her friend. 'You're not dead, Maya. You're here and April Rose is fine. Tell her, Tom.'

'Of course she is. I told you. She's perfectly happy and fast asleep in her cot.' He put a hand on Maya's shoulder. 'I think you could both do with a tot of brandy. I'll fetch that Calvados I brought from London.'

Loveday nodded. 'I think that would be a good idea.'

Tom disappeared into the kitchen. They could hear him opening and closing cupboards followed by the sound of the tinkling of glasses as he poured the drinks.

'It was her, Tom,' Maya said as he came back into the

room carrying their drinks. 'The woman from church. You remember I asked you about her when we were outside?'

'Well, yes.' Tom slid Loveday a look. 'You asked, but I didn't see her.'

'Maybe you could help the police construct a photofit,' Loveday said quickly.

'I could try,' Maya said, her eyes still on Tom. 'Are you sure you didn't see her? She *was* there. I didn't imagine it. Other people must have seen her too.'

Tom put a glass into her hand. 'Sip this. It should help steady you. I can stay the night if you like. Those meetings in London aren't that important. You and April Rose come first.'

Maya shook her head. 'Thanks, Tom, but you don't have to do that. I'll be fine, really I will.'

'I can stay over if you like,' Loveday offered. She could see Maya was wavering at that suggestion and turned to Tom. 'That's settled then, I'll stay until morning. Everything will look so much better in the morning.'

All three heads turned as the doorbell rang. 'That'll be Sam,' Loveday said, getting up. 'I'll let him in.' She went to the door, brushing rain from Sam's shoulders as he and Will came in. 'We're in the sitting room,' she told them.

The new arrivals made the tiny room look smaller than ever. Maya signalled for them to sit, but they declined. 'We won't keep you long. Rotten business this,' Sam said.

Tom stepped forward. 'I've just poured the girls a glass of Calvados. Would you like one?'

SAM SHOOK HIS HEAD, glancing at Will. He didn't miss Will's look of disappointment, but even a small glass of brandy would not have been a good idea when they were on duty. They needed all their wits about them tonight.

'I can imagine how difficult this must be for you, Maya. But it would be helpful if you could possibly take me through it again,' Sam said. 'Start at the beginning and tell us what happened.'

Maya took a breath, gathering her thoughts. 'It would have been about five o'clock when I drove into the car park. We'd had a busy day on Saturday and it's part of my routine to look in on the centre on a Sunday to check everything is OK.' She swallowed. 'When I got to the door I was surprised to find it was open. I knew I hadn't left it like that and then I remembered the cleaner. She doesn't usually come on a Sunday, but Jess likes to do her own thing and we leave her to it.'

'So it didn't surprise you then that the centre was insecure?' Sam asked.

'What? No, of course it did. I was furious. How could the cleaner have been so irresponsible as not to have locked up after herself? I was making a mental note to have a word with her about that. But then I thought about it and it didn't feel right. Jess Tandy is normally so reliable. It would have been totally out of character for her to be that careless.' She looked up. 'That's when I began to feel uneasy.'

Sam nodded encouragement for her to go on.

She continued. 'I went inside and put the lights on. I glanced around the display area and everything looked fine. I really had been worried it might have been a burglary and I would discover the place had been ransacked, but as I say, it all looked normal.'

'What happened then, Maya?' Sam asked. 'Did you go in to the office to check things out there?'

Maya frowned. 'God, yes, I forgot about that. I did go into the office. Not right into it, but I poked my head in. There seemed to be nothing out of place. That's when I headed for the cottage.' Sam could see Maya's hands trembling. 'I still can't believe what I saw in there.'

They waited as she ran the tip of her tongue over her lips. 'She was just sitting there, in the rocking chair, staring at me with that one green eye.'

Sam and Will exchanged a look. 'Green eye?' Sam asked.

'Yes, she had a hood pulled over half her face. It was only the eye I saw. It was staring at me.'

'How did you know she was dead?' Will asked.

Maya put her hand to her forehead. 'You think she might not have been dead? Oh my God. Why was she sitting there then staring at me that way?' She shook her head. 'No, she was dead.'

Sam smiled. 'I know this can't be easy for you but try not to get upset.'

'Tell them about the woman you saw in church today,' Loveday said.

Maya repeated what she'd told Loveday. Sam could see Maya hadn't missed Tom's frown. It made the whole incident sound even more bizarre.

'Did you see her leave?' Sam asked.

Maya shook her head. 'I did look for her as we were coming out of the church, but she seemed to disappear.'

'Think, Maya. Could you have seen her about the village before?'

Maya frowned. 'I may have. I'm not sure.' She shook her head. 'I'm sorry, Sam. I don't know.'

Loveday reached out for her. 'It's fine, Maya. I'm sure this is helping Sam a lot.'

Sam nodded. 'We'll need a list of keyholders from you if that's OK?'

'It will be in my desk drawer at the centre. Do you need me to come back with you?'

'No, it'll be fine,' Sam said. 'I'm sure we'll find everything we need. We'll leave this for the moment but if you remember anything, anything at all, ring me.'

She nodded.

Sam and Will turned to go, but Sam swung back. 'What about the CCTV? I don't suppose you checked that when you were in the building?'

'No, I didn't hang around. After I saw her I got out of there as quickly as I could. It's controlled from the office. There's a list of instructions in the desk drawer.' She got up to find her bag. 'You'll need this to get into my desk,' she said, handing him a key.

'Thanks, that's a great help,' Sam said, nodding to Tom as they left. Loveday followed them to the door. Out of Maya's hearing she said. 'I'm going to stay here tonight. You don't mind if I do that, Sam, do you?'

'Of course not.' He paused, tilting his head at her. 'Don't get too involved. We don't even know if there was a body.'

Loveday stared at him. 'If Maya says there was a body then there was body. What happened to it is your business, Sam.'

He put up his hands laughing as though to protect himself. 'Go support your friend, Loveday.' He bent to kiss her cheek, conscious that Will was looking away. 'Don't get too fond of these sleepovers. I need you at home,' he whispered in her ear.

Loveday slapped his shoulder, laughing. 'I'm sure you'll manage.'

He nodded. 'Ring me later if anything new turns up.'

'Of course I will,' she said as he walked away.

CHAPTER 4

*L*oveday was pensive as she watched Maya leave the room to check on her daughter. Somehow the thought of this horrible thing happening in the cottage area of the centre made the whole thing feel even more sinister. Admittedly the building was only a reconstruction of how things would have been in the old days, but it was still Martha's cottage, built on the very site where her great aunt and her family had lived. Things like this shouldn't happen, not here where her ancestors had scratched a living from the land. The thought made Loveday shiver.

She hadn't heard Tom speaking to her at first. It was only when he repeated how worried he'd been about Maya that she sat up and took notice.

'Something's not right,' he said. 'Maya's not been herself for weeks.'

'She's probably just tired,' Loveday said. 'She's recently found a body in the place where she works. She's bound to be unsettled.' But somewhere inside her a worry was nagging. It wasn't that she didn't believe Maya, but if there

29

really had been a dead woman in that chair, where had she gone?

Tom sighed. 'I wish it was that simple.' He looked away, unsure how much to share.

Loveday met his worried stare. 'What do you mean? If you know something you have to tell me, Tom.'

He paused for a second before swallowing. 'I think Maya is ill. This business of finding a body is the latest thing in a string of incidents she says happened.'

'Says? Don't you believe her?'

Tom shook his head. 'I don't know what to believe. So much of what Maya says at the moment doesn't make sense.'

Loveday raised an eyebrow, waiting for him to continue.

He sighed. 'Things have been going missing from the heritage centre, artifacts are being moved around. Maya came home the other day convinced someone had been rummaging through her desk drawer.'

'Had they?'

He shrugged. 'Who knows, but that's not the point. Maya believes these things are real.'

'And you don't?' Loveday wasn't liking the sound of this. 'Are you saying Maya is imagining all this?'

'I don't know. Maybe. You must have noticed how distant and distracted she's been lately. And now there's this business of the woman in church. Maya was upset enough that I hadn't seen her come out.'

'Why was she upset?'

'I don't know. It was only a young woman sitting by herself at the back of the church. For some reason Maya thought that was odd.'

He scratched his head. 'And then finding this body. No one else saw it. I don't know what to believe.'

Maya had certainly seemed more distracted recently but Loveday had put it down to the responsibilities of being a single mum. Juggling parenthood with her full-time work at the heritage centre couldn't be easy.

'Have a word with her, Loveday. She'll listen to you. She thinks I fuss too much.'

Loveday wasn't sure Maya would appreciate her intervention, but Tom was right, something was going on and they had to get to the bottom of it.

'Have any of these incidents at the centre been reported to the police?' she asked.

Tom shook his head. 'Maya wouldn't hear of it. She said the police have better things to concern themselves with.'

'What about the rest of the staff? Are they aware what's been going on?'

'No, Maya was adamant about that. She said it was too trivial to bother the others with.'

'But that was before she found a body,' Loveday said.

Tom looked up and met her eyes. 'If she did find a body,' he said quietly.

They fell silent as Maya came back into the room. 'April Rose is fast asleep. She didn't need me at all,' she said. 'You settled her well, Tom.'

'She settles well because she's a happy, relaxed child. And that's down to how you care for her,' Tom said, getting to his feet. 'I'll put the kettle on.'

But Maya stopped him. 'I'm sure Loveday and I can manage to fill the kettle. You need to get back to London. I've kept you here long enough.'

'London can wait. I'm not leaving you like this.'

Maya smiled at him. 'I know you just want to help, but you must stop worrying about me. I feel guilty enough causing all this fuss. You have things to attend to in London, Tom. You must get back.'

She turned to Loveday. 'Tell him, Loveday.'

Loveday smiled. 'She's right, Tom. You go. We can look after ourselves.'

Tom didn't appear convinced. 'I really don't like leaving you like this.'

'Nonsense,' Maya said. 'You get yourself back to London. I know how important those meetings tomorrow are.' She smiled up at him. 'And as far as your good news is concerned. I'm delighted for you.' She patted his shoulder. 'Now go and do what you have to, but keep in touch. I'll want to know everything about those plans to come back to live in Cornwall.'

Loveday's brow creased. 'You're moving back to Cornwall?'

'I'm thinking about it. I'll leave it for Maya to explain.' Tom's weekend bag had been packed earlier and he stepped out of the room to pick it up.

He came back, looking from one to the other. 'Can I trust you two to stay out of trouble?'

Maya shooed him away, laughing. 'Drive carefully,' she called after him. She went to the window to watch his car pulling away. Her expression was wistful.

'What was all that about important meetings?' Loveday asked. 'Anything you can share with me?'

Maya turned, sighing. 'Tom's got himself a girlfriend.'

Loveday raised an eyebrow. 'That's good, isn't it?'

'Of course, it is. I want him to be happy, he's important to me.'

Loveday didn't miss the second's hesitation. 'And?' she said, watching her.

'And nothing. It's all good news. He's planning to give up his business in London and move down here full-time. That's what the meetings are about.'

'With his new lady friend?' Loveday asked.

Maya shrugged. 'I suppose so.' Her gaze went to the

glowing wood burner and Loveday wondered if her friend was fonder of Tom Scobey than she was admitting.

'Tell me more about this woman you saw in church.'

Maya shrugged. 'Oh I don't know. I thought she was the body at the heritage centre, but that was only because of the green cloak. The woman in church was dressed like that too, but I'm not certain. Maybe I shouldn't have mentioned that to Sam. It's set them off on a whole different line of investigation. What if I've wasted their time?'

'I wouldn't think twice about that,' Loveday said. 'That's the job. And to be honest, Maya, I think Sam would be pleased to get any piece of information at this stage.'

'I understand that,' Maya said. 'I want them to get to the bottom of this more than anyone. I won't be happy about going back into the centre until this is cleared up.' She frowned. 'I suppose Sam or one of his officers will be back tomorrow with more questions.'

'I imagine so,' Loveday said. 'That won't be a problem, will it?'

'Of course not.' Maya swallowed, gazing into the fire. 'But I don't know I can tell them anything more.'

Loveday was thinking. 'The woman from church, think again, might you have seen her around the village?'

Maya screwed up her face. 'I don't know.'

'What about in the pub?'

'No, I haven't been to the pub in weeks.'

Loveday was still trying to work things out. 'So we're none the wiser about what she was doing there at the back of the church? From what you've said she wasn't one of the regular congregation.'

'No she wasn't, at least I didn't think so. It was just odd to see her there. I imagine she choose that pew at the back so she could slip out before everyone else left. I know that's what I would have done if I hadn't wanted to meet anyone after the service.'

Loveday frowned. 'She could have rented a holiday cottage around here or been staying in a caravan. Going to church on a Sunday might be part of her routine. And as far as her attire goes, well, it was only an old cloak. Lots of people like to be different.'

But Maya was still deep in her own thoughts. 'I found her body,' she said. 'I didn't imagine that. And someone took her.' She shook her head. I don't understand. Where could she have gone?'

'I wouldn't worry about it, not tonight.' Loveday got up and moved to the window. 'It's still raining out there.'

'It's probably settled in for the night.' Maya yawned.

Loveday gave her friend a concerned look. 'You've had a very eventful day, young lady, but now I'm insisting you have to get some sleep. How are you going to look after April Rose if you're exhausted in the morning?'

The mention of her daughter brought a smile to Maya's face. She gave a little stretch. 'You're right. I should at least try to sleep. Maybe the brandy will help that.'

'It probably will,' Loveday said. 'But just to make sure, I'll bring you up a cup of cocoa. How does that sound?'

Maya laughed. 'It sounds very much like you're spoiling me.'

'Nothing wrong with that,' Loveday said. 'We all need a bit of spoiling sometimes.'

CHAPTER 5

*T*he cottage was quiet when Loveday woke next morning. She got up and drew back the curtain. The first tinge of dawn was creeping into the sky. The heritage centre was less than a mile as the crow flies, although not visible from Maya's cottage, but the view across the clifftop looked inviting. Loveday was used to her morning jogs along the beach in Marazion. It was an important part of her routine and set her up for the day ahead. She looked out, wrinkling her nose, wondering if yesterday's rain had left the grass too muddy to run on, but getting out in that early morning light was inviting.

She pulled on the tracksuit she'd been wearing the previous night and quietly left the cottage, pausing at the gate to look around her. Nothing was stirring, the village was still asleep. It was exactly as she liked it. She turned towards the sea, jogging past the old granite cottages. The air smelled sweet after the rain and there was that ever present salty tang.

A new access road had been built to the heritage centre

and she turned into that, planning to follow a track she could see ahead across the clifftop to the cliff path.

She slowed to a walking pace as she passed the centre. The whole side of the building was glass. The architect's intention to invite the outdoors in and create the impression that the place was a natural part of its surroundings had worked. Her eye was taken to the far end of the building where she could see the reconstruction of her great aunt Martha's cottage. No matter how often she saw it the sight always caused Loveday's heart to stir. That morning it felt more like an alarming somersault. The cottage had been recreated on its original site and made to look as it might have done in Martha's day. The granite walls had been aged by including some of the original stones and the little windows sparkled. She wondered if her relations of generations ago would have been as meticulously houseproud. Scraping a living from the land and managing to survive would have been their priority.

She jogged on, leaving the cottage behind and took the track across the clifftop. It wasn't as muddy as she had feared. Loveday slowed to a walking pace again, breathing deeply as the ocean came into view. The sun was coming up behind her, glinting on the waves and making the new day brilliantly beautiful. She reached the cliff path and paused, looking around her. It always felt good to be alive on days like this.

Loveday hadn't intended coming this far, but since she was here there seemed no point in not continuing. She picked up her jog again, settling into an easy pace as she ran along the cliff edge. The tide was out but she could still hear the waves breaking over the outcrops of rock below. A seabird wheeled above her, stretching its wings and making leisurely circles above her head. She paused, watching it, wondering what the world looked like from up there. Other bird sounds drifted up to her from the rocky shore below. She closed her eyes, enjoying the vibrancy of the early morning as it swept over her. Being alone and at one with nature felt good but lingering any longer would be pure indulgence. She needed to get back. If Maya woke up and realized she wasn't there, she might worry. She chastised herself for not leaving a note.

Loveday was on the point of turning back when something below caught her eye. She moved to the cliff edge and peered down. It was difficult to see what had caught her attention because the rocks were covered in seaweed. She blinked, staring harder as the shape came into focus. Her hand clutched at her chest. *Please no*, the voice inside her silently yelled. *Please don't let this be what I think it is.*

The green cloak was being tugged by the breeze. It didn't require much imagination to visualize a body trapped in the rocks beneath it.

Loveday staggered back, not wanting to see the thing again. She was trembling, but had to be sure. Forcing herself to move back to the cliff edge and look down, she could still see only the top of the cloak, but that was enough. No point taking chances. There could easily be a body down there. This was something Sam had to know about.

She reached into her pocket for her mobile phone. It was a moment before he picked up. Loveday could tell by the slight slur in his voice that she'd woken him. 'Sam, you'd better come. I think I've found a body…down by Carn Hendra.'

There was silence for a split second and she could imagine him struggling up in bed, blinking himself awake.

'Is it our missing woman?' His words were abrupt.

'Maybe. It's at the bottom of the cliffs on the rocks.'

'What's the situation with the tide?' he demanded.

'It's out at the moment.' She knew he would be mentally

estimating how long his team would have to recover a body before the waves came and snatched it away. She gave him her location as far as she could work out. She was quite a distance from the heritage centre. Loveday was imagining the woman's killer stumbling along the cliff path under the weight of the poor woman's body.

'OK, I'm on my way. Go back to the heritage centre, Loveday.' Sam's instructions cut through her thoughts. It was comforting to have him take charge. She nodded silently, reluctant to end the call. But he had gone.

Her eyes were on the far horizon, anywhere to avoid seeing what lay below again. Sam's question about the tide was making her think. If the body had been dropped over the cliffs the previous night the tide would have been right up to the base of the rocks. So why hadn't she been washed away? Loveday bit her lip, her gaze travelling out over the waves to the white crests she could see in the distance.

What if this woman's killer had brought her here early this morning, before she had arrived herself? She thought about that but it hardly seemed likely. There was another possibility though, one she hardly dared think about. She drew back from the edge and turned away. If this poor woman hadn't been dead, but only injured when Maya saw her in the cottage yesterday was it possible she could have struggled across the fields and ended up on the cliff path? If she'd been injured she might have been trying to find help. If she had stumbled onto the cliff path she might not have known she was heading to her death. Loveday shivered. She hoped that's not what had happened.

The path ahead was only visible for about thirty yards before it turned inland, away from the rocky contours of the coast. There was no one else in sight as far as she could see. But then why would there be at this hour?

She turned away and headed back to the heritage centre.

Even though Sam had asked her to stay put, Loveday was growing increasingly uneasy about this. It would take him a while to arrive. If she went back to Maya's place she could ring him on the way and tell him to meet her there. It felt like a plan.

As she approached Carn Hendra her attention was drawn the gap in the hillside. It was the fogou, the ancient Cornish cave where she and Sam had found Jamie Roscoe's body that awful day. She could still remember the horror of it. They had been out searching for the ruins of Martha's cottage. An old farmer who lived locally had spoken to them. The rain had come on, just as it had yesterday. Loveday remembered pointing to the cave suggesting they could shelter there. The farmer had warned against it, saying no one went into the fogou. It was dangerous. He told them to stay away, but getting wet had been no fun, so Sam had grabbed her hand and they'd made a run for it.

They'd found Jamie's body a few yards from the entrance. She turned her head away, trying not to dwell on the memory. Maya would almost certainly see this fogou every day when she arrived at Carn Hendra. Loveday hadn't thought of it before but now she wondered how her friend managed to cope with that.

The centre's car park was still deserted as she approached and got her phone out. She tapped in a text message.

Hi Sam, I'll see you at Maya's cottage and go back with you to the cliff path. I'm not happy about waiting here on my own.

Sam answered his phone. 'Are you OK, Loveday?'

She nodded at her phone. 'Yes, of course. Just get here quickly.'

'I'm on my way. I'll pick you up from the cottage.' He paused. 'If you can't cope with going back to the cliff path don't worry. I rang Will. He's already in his car. We'll find the place on our own.'

'No, Sam, I'm fine. Pick me up.'

It took only minutes to walk back to the cottage and from the plinkety plink sound of nursery music coming from the kitchen Loveday knew the family was up and about.

April Rose was bouncing energetically in her high chair, waving a spoonful of porridge around the room. Maya leapt forward, making a grab for the cereal bowl before it was hurled to the floor.

'She's enjoying that.' Loveday laughed.

Maya looked up, still in her dressing gown. 'I thought you were in bed, Loveday. Where on earth have you been?'

'I went for a run out to the clifftop.' She swallowed, wondering how much she should say. But her discovery was like the elephant in the room and besides, Maya would know about it soon enough. She sat down at the kitchen table, waiting for April Rose to finish her breakfast.

'Any more news from Sam this morning?' Maya asked, wiping the child's face with a tissue after she'd spooned the last of the porridge into her mouth. April Rose was still in exuberant mood, waving her arms about and giving Loveday one of her irresistible smiles. Loveday grinned back. Maya looked at her, waiting for an answer.

'I've asked Sam to join us. He's on his way here.'

'Really?' Maya frowned. 'Why so early? Has something happened?'

'Actually, yes.' Loveday spoke quietly. She had no idea how this latest news would affect her friend. She took a breath. 'When I was out on the cliff path this morning I saw something…down on the rocks.'

Maya's eyes were full of dismay. 'It was her, wasn't it? I didn't imagine that body.'

'I'm not sure,' Loveday said. 'We should try not to jump to conclusions.'

'I don't understand.' Maya was shaking her head. 'You said you saw something out there. What else could it be?'

Loveday was remembering how she'd taken off when she saw that cloak being tugged by the breeze. Had she overreacted? She hadn't actually seen a body. Now she wasn't even sure it had been a cloak. It could have been any old rag. She shouldn't have said anything to Maya.

'Sam's on his way.' Simply saying that was making her feel better. 'He'll get more officers out on the cliff path and they'll do a proper search. We should try not to jump to conclusions until we know what they find.'

Maya bit her lip, nodding. 'You're right,' she said. But the distracted look was still clouding her eyes.

CHAPTER 6

*L*oveday jumped up when she heard Sam's car pull up. 'Will you be OK until I get back?'

'I will if everyone stops treating me like fragile china,' Maya said, but she was giving her friend a teasing smile. 'Call me as soon as you know anything.'

'I will,' Loveday said as she ran out to meet Sam.

He leaned over and opened the car door as she approached. 'Are you sure you want to do this?' he said, making no attempt to hide his worried frown as she climbed in. Loveday nodded. She wasn't looking forward to standing on that cliff path again but she knew she had to do it.

They drove on, reaching the heritage centre within minutes. Will was already in the car park waiting for them.

'I'll run ahead. You two follow me,' Loveday said, jumping out and striding ahead. She began to retrace her steps with the two detectives close behind. When she reached the spot where she'd seen the green cloak caught up on the rocks, she stopped, pointing. 'Down there.' She averted her eyes, stepping back.

Sam was already on his phone instructing DC Amanda Fox to find someone local with a boat.

The wind had got up and Loveday's eyes were stinging. She pushed her long hair from her face. 'Is it her, Sam?'

'All I can see at the moment is a rag caught up on the rocks.' He turned to Will who had stepped closer to the cliff edge. 'Can you see anything?'

Will shook his head. They both knew any body that might have been down there was now long gone.

'What exactly did you see, Loveday?' Sam asked.

'I told you. I saw this thing on the rocks. It looked like the cloak Maya described seeing on this dead woman.'

'You definitely didn't see a body then?'

Loveday sighed. 'If I'd seen a body I would have said so.' She stepped forward and peered down at the waves breaking on the rocks. 'It's not her, is it? I've brought you and Will on a wild goose chase and upset Maya for nothing.'

Sam put a hand on Loveday's shoulder. 'Maybe not. We'll know more once we recover what's down there.' His mobile rang and he answered it. 'Yes, Amanda. Did you get that boat?'

'The local inshore lifeboat is launching as we speak,' she told him. 'It should only take them a few minutes to reach you. The coastguards will link you up with them. I'll text you the number.'

'Thanks, Amanda. You'd better get yourself down here too.'

'On my way, boss.'

Loveday was by Sam's side, staring at the waves. 'You don't believe Maya's dead woman is down there, do you?'

'I don't know, Loveday. Let's see what the lifeboat crew finds.' He nodded below to the rocks. 'We're not even sure that's her cloak.'

In the distance they could see the lifeboat powering towards them and watched until it was just offshore. As the little boat drew closer, Sam waved, indicating the garment below. One of the crew raised an arm in acknowledgement as the lifeboat inched closer to the rocks. A long pole was produced. The crew made a few unsuccessful attempts to snatch at the fabric before they managed to recover it.

Sam and Loveday had been so focused on the lifeboat activities they hadn't noticed Will walking off. They both turned at his urgent shout. He'd cupped his hands to his mouth, yelling out against the wind. 'Over here, sir! You need to see this.'

Sam turned and walked towards him with Loveday hurrying behind.

Will was pointing. 'I almost missed it. It was the interest of the crows that made me take a second look.'

They moved closer. When Sam saw what Will was indicating he threw out his arm to prevent Loveday advancing further. But it was too late. He could see she was already staring wide-eyed at the woman's body.

'If you're going to throw up move away from the site,' he said, seeing the blood drain from Loveday's face.

* * *

BUT SHE STAYED BEHIND HIM, not sure her legs would even move. The woman's body was curled into the foetal position as though she had settled comfortably for the night behind the big rock. It had protected the body from the weather. The gory-looking gash on her forehead was still bloody.

Loveday covered her mouth with her hand. Both Sam and Will were on their mobile phones barking out instructions to get the team together.

'Look there,' Will said, pointing to a stone near the body. 'Is that blood?'

'It is,' Sam said grimly. 'We might have found a murder weapon.'

Loveday also saw where the detective had pointed and shivered. 'Poor woman. If this is the same person Maya saw at the centre, could she have been mistaken in thinking she'd been dead?' She was trying not to look at the horrifying scene.

Sam spun round to stare at her. 'So what are you saying? That she came across the clifftop in that horrible weather yesterday, stripped off her cloak and battered herself to death with that stone?'

'I don't know. If she was injured she might not have known what she was doing.'

'Or we could go on speculating all day long,' Sam said. 'Let's wait to hear what the pathologist has to say.'

He had already rung the Home Office pathologist, Dr Robert Bartholomew.

He glanced back in the direction of the heritage building. 'We'll use the centre as a base and get a team out door knocking in the village. Someone may know who this woman is.' He turned to Loveday, his expression softening. 'I'm sorry you've been caught up in all this, love.'

'I don't need protecting, Sam. I'm here to help.'

'I know,' he said, glancing back to the woman's body. 'There is something you could do. Go back to Maya and let her know she won't be able to open the centre today. She needs to stick around though. We'll need to speak to her later.'

Loveday knew he was trying to get her away from the site, but she nodded anyway, her eyes also going back to the body. 'It's her, isn't it…it really is the woman Maya saw.'

Sam's grim expression gave nothing away.

'At least we know Maya is not going doolally,' Loveday said.

Sam looked up. 'Did somebody suggest she was?'

'Tom's been worrying about her. I'm not sure he believed all the odd things she told him had been happening at the centre. But that body is real enough. She didn't imagine that.'

'Maybe not,' Sam said. 'But I don't want you discussing this with her, not yet, not before we establish what's happened here.'

'I promised to ring her if we found anything. How can I not tell her it's a body?'

Sam's sigh sounded frustrated. 'Tell Maya I'll be calling, but I need your word that you will give her no details.'

'You have it,' Loveday said.

His eyes narrowed as he watched her walk away, then he turned as Will came to join him. 'What do you think, Will? What's going on here?'

His sergeant shrugged. 'How well do you know Maya?'

'Maya? She's a friend. Why do you ask?' He caught Will's expression and stared at him. 'You're not suggesting Maya could have done this?'

'I'm not suggesting anything, just throwing in a few ideas to consider, but it's not impossible. We only have her word for it that there was a body in the centre. She could have met the woman by arrangement and walked out here with her. Maybe they argued and Maya lifted a stone and clouted the other woman.'

Sam threw him a disbelieving look. 'Why would she do that?'

Will's shoulders rose in another shrug. 'I don't know. Maybe she was being blackmailed.'

Sam didn't like the turn this was taking. 'I think that's highly unlikely,' he snapped, but he knew it was something they would have to investigate.

* * *

MAYA AND APRIL Rose were on the sofa, a colourful children's book spread out between them. They looked up when Loveday walked in.

Maya's face was instantly alert. 'What's happening, Loveday? What's this all about? Have you found the body or not?'

Loveday bit her lip. She was under instructions from Sam not to discuss this, but surely Maya had a right to know? On the other hand… 'I know it's asking a lot, but please bear with us a little longer. I'm sure Sam will explain everything when he gets here.'

'Why do I have to wait?' Maya said crossly. 'I don't understand. Either you've found the woman's body or you haven't. What's the big secret?'

Loveday tried a placating smile. 'Sam says would you mind not opening up today, I think they are going to use the place as a kind of base. They'll want to do a door knock around the village to see if anyone knows who the woman is.'

'So it is her,' Maya said quietly.

'I didn't say that. Let's wait for Sam.'

Maya pulled a face. 'OK, but we don't have to be confined to the cottage, do we?' She lifted April Rose high and wrinkled her nose at her. 'What do you say, my darling? Shall we go for a walk?'

April Rose giggled. 'I guess that's a yes from her,' Maya said.

* * *

THE CHURCH DOOR was open as they passed and they could hear movement coming from inside. 'Somebody's in there,' Loveday said.

'It's probably the cleaner. She likes to get things done early,' Maya said.

'Let's take a look.' Loveday bent to help lift April Rose's buggy up the steps.

Inside the church they paused, feeling the tranquility of the place settling around them. Ahead by the font a woman was standing, staring into space.

'Jess,' Maya called. 'We thought it might be you in here.'

The woman jumped, a hand flying to her chest. 'Who's there? Come out where I can see you.'

'It's only me, Jess. It's Maya.' They didn't see the bruises on the woman's face until they drew closer.

'Whatever's happened?' Maya's voice was shocked. 'Your poor face, Jess.' She reached out for the woman's arm.

But Jess Tandy snatched it away. 'I had a fall,' she said, touching her cheek.

There was an angry-looking gash under the woman's eye. 'Have you seen a doctor?' Loveday asked, her voice full of concern.

'I don't need a doctor. I told you, I tripped.' She winced as her fingers touched her face again. 'It's only a scratch.'

Loveday frowned, her eyes examining the woman's injuries. She was willing to bet there were more unseen bruises.

'That's more than a scratch,' Maya said. 'I think you should let us take you to A&E.'

'No!' Jess bit her lip. 'I know you and your friend are trying to be kind but I really don't need any help. This looks worse than it is.'

Loveday doubted that. The woman looked like she'd been badly beaten. 'Has someone done this to you?' she asked gently.

Jess reached for the font, steadying herself. 'I can see you won't leave me alone until I tell you what happened.' She looked from one to the other. 'I wasn't doing anything wrong. You do understand that, don't you?'

'Of course we do,' Maya said. 'Now just tell us.'

Jess swallowed. 'I came back to the church last night, late last night.' She hesitated, and Loveday wondered if she was considering how much to tell them.

'I'd been here cleaning earlier in the evening and thought I might have left the lights on. I couldn't sleep for worrying about it, so I came back to check.' She blinked, frowning. 'There was a car parked at the bottom of the steps. I knew straight away something wasn't right. I mean, what was it doing there? I should have turned around right there and then and come home, but I didn't.

'I had the keys to the church. I remember how heavy they felt in my hand. It was so quiet, and then it wasn't. A man.' She frowned again touching her head. 'Maybe more than one. I'm not sure. Somebody rushed at me and then I felt this crack on my head. I can remember falling. Maybe my face struck one of the headstones, I don't know.

'When I came to I was lying on the path. My head hurt but the men had gone. Everything looked normal.' She winced as she touched her head again. 'My cottage is in the lane right by the church. I knew I was staggering a bit but I wanted to get home.'

Maya couldn't hide her shock. 'And didn't you call the police?'

Jess looked embarrassed. 'What if I'd taken a bad turn and collapsed outside the church?'

'You said there was a car,' Loveday said.

'There was,' Jess said thoughtfully. 'That's why I came back today. There was nothing on the news about any burglary at the church. I decided to come in myself this morning to check. I wanted to make sure none of the church's old treasures was missing.' She looked up at Maya and Loveday. 'That's what I was doing when you two got here.'

Her expression changed. Talking about her previous night's experience seemed to have helped her. 'You had a nasty shock too yesterday,' she said to Maya. 'I hear you found a body over at the centre.'

Loveday raised an eyebrow. News travelled fast in these Cornish villages.

'The vicar rang me last evening,' Jess explained.

Loveday nodded. 'Were you in the centre yourself yester-day?' she asked.

'No, not yesterday. I nipped in early Saturday morning to do my work.' She met Loveday's eyes. 'I don't think I know you.'

'This is my friend, Loveday,' Maya explained. 'She's been keeping me company while all this is going on.' She hesitated. 'The thing is, Jess, the centre was unlocked when I got there yesterday. It hadn't been broken into or anything like that, but somebody who had a key had obviously gone in there and not locked up after them.'

Jess Tandy gave her an indignant look. 'You're not suggesting that was me?'

'No of course not, I know how careful you always are. I was only mentioning it because you can probably expect a visit from the police today.'

Jess looked worried again. 'The police? Why would the police want to question me?'

Loveday smiled. 'There was a woman in church yester-day.' She turned to the faraway back pew. 'Sitting right over there, I believe.' She looked at Jess Tandy. 'Were you at the service yesterday by any chance?'

'Yes, but I don't see what that has to do with anything.'

'I was wondering if you happened to notice this woman.'

She could see Jess was thinking about that. She was still

wondering if the woman was involved in this business and trying to get her story right.

At last Jess nodded. Her eyes going to the back of the church. 'Now you mention it, there was somebody sitting back there. That pew is usually empty. Most of us sit up front because you can hear the vicar much better from there.' She pulled a face. 'It did look a bit odd her sitting at the back on her own. Pretty young thing like that shouldn't be on her own all the time.'

Loveday and Maya exchanged a surprised look. 'You've seen her before?' Loveday asked.

Jess sat down heavily on the end of a pew. Her shock of earlier appeared to be receding. She looked like she was enjoying the moment. She waved towards the little chapel. 'Over there,' she said. 'I've seen her over there by the carving of the saint. Not that I paid special attention. It's the main attraction for visitors coming to the church. I've noticed her about the village too, but Sunday was the first time I saw her wearing that green cloak thing. We get all sorts here.'

Loveday glanced about her. 'I'm not surprised. It's a beautiful church. You keep it sparkling.'

The woman beamed at her. 'I do my best.' She turned back to the font. 'You should speak to the vicar. I've seen her speaking to the woman. Maybe she knows who she is.'

Loveday's heart skipped a beat. Sam needed to know about this.

Jess was getting to her feet, puffing. 'I'll get off if you don't mind. I'm looking forward to a good strong cup of tea.'

Loveday watched her go. 'How well do you know Jess Tandy, Maya?'

'I don't, well not really. She was recommended to me when we were looking for a cleaner for the centre. She's a bit odd, isn't she?'

Loveday was pensive as she stared after the woman. If

Jess Tandy didn't report what had happened in the church-yard the previous night then *she* certainly would.

April Rose had begun to chunter impatiently and Maya bent, touching her daughter's cheek and speaking softly to settle her as they strolled out and went back to the cottage.

CHAPTER 7

*S*am's silver Lexus was pulling up as they arrived back at the cottage. Loveday gave him a wave. 'No DS Tregellis?' she asked, glancing along the lane as they went up the path.

'I've left Will in charge at the site. Dr Bartholomew's still there.'

Maya looked up, frowning, as they went into the sitting room. 'Dr Bartholomew? Isn't he the Home Office pathologist?' She didn't miss the look that passed between Sam and Loveday. 'You've found her, haven't you? She wasn't a figment of my imagination at all.' Maya's face was alight with excitement.

Sam drew a breath. 'We've found a body, yes.'

'Is it her? Was she wearing that long green cloak?'

'I'm sorry, Maya. It's an ongoing investigation. I can't share information with you, but it would be helpful if you could answer a few questions.'

'Of course. Ask me anything.' She turned as April Rose began to cry. 'She's hungry. I was going to boil an egg for her lunch.'

'I can do that,' Loveday said, bending to scoop April Rose from her buggy. 'Let's leave Mummy and Uncle Sam to have their chat while we find something to eat.'

Sam waited until Loveday had left the room before turning to Maya. 'I need you to think, Maya. Think!' He gave her a second. 'You're back there in that room. The dead girl is in the rocking chair in front of you. You can see her now. She's staring up at you.'

Maya covered her face with her hands.

'You can see her, Maya,' Sam persisted. His voice was gentle, persuasive. 'You've seen her before. Who is this woman, Maya? Who is she?'

Maya's hands slipped from her face. Her eyes were wide. 'It was her. I remember. She came to the centre. She brought a class of children with her.' She looked up, staring at Sam. 'She's a teacher!'

'A teacher? Are you sure?'

'I think so. I think it's her. I hope it's not, but…' She touched her head. 'Yes, it's coming back to me. If she's the same person, I think she was from a primary school in St Ives. She was really into the history, explaining to the children what the heritage centre was all about, what the exhibits meant. I was impressed that she knew so much. The children loved it.'

It was a long shot, but Sam hoped it was worth a try. 'I don't suppose you would have her details?'

Maya nodded. 'They'll be in my office. Visiting schools have to be booked in. The teacher's name will be there with her school.'

Maya sank down onto the sofa, her hand at her head. 'Why didn't I recognize her? I should have recognized her.'

'It doesn't always work like that.' Sam was wishing he'd brought Will with him. Maya's innocence was obvious. If she'd been putting on an act he would have seen straight through it. This young woman was no more a murderer than he was.

'What happens now?' Maya asked.

'It's imperative we identify the body. We'll go to the school and take things from there.'

Loveday poked her head into the room as Sam was getting to his feet. 'Did you tell him about the cleaner?' she asked.

'Gosh no. My head's all over the place.'

From the kitchen April Rose had begun bashing her spoon on her high chair. Loveday turned to attend to her but Maya was instantly on her feet. 'Can you tell Sam about that? I'll see to April Rose.' She pointed to a small desk by the window. 'My keys are in the drawer. You'll need them to get into my office desk.'

'What's this about a cleaner?' Sam asked, fetching the keys as Maya hurried from the room.

'It's probably got nothing to do with your case.' Loveday recounted Jess Tandy's story.

Sam's eyebrows came together. 'And there was nothing missing from the church?'

'I don't know. Jess was kind of all over the place. You'd have to talk to the vicar.'

'We'll check it out.' He smiled down at her. 'Are you OK to stay here with Maya for the moment?'

'Of course.' Loveday moved forward and put her arms around him. 'The magazine can manage without me for a day. I've explained the situation to Merrick. He said he would cover for me.' She brushed a strand of hair from his shoulder. 'You should get off.'

'I'll keep in touch,' he said, turning to leave.

Of course you will, she thought, smiling after him.

* * *

THE CENTRE CAR park was busy with police activity as Sam arrived. He found Will heading back from the cliff path.

'You've just missed Dr Bartholomew. He's scheduled the post mortem for this afternoon.'

Sam got out of the car and was walking briskly to the centre. 'We might have an ID before then,' he said. 'Maya's had a think and she believes she might have recognized the woman.'

Will threw him a look as he walked beside him. 'Really?'

'She could be a teacher at a primary school in St Ives.'

'And Maya has just remembered this?' He sounded cynical.

'They keep files of the bookings. The information should be in the office.' Sam glanced around him as he strode through the building. New desks had been brought in and his team of detectives were already settling in to their temporary HQ.

'The bookings journal should be in this desk,' he said, unlocking the drawer and flicking through the contents. 'Here it is. Maya thought the booking was only a few weeks ago.'

Will slapped his hand down on a page. 'St Ives you said?'

'That's it. Well spotted.' Sam ran his finger down the columns of information and stopped at *Organizer*. 'That's her,' Sam said, a flutter of excitement jabbing through him. 'Morwenna Chenoweth, St Ives Primary School.'

'This is a bit of a long shot, isn't it?' Will commented.

'Possibly,' Sam said. 'But it's all we've got and we urgently need to identify the body.'

'What about going back to the church? Maybe the vicar knows the woman,' Will suggested.

'We'll be calling in there soon,' Sam said. 'Let's see about this teacher first.'

· · ·

AN INQUISITIVE-LOOKING woman in a cherry red cardigan and tightly permed silver grey hair approached as they arrived. The buzz of children's voices drifted from the open door of a classroom. Sam and Will produced their warrant cards.

The woman offered her hand. She looked flustered. 'Marion Logan. I'm the head teacher.' She glanced back to the unattended classroom. 'We're not usually as disorganized as this. One of our teachers hasn't turned up and I'm supposed to be taking her class…amongst other things.'

Sam shot Will a look. 'Can we go to your office?'

Marion Logan's fluster turned to concern. 'Of course, it's this way.' They followed her along the corridor and took the seats she offered. 'This isn't about Miss Chenoweth, is it? Has something happened to her? It's not like her not to turn up and we haven't been able to contact her.'

Sam hesitated. 'Do you have a staff list, Ms Logan?'

The head teacher went to a wooden filing cabinet, slid open the bottom drawer and extracted a file. She opened it and selected an item, handing it to Sam. 'This is Morwenna's file.'

Sam and Will stared at the photograph of the pretty young blonde woman. She didn't look like that the last time they'd seen her on the cliffs at Carn Hendra, but it was definitely the same woman.

'What's all this about?' Ms Logan was looking seriously worried.

Sam glanced at the file. 'I'm afraid we have some bad news for you. A body was found at Carn Hendra this morning and we believe it might be this young woman, Morwenna Chenoweth.'

Marion Logan stared at them, her eyes wide with disbelief. She put a hand to her throat. 'Surely not? Are you certain?'

'We believe so,' he said. 'Anything you can tell us about Miss Chenoweth could be helpful.'

'I don't know what I can say other than she was a dedicated teacher. She has a house in Penzance. I understand she lives alone. Her parents are both dead.' She screwed up her face. 'Morwenna didn't talk much about herself although she did once mention she'd been brought up in a children's home…in Plymouth I think she said.'

'Was she popular?' Will asked.

Marion Logan nodded. 'Everyone loves Morwenna. She's that kind of girl.'

'What about boyfriends? Has she ever mentioned anyone to you?' Sam asked.

'I wouldn't know. I don't pry into the private lives of my staff, Inspector.'

'How about the rest of the staff then? Was she close to anyone in particular?'

'We only have two other teachers and they are both older and married. Everyone gets on of course, but I wouldn't say any of them were particularly close friends.'

'What about Miss Chenoweth's interests?' Sam asked. 'I understand she took her class on a visit to the Carn Hendra Heritage Centre recently.'

'Morwenna loved her Cornish heritage and she wanted her young charges to have the same pride in the place where they lived. She also took them on a visit to Carn Euny, one of the Iron Age settlements above Penzance. I wasn't sure how sensible it was for eight-year-olds to go trekking across those fields and over stiles to get to the site, but that's what she did. As far as I know the children loved it.'

Sam was looking around him. This was clearly the head teacher's office. 'Is there a staff room?' he asked.

'We have a little room next door where the teachers

gather at break times. Would you like to see it?' Marion offered.

The officers nodded and followed her next door. Sam's eye went instantly to a set of lockers. 'Does one of these belong to Miss Chenoweth?'

'Yes, I'd forgotten about them. I'll fetch the key.' Ms Logan left the room and returned moments later with a bunch of tiny silver keys on a ring. 'I'm not sure which key is Morwenna's.'

The locker door opened with the second key and they found themselves staring at a photo of a young couple taped inside the door. The woman was pretty, her long blonde hair cascading over her shoulders as she smiled at the camera. The slightly older-looking man by her side was glancing away, scowling as though he didn't appreciate having his picture taken. Sam turned. 'Is this Morwenna Chenoweth?'

Marion gave a sad smile. 'That's her.'

'Do you recognize the man?'

The woman scrutinized the photo. 'I couldn't be certain, but he looks like one of the men who did some work on the school roof last year. It was a Penzance firm…James Bluitt Builders, something like that. They did a good job. The receipt for the work will be in my files.'

'But you don't know this man's name?'

'No, sorry. I have no idea.'

'OK,' Sam said, removing the photo and reaching into the locker for the contents. There was a long filmy green scarf, a pen, notebook and a small card, still in its cellophane wrap. There was an image of St Piran on the front.

'We'll take these,' he said. 'Sergeant Tregellis will give you a receipt for them.'

Will got out his notebook and jotted a few lines which he tore out and handed to the head teacher.

She took it hesitantly, shaking her head. 'I pray that you

come back and tell us all this has been a terrible mistake and that you found Morwenna at home with the flu or something. I can't believe anything as awful as this could happen to her.'

Under normal circumstances they would ask a member of the family, or someone close, to make an identification, but in this case they had no one. 'How would you feel about identifying the body?'

Marion Logan's eyes widened. 'Me? You want me to identify her?'

'It would help us enormously and at least you would know one way or the other.' Sam's expression was sympathetic. 'I could arrange for you to be collected later this afternoon.'

The woman's slow nod was almost imperceptible.

Sam thanked her, passing Morwenna Chenoweth's file to Will as they left.

The school was in a built-up area high above St Ives Harbour but there was no view of the harbour from this spot. It didn't stop Sam visualizing it, and the pub down there where his late wife, Tessa, spent her last hours with a friend before she was mown down by a drunk driver. It was always difficult for him coming to St Ives without those terrible memories flooding back.

Sam wished he could concentrate on all the good things in his life. He had a great relationship with first wife, Victoria and their children, Jack and Maddie. Victoria had married again but they all still lived in Plymouth and he and Loveday saw all of them often.

A smile crossed his face. Loveday! They were happier than he ever dared to believe possible. But every now and then the dark days of the past came swirling back into his head.

'Everything all right, boss?' Will's voice brought him back to the present.

'Yes, fine,' he said. 'Let's check out this Penzance address.'

* * *

Morwenna Chenoweth's house was a mid-terrace in a quiet cul de sac above The Causeway, one of the town's busy shopping streets. No one answered their knock, but an old woman appeared from the door of the adjoining property. 'If it's Morwenna you're after she'll be at the school. Although come to think of it,' she wrinkled her nose, 'I haven't seen her all weekend.' She nodded to the door. 'He's been here though.'

'Who would that be?' Will asked.

'The boyfriend. He was here yesterday.'

Sam took the photo from Morwenna's locker from his pocket. 'Is this him?'

The old woman's face lit up. 'Yes, that's him. Shifty-looking devil, isn't he?' She turned piercing blue eyes on Will. 'What's your business with Morwenna?'

Both officers produced their IDs. She frowned at them. 'Well that tells me who you are. It doesn't say what you want. Has something happened to Morwenna?'

'We're here as part of an investigation,' Sam said quickly, hoping she would be satisfied with that. 'I don't suppose you have a key to the house?'

But there was no fooling the old lady. 'It's serious, isn't it?' She looked from one to the other. 'Morwenna has left a key with me. I'll get it.' She moved slowly back indoors and returned with the key.

Sam smiled as she handed it over. 'You didn't tell us your name.'

'You didn't ask,' she said, folding her arms. 'It's Annie Gemmel. *Miss* Annie Gemmel.'

'Thank you, Miss Gemmel. We'll give you a knock when we're finished,' Sam said, waiting as she finally took the hint and returned to her property.

They pulled on their blue nitrile gloves before stepping inside the house, careful that any fingerprint or other forensic evidence should be protected. The place smelled faintly of incense.

Morwenna Chenoweth's house didn't exactly look as if it had been burgled, but someone – possibly the young man Annie Gemmel had described as 'shifty looking' – had definitely searched the place. Drawers had been rummaged through and not properly closed, cupboard doors lay open. Sam wondered what the searcher had been looking for.

Will pointed to the cable snaking across the floor and what looked like a battery charger. 'The computer's gone,' he said.

Sam nodded. 'See what else you can find down here. I'll check upstairs.' The house wasn't spacious. A sitting room and kitchen on the lower floor and two small bedrooms and a bathroom above. He poked his head round the door of what appeared to be the spare room before moving on to what he assumed had been Morwenna's bedroom. There was a prettiness about the place, an intimacy that gave Sam a feeling he was intruding into Morwenna's private world.

The bed was unmade, the duvet cast carelessly aside as though whoever had slept there cared nothing for order. In the wardrobe clothes hung neatly on hangers and had been grouped according to colours. The skirts he could see were long, and most of the dresses appeared to be of filmy materials. Several pairs of sandals had been arranged neatly at the bottom of the wardrobe. There were no trainers.

Long strands of coloured beads hung from the dressing table mirror and there were pictures of fairies on the walls.

There was only one toothbrush in the bathroom and no evidence of a man also living here, but that could be what they were meant to believe.

Sam went back downstairs. Will was examining the contents of a desk in the small sitting room. 'It looks like Morwenna was writing a book,' he said, holding up a sheaf of printed papers. '*Folklore of Ancient Cornwall*, not exactly bodice-ripping stuff.'

'Not everyone has your taste in fiction, Will.' Sam was lifting out some more papers. 'This is interesting. It's the story of a Cornish saint, St Piran.' Somewhere in the back of his mind he could remember an old carving of a St Piran in the church near Carn Hendra…the church where Maya had seen the cloaked woman. He was now sure it had been Morwenna Chenoweth sitting at the back of that church.

Knocking on the elderly neighbour's door had been more of a nod to courtesy and to say they were keeping the key than any expectation she might have helpful information for them. But she surprised them by producing a small black notebook.

She held it out to Sam. 'This is Morwenna's. She left it here.'

Sam took it, raising his eyebrow.

'I don't expect it's important. It was somewhere to scribble her notes. Morwenna was interviewing oldies like me about their memories of growing up in Cornwall. I think it was her intention to put it all into a book.'

'I'm sure it will be a great help. Thank you.'

'I hope Morwenna is OK,' she called after them. 'Such a lovely girl.'

CHAPTER 8

*J*ames Bluitt Builders was a small family business housed in a yard next door to a used car dealership on the outskirts of Penzance town centre. A red pickup drove up as Sam and Will crossed the cluttered yard and a middle-aged man jumped out. 'Can I help you?' he called, coming towards them.

'Mr Bluitt?' Sam asked.

The man nodded.

Will produced his warrant card and Sam held up the photo they'd taken from Morwenna Chenoweth's locker. 'We understand this man works for you.'

Bluitt glanced at the photo and back to Sam. 'What's he supposed to have done?'

'Then you do recognize him?'

'It's Joss Teague. He works for me. Why do you want to see him?'

Sam ignored the question. 'Where can we find him?'

James Bluitt hesitated, his body language suggesting he was weighing up whether or not to co-operate with these people. He nodded to a scruffy-looking caravan at the back of the yard. 'You'd better come into the office.' He strode ahead of them and threw open the door, leaving Sam and Will to follow him in.

The inside looked a lot more organized than the unkempt exterior had suggested. Sam's attention went to the grey metal filing cabinet. 'We'd like Joss Teague's address please, Mr Bluitt. I presume you have it?'

Bluitt sucked in his cheeks. 'You still haven't told me what you want with Joss.'

Sam's uncompromising stare didn't change. 'We need to talk to him in connection with an ongoing investigation.' He waited while the other man frowned. He moved closer. 'The address please, sir.'

James Bluitt turned and slid open a drawer of the filing cabinet. Flicking through the files he extracted one, holding it out to Sam. 'This is supposed to be confidential, you know. Joss is a good lad. I won't have anything said against him.'

The address in the proffered file was on the Penzance seafront. Sam looked up. 'How long has Teague worked for you?'

'I took him on as an apprentice two years ago. He's not frightened to put his shoulder into a job, which is what a small family business like this needs. I can rely on him.'

'Is he out on a job?'

Bluitt shook his head. 'He asked for a few days off. He said he had personal stuff to attend to. We don't have much on at the moment, so I said yes.'

'Did he say what this personal stuff was?' Will asked.

'He didn't, and I didn't press him.'

Sam held out the photo again. 'Do you recognize the young woman with Teague in this photo?'

James Bluitt screwed up his face. 'She's a teacher at a school in St Ives, but I don't know her name. We did a job on the roof there a while back.' He was still looking at the photo of the couple, smiling into the camera with their arms wrapped around each other. 'I didn't know that she and Joss were an item.'

* * *

THE ONE THOUGHT in Joss Teague's head was to get out of Cornwall. He was in trouble again. He thought about lying low in the tiny one-roomed flat he rented in Penzance, but that was the first place they would look for him. In the end, after a sleepless night, he'd bundled some clothes into his backpack and got out of there at first light. Joss had thought about taking Bluitt's van but decided against it. The police could easily get the registration number and from that they could track him wherever he was. He had no choice but to get away on foot.

Living rough was not something that came easily to him, but wild campers and walkers were nothing unusual in Cornwall.

The first night he'd slept in a field, behind a wall. It was the most uncomfortable night of his life and when he woke at first light it was to find himself under surveillance by the black eyes of a distinctly unfriendly looking bull. The threat in the animal's stare had Joss grabbing his belongings and scrambling over the wall to safety. He ran and kept running until the field and its ill-tempered occupant were far behind him.

His legs were still shaking as he approached a village. He glanced at his watch – 5.25am – and reached into his pocket where his fingers closed over a solitary £20 note. It was all the money he had in the world, but at least it could buy him a bun if he could find a bakery open at this hour.

He sat down on a bench in the deserted village square, wondering what to do next. In the distance he could hear a vehicle approaching. His first instinct was to run and hide, but where would he go? So he sat watching the blue van as it got closer. It pulled up outside what looked like the village store. If the driver had noticed him sitting there he hadn't shown it. He got out and flung open the van's back door. Joss could see it was stacked with newspapers. The man slid out two bundles and carried them to the shop, dropping them at the door before returning to the vehicle and driving off.

Joss stared at the bundles of newspapers, wondering if his picture would be on the front page. Could he risk getting out and taking a look? But before he had even processed the thought the shop door opened and a middle-aged woman came out and grabbed one of the bundles. She heaved it inside and returned seconds later for the other one. He chewed his nails, wondering if he should risk going in. His rumbling stomach reminded him again that he hadn't eaten since the previous afternoon. If he was to spend the day – and God knows how many more days – on the run then he might not get many more opportunities to buy food.

He crossed the road, looking about him as he went. No one appeared to be around. A bell tinkled as he went into the shop. If the woman had thought it unusual to have a customer at this time of day she didn't show it. Joss glanced at the newspapers. He wasn't on the front page – at least that was something. He pointed to the shelf of cellophane-wrapped pasties and asked for two. The woman glanced at the £20 note he offered and scowled. 'Is that all you've got?'

'It is, unless you don't want to charge me.'

The woman slid a look to her till. Changing the note would take all her loose cash. She decided against it, flapping a hand at the door. 'This is your lucky day, lad. Now get out of here before I change my mind.'

Joss didn't hang about. He nodded a thanks, stuffing the pasties into his pockets as he made a swift exit. Back in the square he spotted a copse of trees and made for it. At least it would provide some cover while he worked out what to do next. The wooded area was on a slope and through the trees Joss could just make out a clearing. It looked deserted. He could feel his spirits rise as he ran through the trees, peeling off his backpack as he went. He found a large rock and sat there, greedily devouring his pasties. When they were finished he brushed the crumbs from his jeans and fished the note from his pocket. He still had his £20 but it wouldn't get him far and when he'd spent it, how would he manage then? He couldn't go on running forever.

He had no idea where he was, other than being out on the moors. He guessed maybe close to Land's End. The remoteness of his surrounding was intimidating. He could still see Morwenna's face, her teasing smile. He'd been secretly impressed by her plan to discredit the girl from the heritage centre. Whether it would have worked or not was another matter. He shouldn't have left her like that. He tried to shut out the images that were reeling through his head, but they wouldn't go away. Keeping his eyes tight shut didn't help. The pictures were still there. They would always be there.

He couldn't run away from that. It had happened and he would never be free of the guilt he was feeling.

Joss spent the rest of the day stumbling through the gorse, wedging himself in a crevice between two rocks when darkness fell. It was another uncomfortable night and pangs of hunger gnawed at his insides. Was this what his life was to be now?

The sky looked dark and ominous when he woke. He felt safe enough in this place but how long could he go without food? The rain arrived at noon and came with such force that Joss abandoned his rocks in search of shelter. By his estimation it was Tuesday. He wondered how much interest anyone would take of a man with a backpack walking the moors. He had stayed off the beaten track until now but he needed to find food. Could he risk the main road? Maybe not. He wished he knew where he was. He'd watch out for road signs or even fingerposts to give him some clue. He had headed up into the hills when he left Penzance and reckoned he must be somewhere around Chysauster but the ruins of an ancient settlement would provide no safe haven.

His empty stomach rumbled and he wondered if he could buy food from the farmhouse he could see across the field. He stomped across the grass, steering clear of cows he could see sheltering under the trees until he reached the back door of the farmhouse. Rain was dripping down his neck and he shivered as he knocked. The door was opened by a short, homely looking woman who stood there giving him an inquisitive stare. Her brow creased at the sight of the exhausted looking man who was dripping rain all over her doorstep. Without waiting for an explanation she reached out and pulled him inside. Joss found himself in the cosy warmth of a kitchen where the aroma of roasting meat had him almost fainting from hunger.

'You look half-starved, boy. What are you doing wandering the lanes in this weather?' She got a towel from the cupboard and threw it to him. 'Get yourself dried and tell me what you were doing out there.'

Joss started to dry his hair, muttering something about having lost his way. He said he'd stopped for directions back to the main Penzance Road and to ask if he could buy some food.

'We can do better than that, boy. My Andrew and I were about to have dinner and there's plenty for another little 'un. You can call me Rosie.' She nodded to the fleshy, outsized man who had shuffled into the kitchen. 'This is Andrew. He's not out in the fields today on account of the weather.'

The man raised his arm in acknowledgement as he went

to the sink to wash his hands. 'Where are you making for, lad?' he called over his shoulder.

Joss swallowed. 'Truro,' he said. It was the first place that came into his head.

'Truro?' Andrew surveyed him from under straggly white eyebrows. 'You'll take a hell of a time getting there if you keep on in this direction.' He nodded to the outside. 'You need to be going right for Truro. Walk across the fields but keep the main road in sight.'

'You didn't give us your name,' Rosie said, her chins wobbling as she tilted her head at him.

Joss hesitated. He couldn't give his own name. 'James Bluitt,' he said.

'Well sit yourself down, James,' Rosie said. 'We don't get many visitors hereabouts. She heaved an enormous tin of roast beef from the oven and smiled at Joss's wide-eyed stare. 'Aye, I know it's a lot, but Andrew and I like our good healthy portions,' she said.

It was the best roast dinner Joss had ever tasted. He felt guilty accepting these people's hospitality, but folk like this would never understand the truth.

'My Rosie bakes the finest apple pie in all Cornwall,' Andrew informed him, giving his wife an adoring smile.

'I wouldn't question that,' Joss said, shovelling another spoonful of melt-in-the-mouth pastry into his mouth.

The rain was still lashing the window when Joss stood to leave.

'You can't go now!' Rosie struggled to her feet. She looked shocked. 'You'll catch your death out in this.'

Joss shook his head, reaching for his hoodie. 'I have to get on. I'm grateful for your hospitality.'

'Stay,' Rosie urged.

Andrew put his arm round his wife's shoulder and grinned. 'You know where we are now, lad, no need to stand on ceremony. It's not often my Rosie gets the chance to feed a stranger.'

The hospitality of this couple was not something Joss was used to. It made him feel even more guilty for leaving Morwenna. He didn't like that.

Nor did he like Rosie standing by the door shaking her head as she waved him off, even if she did stuff a large slice of pie in his rucksack.

It was early evening before the rain finally eased. Joss found himself a dry, straw-filled barn. He'd thought a lot about what had happened over the previous days and couldn't believe how stupid he'd been. He should have stayed and made sure he was doing the right thing, but guilt was taking him back to that clifftop again. Morwenna's green eyes bored into his mind.

Poor Morwenna. He shouldn't have left her but his first instinct had been to run. It was time to make amends for that mistake.

CHAPTER 9

'What about the church cleaner?' Will asked. 'You mentioned her earlier.' They were back in the car park at the heritage centre.

'I'll handle that,' Sam said. 'Although from what Loveday said I doubt if it has anything to do with our case. Anyway, you get off home, Will, something tells me tomorrow is going to be a busy one.'

He had already spoken to the Reverend Sara Corey and arranged to meet her and the cleaner Jess Tandy at the church.

'She'll hate this, you know. She already thinks too much of a fuss has been made,' Loveday said after they'd left Maya's cottage and were walking to the church.

'If the woman was attacked she needs to report it,' Sam said.

'She won't do that.'

'That's why I've asked the vicar to be present when I interview her. We need to inject some common sense into whatever this is.'

Loveday slid him a look. 'And you think a vicar you've

never met will do this?'

'Why not? She knows the woman.'

Jess and the Reverend Sara were already in the church when Sam and Loveday walked in.

'You know of course that this is a complete waste of time.' The cleaner's tone was huffy. 'I tripped and fell on the path outside the church. I'm sure that's what happened.' She touched the gash under her eye. 'I must have hit it on a stone. It's really dark out there at night.'

'But you said there were two men. You said you'd been attacked. You came back this morning to make sure the church hadn't been burgled,' Loveday said.

The cleaner looked embarrassed. 'I was just…' She hesitated. 'I was making sure.'

'And you did right, Jess, but you should have called me. We could have checked the church together.' The Rev Sara Corey's response was only mildly chiding.

She turned, her smile travelling from Loveday to Sam as she introduced herself.

'I take it you found nothing amiss in the church?' Sam said, looking around.

'Everything appears to be normal. If there had been an intended break-in last night, Jess's arrival could have frightened them off.'

Jess tutted. 'I told you. There were no burglars. I imagined that. This is a scary old church.'

The vicar touched her arm. 'Our church is home to many precious artifacts.' She pointed to an ornately framed painting of a mermaid on a rock.

'Locals still tell the tale of the local lad who was so entranced by the mermaid's song that he followed her into the sea. That fable lives on to this day.'

Her eyes were still on the painting.

'You surely don't believe it,' Sam said.

Sara shrugged. 'Who knows. The legend has inspired many works of poetry, literature and art.'

She turned, indicating a carved image on the wall of a side chapel. 'That's St Piran. You must have heard of him, Inspector?'

'The patron saint of miners, yes I've heard of him.'

'DI Kitto is from Redruth,' Loveday said. 'Plenty of mines in that part of the world.'

Sam's eyes had rested on the carving.

'Beautiful, isn't it?' Sara said, following his gaze.

'Is it valuable?' Sam asked.

'Not in the way you mean,' Sara said. 'But to us it's priceless.'

Sam walked over to the little chapel. He could see no sign of any security protection for the St Piran. The carving was mounted on a wooden plinth bolted into the stone wall.

'How did this come to be in your church, vicar?' Loveday asked. Her knowledge of Cornish history was adequate for a journalist working in the county, but it would never match Maya's expertise in the subject. She would know all about this.

Sara was nodding. 'West Penwith was a very important mining area at one time. The people here believed in the teachings of St Piran.'

'He came to Cornwall from Ireland, didn't he?' Loveday interrupted.

'So the story goes,' Sara said. 'Way back in the fifth century, St Piran is reported to have been flung into the sea in Ireland.

'Despite having been cast aside with a millstone around his neck he miraculously floated across the water to Cornwall and landed on Perran Beach at Perranporth. It was here he built his oratory amongst the sand dunes. People would come from miles around to hear him preach there.'

'So this carving is very old,' Sam said.

Sara sucked in her bottom lip considering this. 'No one knows how old it is, but certainly centuries.'

'Doesn't that make it vulnerable to theft?'

'It's not something the church has ever seriously considered. I mean, an ancient Cornish saint? Who, apart from us, would be interested in taking that?'

Sam raised an eyebrow. 'You'd be surprised.'

He reached into his pocket and drew out the photo of Morwenna Chenoweth and her boyfriend Joss Teague. He showed it to both women. 'Do you recognize either of these people?'

Jess leaned forward for a better look at the images. 'That's her,' she said, pointing. 'That's the woman who was in church on Sunday. The one that sat at the back there.'

'I thought you didn't get a good look at her.' Loveday was remembering what the woman had told her and Maya earlier. It confirmed Maya's description of how the woman had kept her head down and the hood of her cloak pulled over her face. It had sounded deliberate as though she'd been trying to protect her identity.

'It's true I didn't see her face, not then, but there had been something familiar about her. Looking at this photo now I'm sure she's the same young woman I've seen about the church.'

'Other than when a service was taking place?' Sam wanted to know.

Jess nodded. 'The vicar will tell you. We get a lot of visitors coming to see our church and this girl has been here more than once.'

Sara took the photo from Sam. 'Yes. I've seen her wandering about the church too.'

Loveday was looking at the photo over Sam's shoulder. 'You won't believe this, but I think I've met this woman.'

Sam spun round to stare at her. 'You know her?'

Loveday gave a hesitant nod. 'I think so,' she said slowly, her eyes on the photo. 'No, I'm sure. This woman was a candidate for Maya's job.'

* * *

SAM WAS quiet later as they drove to Marazion. Maya had confirmed previously meeting Morwenna when she'd brought her class of children to the heritage centre. At the time he'd thought it strange that she hadn't recognized the same person in church, even if she hadn't seen the woman's face. He'd been shocked when Loveday confirmed Morwenna had been a candidate for the job that had been awarded to Maya. Earlier he had dismissed Will Tregellis's suggestion that Maya had somehow been involved in the teacher's untimely death. This was Loveday's friend. How could she possibly have been involved in a murder? He needed to think about this.

He was aware of Loveday studying him as they turned into their drive. 'OK, Sam,' she said. 'Are you going to share what's bothering you, or am I to be kept in the dark?'

'You know I can't discuss the case.' There was no way he was going to tell her that Maya could be more involved in this than she was saying, however, questions had to be asked. He needed to choose his time, but Loveday wasn't about to let it go.

In the kitchen her hands were on her hips, her pose defiant as she faced up to him. 'Are we forgetting who led you to finding Morwenna's body in the first place?'

Sam sighed. 'Don't make this difficult for me, Loveday.'

'I'm not,' she said, shrugging off her jacket and hanging it on the hook behind the door. She tried a coy smile. 'I only want to help.' She slid her arms around his waist. 'Let me help,' she coaxed.

Sam looked down at her, tilting his head. 'You can't get round me that way, Loveday.'

'Can't I?'

He laughed. 'Behave yourself.' But he pulled her arms tighter around him. 'There is something you can do.'

She raised an eyebrow.

'Tell me about those candidate interviews,' he said. 'I'd forgotten you were on the panel.'

'I was there more as a courtesy because I had donated the land. It wasn't for my limited historical knowledge. The other two panel members were from museum backgrounds. They knew their stuff. Maya was chosen on her merit and experience. It had nothing to do with us being friends.'

'OK, I get that,' Sam said. 'How many candidates were there?'

Loveday screwed up her face, thinking. 'Six.'

'Did they meet each other before the interviews?' He hoped he'd slipped in the question casually, but Loveday immediately seized on it. '

'If they had met then Maya would have recognized Morwenna. So no, they didn't. If I remember correctly the six candidates were split into two sessions, three in the morning and three in the afternoon. Maya and Morwenna were interviewed at different sessions.'

'Can you recall Morwenna's interview?' Sam asked.

'I can, as it happens. She was impressive. It was a toss-up between her and Maya who got the job.' She paused. 'I think Morwenna took it hard when she wasn't successful.'

'Why do you say that?'

'She asked for feedback of the panel's decision. In fact she basically demanded to know why the job had gone to Maya and not her.'

Sam needed to think about this. He would discuss it with Will in the morning.

CHAPTER 10

On Tuesday evening Joss Teague walked into Penzance Police Station. The sergeant at the reception desk raised an eyebrow.

Joss swallowed and squared his shoulders. 'I think you've been looking for me,' he said.

Sam had been about to leave for the day when he was told the man was in the building. His spirits rose. Could this be the breakthrough they needed? He instructed that Teague be put into an interview room where he could be viewed from the other side of a two way mirror. Sam's mouth pursed into a hard line as he stood watching the man.

His restless pacing was interesting. He was clearly agitated, but then his girlfriend had been murdered and now he was about to be interviewed by the police. He was bound to be distressed, but was this something more?

'What d'you think, boss?' Will said as he came into the viewing room and stood beside Sam. 'Does he look guilty or what?'

'If we could charge suspects on how they looked our cells

would be bursting at the seams.' Sam sighed. 'Let's hear what Mr Teague has to say for himself.'

Joss Teague eyed them suspiciously as they entered, but he took the seat Will was indicating.

'You're a difficult man to track down, Mr Teague,' Sam said. 'I'd go so far as thinking you've been trying to avoid us. Why would that be?'

'I had nothing to do with Morwenna's death.' Joss's wild look went from one to the other. 'I just wanted to make that clear.'

'How did you know she was dead?'

'I read the papers,' he lied. 'It was all over the news.'

Sam raised an eyebrow. The body had only been found yesterday. She hadn't even been officially identified. So why this ridiculous lie? He took a breath. 'And yet you didn't come forward? You must see how that concerns us.'

Joss pushed his fingers through the tangle of long curly dark hair and shook his head. 'You don't understand. I couldn't come forward. If that man knew I'd seen him kill Morwenna he would have come after me too.'

Sam and Will exchanged a look. 'You witnessed the murder?' Sam said.

Joss gave a miserable nod. 'I should have tackled him, brought a rock crashing down on his head or something, but I didn't. I couldn't move. I just crouched there behind that headstone, trembling.'

'Headstone?' Sam repeated.

'Fenwick churchyard. Morwenna was obsessed with the place. There's a carving of an ancient Cornish saint. She was fixated on it. She went there all the time to sketch it and take photos for the book she was writing. She was into history, everything old interested her, especially ancient tales of Cornwall.' He looked up and met Sam's gaze. His eyes showed he was back there in the churchyard with Morwenna.

'It's a lovely old church. I could understand why Morwenna was so drawn to it. We were wandering amongst the headstones and taking photos when we noticed two people cowering behind the church. They were whispering to each other but occasional phrases drifted in our direction.'

'What phrases?' Will asked.

'They were whispering about breaking into the church and stealing the carving. Morwenna was horrified. If it had been up to her she would have stormed over there and tackled them, but I grabbed her arm and got her away.

'She wanted to go straight to the police. I persuaded her not to, not until we had more information.' Joss hung his head. 'I didn't realize she would translate that into staking out the church every night. She had this idea of getting a picture on her phone, catching them in the act so to speak. I told her she couldn't go there alone, which is why I was with her that night.'

Sam was still curious to know why the man had been so against reporting what they'd heard to the police, but he didn't want to interrupt his flow. Joss continued.

'We were hiding in the churchyard when the pub across the road closed. I'd been beginning to wish I'd brought a flask or something stronger.

'We crouched lower behind the headstones when we heard the car turn up. Two people got out. I'd already warned Morwenna against any heroics. I told her we were only there to observe and get evidence.'

'Go on,' Sam said.

'Morwenna must have stirred or something because one of the people suddenly swung round and spotted her. She sprang up, pushing me back down behind the headstone. The man grabbed her but she wouldn't stop struggling. He had a spanner or something in his hand and he brought it down on Morwenna's head.

'I froze. I couldn't see too clearly in the dark but I knew she was on the ground and not moving. I didn't know what to do. I couldn't help Morwenna. I couldn't tackle both of these people.

'I saw one of them bundling her into the boot of the car. If I showed myself they would have bludgeoned me to death.'

He looked up, his eyes glistening with tears. 'I know what you're thinking. You think I should have tried to help Morwenna.'

Sam shrugged. 'Who knows. You made a judgement call. We could speculate all day on the *what ifs.*'

'Why did you stop Morwenna from coming to us in the first place?' Will asked.

Joss rolled his eyes in a gesture of frustration. 'Because it wouldn't have helped.' His voice was rising. 'You would have asked us to identify the two people we overheard doing the plotting. We might even have had to take part in an ID parade.' His eyes were wild. 'I couldn't do that. Don't you understand? I couldn't get involved again.'

Will screwed up his face. 'No, we don't understand. Suppose you tell us exactly why you couldn't get involved?'

Joss put his hands on the table and splayed his fingers, staring at them as though he would somehow find the answer there. He looked up and nodded to the recording equipment. 'Can we have that off?'

Sam's hard stare never left the man's face. 'We'll take a comfort break,' he said, nodding to Will to switch off the recorder.

Joss's gaze travelled from one detective to the other. He swallowed. 'I'm not Joss Teague. It was the name they gave me.'

Sam blinked. 'Who gave you?'

'Your lot. It was part of the deal if I gave evidence in a court case.'

Realization was starting to dawn. 'You're on a police protection programme,' Sam said. 'You should have told us.'

'That would have defeated the purpose, don't you think?' Joss sighed. 'Before I walked in here, Morwenna was the only one who knew about my past. Now you two know as well. It's only a matter of time before the rest of the world knows and I'm a dead man.

'It was my evidence that put Abel Caplan away for thirty years. His brother, Aaron, yelled across the courtroom that I would pay for what I'd done. I can still see his eyes bulging at me. Pure hatred it was. *"I'll get you, Prentice,"* he spat at me. *"When you least expect it, I'll be there."'* He shuddered.

Sam was silently chastising himself for not realizing sooner that the man was on a protection programme. All the signs had been there – no details about any employer before the Penzance firm, no trace of any family, in fact nothing beyond two years ago.

'If what you tell us has no bearing on our current investigations it will remain in this room. You have my word on that,' Sam said.

The man sat silently for a few moments, his head bowed as though he wasn't sure where to begin.

'Take your time,' Sam said. 'Start at the beginning.'

Joss Teague took a deep breath. 'My real name is Martin Prentice. Before all this happened, I was a porter in a London auction house. I was so keen to learn the trade that I used to stay on after everyone had gone home. I know it will sound strange but I liked to set myself the challenge of valuing antiques that had come in that day. Cutting to the chase, one evening, I found a stash of drugs hidden in a bureau.' His voice was shaking. 'Everything happened so quickly after that. I suddenly realized I wasn't alone. Somebody was creeping about amongst the antiques. I stuffed the package back into the bureau and found a hiding place. My heart was thumping.

'I watched the intruder come closer. He found the bureau and began to yank out the drawers. I knew he was looking for the drugs. And then he found them. He snatched up the package and made for the back door into the lane.

'I followed him. Well, I wanted to make sure he had gone. There was a car in the lane. The driver got out. I saw him knife the intruder and bundle him into the boot before driving off at speed with the drugs.'

Joss Teague swallowed. 'If I'd thought about it I would have got out of there, not told anyone what I'd witnessed, not got involved.'

'But you didn't,' Will said. 'You called the police and reported it. You did the right thing.'

Joss frowned. 'Did I? You can't imagine what it's like to be constantly looking over your shoulder, to shake with fear every time you see somebody looking at you. Once I'm recognized I'm a sitting target for getting a knife in my back.

'You'll never know how often I wished I had looked the other way that night. I should never have identified that killer as Abel Caplan. I didn't know he and his brother, Aaron, were big-time London drug barons.'

He paused, taking a breath. 'The police assured me if I gave evidence and helped convict Abel they would protect me. I wasn't happy about going to court and pointing the finger, but they persuaded me it was the right thing to do.

'I was to be put on a witness protection scheme and given a new identity.' He touched his hair. 'It used to be blond, but they suggested I dyed it brown and let it grow. I was no longer Martin Prentice. I was Joss Teague. My parents were dead, but my dad was from Cornwall, which is why I moved here. It was a long way from London and I suppose I felt it would be safer.'

He sighed. 'Anyway, I got a job as an apprentice builder with a Penzance firm, James Bluitt. I met Morwenna when we were working at the school where she teaches in St Ives.' He put up his hands in a gesture of helplessness. 'I still can't believe she's gone.'

Will waited until he got the nod of consent from Sam before taking over the questioning. 'Tell us about Morwenna, Joss. What was she like?'

A wistful smile crossed Joss Teague's face. 'She was beautiful and I don't just mean how she looked. Inside she was beautiful. She was crazy, adventurous, kind. I loved how she cared so much about things.' He shook his head slowly, remembering. 'She changed completely when she didn't get that job at the heritage centre. She would have been perfect for it, but it went to somebody else.'

Sam and Will exchanged a look. Sam said, 'Tell us again about these two men you saw in the churchyard.'

Joss looked up, frowning. 'Did I say it was two men?'

'Wasn't it?' Sam was staring at him.

'I couldn't be sure,' Joss said slowly. 'But one of them could have been a woman.'

CHAPTER 11

*I*f what Joss Teague told them was true they could strike him from their list of suspects, Sam reflected. But then he was hardly likely to admit to murder. They needed to know more about this man.

'You say Morwenna changed,' Sam quizzed. 'In what way?'

Joss spread his fingers out on the table and gave a long sigh. 'Little things. She would pick up on everything I said. She was cross so often that I felt I couldn't do anything right for her.' He shrugged. 'I thought she loved teaching but she was very bitter about not getting that job.'

'Did she talk about it?' Will asked.

'She told me some of the stuff she'd been doing. I thought it was childish.'

Will frowned. 'What kind of stuff?'

'She told me about going into the centre after it had closed and moving things around.'

'How do you mean?' Sam asked. 'What kind of things did she move around?'

'She would shift some of the displays, put them in different places. Rearrange files in the filing cabinet so they appeared disorganized, that kind of thing.' He looked up and met Sam's stare. 'I told you it was childish but Morwenna was determined to discredit that Maya woman.'

'But why?'

'Because she was jealous, of course. If she could persuade people that Maya was not fit for the job they might dismiss her and the job would be advertised again.' He sighed. 'I know it sounds crazy but you don't know what Morwenna has been like lately.'

Sam was remembering Loveday's description of Tom Scobey's fears for Maya's mental health. Parts of the puzzle seemed to be falling into place, but he had no idea how helpful that was going to be.

'How did Morwenna get into the building?' he asked.

'Didn't I say? Bluitt got the contract to do part of the construction work on the new building. I had a key. It had to be handed back when the job was completed of course, but at Morwenna's request I made a copy.'

Sam blew out a long sigh. 'So Morwenna could come and go at the centre as she pleased?'

Joss examined his spread fingers again. 'More or less, but it wasn't all about making mischief. Morwenna was studying the St Piran stories. She said it was easier if she could do that in the evenings and not have to make specific visits to the centre during opening hours when she was teaching anyway.'

Sam was remembering her house in Penzance. The curious artifacts she'd collected were making sense now. 'So Morwenna was interested in the St Piran carving?'

Joss nodded. 'I was into antiques, but for me it was more about the skill, the craftsmanship that went into producing them. That's why I loved working in the antiques house in

London. Morwenna was more concerned about immersing herself in the whole picture. She wanted to know the history, who had owned the piece over the years, what had happened to it in that time.

'She was totally fascinated by that carving in the church. It horrified her that someone had planned to steal it. It belonged there, you see. She knew of course that the saint wasn't real but she said she could feel his presence when she sat in that church.'

He swallowed, the spark of tears returning to his eyes. 'It was that obsession that killed her.'

Sam sat back in his chair. He was still trying to assess whether they could believe this man. Was he putting on a clever show or was he genuinely distressed? 'You'll have to explain that,' he said quietly.

Joss buried his face in his hands and shook his head. 'It's all my fault,' he said. 'I should have protected her, but I didn't. I was a coward. It would never have happened if we hadn't been in the churchyard that night.'

'Tell us again what happened,' Sam said.

'I saw them attack her. I saw her fall. They took her away.'

'You're sure of this?' Sam said.

'Yes, I told you. They panicked when they saw Morwenna. It was chaotic after that but I definitely saw her being attacked.'

Joss held his head and rocked from side to side. 'They killed her,' he sobbed. 'They killed my Morwenna.'

Sam's expression gave nothing away, but his thoughts were in turmoil. Joss Teague's version of events could have been carefully constructed to keep him in the clear. Could they really believe Morwenna's killer or killers had been the ones who were planning to rob the church? If that was true, why hadn't her attackers spotted Teague in the churchyard?

He wasn't sure about any of this and judging by Will's body language, his sergeant felt the same.

Morwenna's body had been found on the cliff top at Carn Hendra. What was she doing there? It didn't tally with what they were being told. If their victim had died in that church-yard they still had to work out why her body had been taken to the heritage centre. Moving her there felt like the kind of thing Joss himself might have done. He looked at the man, weighing up the possibilities. If they went along with his story about Morwenna's attackers, maybe they hadn't carried off her body.

Had Joss waited in the churchyard until they'd gone and then carried her body to the heritage centre? Surely it would have been more appropriate to leave her at the church she loved and call the police?

And now they had to figure out how that broken body came to be found on the cliff path. And her cloak – had it been thrown onto the rocks as a distraction, something to take attention away from the body lying nearby? Sam shook his head. This case got more confusing by the minute.

'Am I under arrest?' Joss's shoulders slumped as his look of misery went from one to the other.

Sam ignored the question. 'Would you recognize these people again?'

Joss shook his head. 'It was dark and I didn't see their faces.'

'Let's put it another way,' Sam said. 'The two people you saw plotting to steal the St Piran carving…were they the same ones who attacked Morwenna?'

'I think so.'

'Just think?' Will said.

Joss Teague threw his arms up in frustration. 'Do you think I haven't gone over this in my mind a million times?'

His voice was rising. 'If I could describe these people then I would. I just don't know.'

Sam was studying the man's body language. His distress seemed real enough. Did he deserve to be given the benefit of the doubt? He would need to think about that.

CHAPTER 12

'Come through to the kitchen. I'm giving April Rose her breakfast,' Maya called over her shoulder as Sam followed her into the cottage. 'Sometimes I think this child is a turbocharged eating machine.' She looked up, frowning at Sam's expression. 'Please tell me this isn't more bad news.'

'It's not,' Sam said, dodging a spoonful of strawberry yoghurt as April Rose banged noisily on the tray of her high chair. 'But you might want to sit down.'

'Sounds ominous,' Maya said, taking charge of April Rose's spoon and feeding her more yoghurt.

'We interviewed a young man yesterday. Does the name Morwenna Chenoweth mean anything to you?'

Maya frowned, trying to remember. 'It's familiar. Can't say I know her though.'

'We think she's the one who brought her class of primary children to the heritage centre.'

'Morwenna,' Maya said quietly, a shiver sweeping through her. 'So that was her name.'

Sam paused. 'She was also a candidate for your job.'

'Was she? I never met the other people on the shortlist.'

She stared at him. 'Is that connected to what happened to her?'

'We don't know. I don't think so.'

Maya's eyes were wide. 'It was definitely her body you found out on the clifftop?'

Sam nodded. 'The head teacher from her school identified her body.'

Maya's head shook slowly. 'And the girl I saw dead at the heritage centre? Was that her too?'

'We believe so. We're still investigating how her body turned up on the clifftop.'

April Rose began to thump on her table, annoyed she was losing her mother's full attention. Maya reached out and absent-mindedly stroked the child's hair.

'We interviewed Morwenna's boyfriend yesterday,' Sam said, watching her. She was still looking shocked. 'According to him, Morwenna was very bitter that she didn't get the job at the heritage centre. From what he told us she was a particularly vindictive young woman who set out to discredit you.'

Maya's brow wrinkled. 'Discredit me? But why? I don't understand.'

'She set traps, moving files around to appear you had misplaced them, altering diary appointments, even moving sets and displays.'

'That was her?' Maya said slowly, her voice incredulous as the implication of what she was hearing sank in. 'How did she get into the building? We were meticulous about security.'

'She had a key. Her boyfriend works with a local contractor who was involved in the original construction of the centre. He said Morwenna persuaded him to make a copy of the key.'

Maya met Sam's eyes. 'So I'm not going mad?'

Sam shook his head, smiling. 'We have no evidence that you're going mad.'

'And I can go back to work?'

'Give it a day or two.'

Maya pulled a face. 'I feel really guilty now, as if it's my fault that this poor girl died.'

'What happened to Morwenna was not your fault. You didn't make her hang around the centre.' Sam shook his head. 'She did her best to discredit you, Maya. I'm not saying she deserved what happened to her, but it had nothing to do with you.'

April Rose let out a demanding yell and began to bang her little fists on her table. Maya turned to her, smiling. 'Oh, baby, are we ignoring you?' She picked up the sticky spoon and began to feed her the remainder of the yoghurt.

'Poor Morwenna,' she said. 'I remember her now. She spoke to me when she brought the children to the centre.'

Sam's ears pricked up. 'She spoke to you?'

Maya nodded. 'Yes, it's coming back to me. She was particularly interested in St Piran. We have a display dedicated to him.'

'St Piran?' Sam repeated. Well at least that tallied with what Teague had told them.

Sam knew the saint's story. Having been born and brought up in Redruth he was no stranger to the mining industry. It once provided most families in the area with a living and St Piran was the patron saint of mining. There was even a special day dedicated to him on March 5 when the local schoolchildren got together to celebrate him.

Pubs across the county also got involved for the Trelawny Shout when everyone sang 'The Song of the Western Men'. It was a song celebrating how brave and amazing Cornishmen were. Sam wasn't about to disagree with those sentiments.

'There's an old carving of St Piran in the church,' Maya

said. 'And we have much more information at the centre.'

Sam nodded. The setting for the carving was appropriate. The fields around the area were littered with mine shafts, and the remains of engine houses dominated the skyline.

'I remember walking around the exhibition with this teacher and her class. The children were fascinated,' Maya said. 'I also remember how surprised I was by her knowledge. We have display boards on show but this Morwenna described the story of how St Piran crossed the sea to Cornwall from Ireland and built a chapel on the sand at Perranporth.' She smiled. 'It was wonderful seeing the little ones' eyes grow wide when she described how St Piran was sitting on the beach in front of his fire when the great firestone cracked and a cross of melted tin oozed out.'

She looked up. 'It's said that white cross on the black firestone was the origins of the Cornish flag.'

Sam was still watching her. 'I take it Loveday has not told you.'

Maya's head swung round to him. 'Not told me what?'

'We think there was an attempt to steal the carving.'

'What?' She frowned, trying to make sense of what she was hearing. 'Why on earth would anyone want to steal it?'

'It's rare antiquity,' Sam said quietly.

'Undoubtedly, and I certainly wouldn't refuse it wall space in the heritage centre, but it's not like the crown jewels. It's certainly collectable but surely not valuable.'

Sam could see April Rose's little brows coming together in an angry frown. She was losing her mother's attention again and she wasn't liking that. 'I think I better leave you two to your breakfasts,' he said, putting up a hand when Maya made to see him out.

'Thanks for coming, Sam,' she called after him as he left. 'And thanks for taking that weight off my mind. I can't tell you how much that means.'

CHAPTER 13

'*I* don't need you to babysit me anymore, Loveday, not now everyone accepts I didn't imagine that body. At least I know I'm not going mad.'

Loveday smiled into the phone. 'No one thought you were,' she said.

'Tom did. I know he asked you to keep an eye on me.'

'He cares about you.'

'Maybe, but it's not necessary. It's time Tom learned I can look after myself.'

Loveday wasn't so sure about that, but arguing the point wasn't likely to help.

'Sam says we can open the centre again in a day or so.'

'Really? That's great news. He tells me nothing.'

Maya laughed. 'It is. I can't tell you how much I'm longing to get back to normal.'

'Don't be in too much of a hurry to do that,' Loveday said quietly. 'You've been through a bad time. Just be kind to yourself.'

'Of course I will. I have April Rose to consider as well.'

94

She paused. 'And speaking of her...' A loud wail went up in the background.

Loveday smiled. 'I can hear you have your hands full. Let me know when Sam says you can reopen the centre,' she added as they ended the call.

The quick knock on Loveday's back door could only be one person. 'Come in, Cassie,' she called.

Cassie Trevillick was her neighbour in the big house on the opposite side of the drive. Her GP husband, Adam, ran his surgery from a room at the back of their house. And her children, Sophie and Leo, called Loveday 'auntie'.

'Got a minute?' she asked, breezing in.

Loveday levelled a look at her friend. 'You're up to something. I can tell.'

Cassie gave her an indignant frown. 'I came to offer you the experience of a lifetime, but if you're not interested I can go on my own.'

'Interested in what?'

'Interested in a sneak peek at how the other half live.'

'Really?'

'That's right. There's a superyacht in Falmouth Harbour and they've only invited me on board to repair some upholstery.' She smiled. 'I was thinking you could be my assistant.'

Cassie ran a successful business refurbishing the interiors of expensive yachts. The fact that she was also more than a little unconventional just added to her appeal.

'You said you were taking time off from the magazine this week. So are you coming or not?' She had already turned and was heading for the back door and the big green four-by-four in the drive.

Loveday stared after her. In her head she was scrolling through the 'To Do' list she had planned in order to make the best use of the time her boss, Merrick Tremayne, had insisted she booked off work. They were nearly halfway through the week and she wasn't remotely close to tackling that list.

'Well?' Cassie called back. 'Are you coming or not?'

Loveday sighed as she grabbed her bag and reached for her jacket. The vehicle's engine was already running. 'Wait for me,' she called as she hurried after Cassie to the Range Rover and climbed in beside her.

They moved off up the drive and past the seafront, heading for the A30 and Falmouth.

'So tell me about this superyacht. How come they contacted you? I would have thought they'd have any number of top interior designers lined up to do repair jobs.'

Cassie slid her an indignant look. 'Quite possibly, but I happen to be the top interior designer they chose.'

Loveday smiled. Cassie's exclusive refurbishing services were always much in demand with Cornwall's wealthy yachting community.

'Besides,' Cassie said, 'I think this is a bit of a rush job. They're expecting the repairs to be completed this afternoon.'

'I see.' Loveday was enjoying settling back into the Range Rover's soft leather upholstery as they sped to Falmouth.

* * *

'WE'RE HERE,' Cassie said, pulling into a parking space at the town's marina. 'And there she is.'

Loveday followed her gaze to the sleek lines of the beautiful white motor yacht anchored outside Falmouth Harbour.

'That's the *Moonflyer*,' Cassie said. 'Forty-two metres of custom-built luxury with guest accommodation for twelve people in five generously sized en suite staterooms. There's a comfortable lounge and dining area with a bar plus a backgammon table and a bridge deck equipped with a range of fitness equipment that can be used as a private gym or yoga studio for early morning workouts.'

'Sounds like you swallowed the brochure,' Loveday said.

'I didn't swallow it, but I did read it. It's part of the job to do your research.'

Loveday couldn't argue with that.

'Over there, look!' Cassie pointed. 'They've sent the tender for us.' She heaved a large sample bag from the back of the Range Rover and handed Loveday her briefcase. They made their way to the high-speed tender where a young man with the *Moonflyer* logo displayed on his pristine white top, took their bags and helped them on board.

Loveday stifled a gasp as they approached the yacht. 'I feel we should be taking our shoes off before stepping onto that.'

A young officer came forward to greet them as they climbed on board. 'James Crawford,' he said, shaking hands with each of them in turn. 'I'm the bosun on *Moonflyer*. I was the one who contacted you, Mrs Trevillick. I apologize for the short notice but we're expecting Mr Cassavetes tomorrow.

'Our main worry is the furnishings in the owner's master suite. One of the maids noticed a tear in one of the cushions. We need you to go over all the soft furnishings on board and make the necessary repairs by the end of business today.' He swung round to look at Cassie. 'I presume you can do that?'

Cassie gave him her professional smile. 'Of course we can. If you could just show us over the yacht, my assistant and I will start our inspection.'

Loveday adopted what she hoped was a knowledgeable expression as she and Cassie followed the bosun on their tour of the *Moonflyer*.

'We can accommodate twelve guests in five generously sized en suite staterooms,' the bosun began to explain.

Loveday hid a smile. The man was quoting directly from the yacht's promotional brochure as Cassie had done.

They followed him into a larger stateroom where the sheets on the bed were soft and creamy as opposed to the crisp white in all the other bedrooms. 'This is the owner's stateroom.' He stepped forward and picked up one of three brocade-covered bolsters from the bed. 'The maid noticed a gap on the side here.' He ran his fingers over the cushion. 'You see here where the seam has come apart?'

Cassie glanced at Loveday and they both nodded.

'This especially has to take priority. Mr Cassavetes is most particular. Everything has to be pristine.'

Loveday's attention had wandered to a small silver-framed photograph on the bedside table. It looked familiar. She edged closer to it, but the bosun was already taking his leave.

'You will find members of our crew everywhere on the vessel. If you need anything just ask one of them.' His smile went from one to the other. 'I'll leave you ladies to get on with your work.' He gave a little bow before turning and leaving them alone in the sumptuous stateroom.

Loveday picked up the photo frame, studying in the picture. She beckoned Cassie over. 'Recognize anyone here?'

Cassie peered over her shoulder. 'No, who is it? I know you're dying to tell me.'

'That's it. I know who it is. What I don't know is what it's doing here beside the bed of a Greek billionaire.'

Loveday had already taken her phone from her pocket and was snapping a picture of the photograph. 'Unless I'm much mistaken, this is a picture of Maya and her mother.'

'Maya?' Cassie was interested now. 'Are you sure?'

'Not 100%, but pretty sure. There's an identical photo in Maya's bedroom at the cottage. I've seen it.'

Cassie's stare was confused. 'If that's Maya then what is she doing here?'

'I don't know, but I think we should find out.'

Cassie put up at hand. 'Wait a minute. What's all this *we* business? I'm not getting involved. Do you want me to lose this very lucrative little job?'

'Of course not,' Loveday said. 'All we have to do is keep our eyes open.'

'You keep your eyes open,' Cassie said. 'I have work to do.' She was already beginning to lay out her repair kit.

'Oh, Cassie. I'm sorry. I came to help and I'm getting under your feet. Tell me what I can do.'

'You can set these things out for me,' Cassie said. 'Put them on that blue linen square so I can see what I'm doing.'

Loveday followed Cassie's instructions and then stood back, watching her needle weave expertly over the damaged cushion creating one invisible stitch after the other. 'There,' she said, sitting up and smoothing a hand over the cushion. 'I challenge anyone to find that repair.'

'I'm impressed,' Loveday said. 'Not that I was expecting anything less than perfection.' She looked around her. 'What's next?'

Cassie was gathering her things together. 'We check out the upholstery in the rest of the yacht.'

The opportunity to explore *Moonflyer* was not something Loveday was likely to refuse, especially if it meant picking up information on the vessel's owner, the mysterious Mr Cassavetes.

Cassie was moving ahead, focusing on her microscopic examination of the sofas, chairs and cushions. They both turned when James Crawford came into the lounge. Cassie invited him to check out the repair she had already carried out in the owner's stateroom.

'I already have,' he informed her crisply. 'What about the

other things that need attention? How long do you estimate that will take? I don't want to hurry you but the owner is returning unexpectedly early and everything must be completed as soon as possible.'

Cassie closed the book she had been jotting notes in and gave the young bosun her professional smile. 'Things shouldn't be hurried if you want them done properly, Mr Crawford.'

'I know and I apologize for this but it's out of my control. Mr Cassavetes is already on his way. He should be here by 7pm, so if you could finish up what you're able to by then we will have to leave it at that.'

'Mr Cassavetes is Greek, isn't he?' Loveday said.

The bosun spun round, raising a surprised eyebrow at the question.

'I was wondering what the *Moonflyer* was doing in Cornwall,' Loveday continued. 'I would have thought most charters would start from somewhere in the Greek Islands.'

She could feel Cassie's eyes on her but it was a simple question.

'I'm not privy to the reasons why Mr Cassavetes makes his decisions. I expect he likes Cornwall. I believe he has family in the area.'

'Family?' Loveday repeated. 'That would explain the photograph of a child in his stateroom.'

Cassie was now staring daggers at her.

'I know nothing of that, Mr Cassavetes does not discuss his private affairs with his crew.' James Crawford was definitely being dismissive. He turned back to Cassie. 'I'm sure you want to get on. Let me know if there's anything you need.'

'Another 24 hours would be good,' Cassie muttered at the bosun's retreating back. She pushed her notebook and pen at

Loveday. 'If you really want to be useful you can write down what I say.'

'Of course,' Loveday said, taking it. 'But you must be curious too about that photo.'

'I'll be curious later,' Cassie said. 'Right now I have other things on my mind.' She had already started to examine seams and run her hand over the luxuriant fabrics and soft furnishings in the yacht's salon. She dictated two repairs needed. 'I need to check the other staterooms,' she said, hurrying off and leaving Loveday to run after her.

Neither of them noticed the time passing as Cassie's hand flew over her work.

Loveday knew it would be perfect, knowing how fastidious her friend was. It was 6pm when Cassie eventually sat back, looking around her. 'I'm not at all confident there isn't more to do here.'

Loveday smiled. 'Something tells me you would always find more to do.'

They sensed rather than heard the shuffle of feet as the crew assembled on the deck. 'I'm guessing that's the welcome party for the mysterious Mr Cassavetes,' Loveday said. 'Shall we go up and take a peek? I'm curious.'

They didn't expect to come face to face with the new arrival at the top of the stairs.

'I'm so sorry, Mr Cassavetes.' James Crawford flashed them an angry scowl. 'These ladies were just leaving.'

Amused brown eyes met Loveday's. 'Are you in such a great hurry?'

'I…err.' Loveday flashed Cassie a look. 'We wouldn't want to outstay our welcome.' Did she imagine she saw Cassie's eyes roll? This young man with the black curls falling over his forehead intrigued her. Surely this wasn't Spiro Cassavetes, the billionaire owner of the *Moonflyer*? She had expected an older man.

'I'm sure you lovely ladies could never outstay your welcome. Perhaps I could persuade you to join me for a cocktail before you hurry away?' He turned to the bosun. 'Show the ladies to the aft salon, James.' His smile included both of them. 'I'll join you presently.'

'I think the lord and master has returned,' Loveday whispered to Cassie as they followed the bosun to the upper deck.

CHAPTER 14

'Why are we here?' Cassie hissed out of the side of her mouth as a barman placed a glass of fizzing wine in front of her.

Loveday picked up her glass and took an appreciative sip. 'Sorry, Cassie. I couldn't miss an opportunity like this. I didn't mean to involve you.'

'I'm not involved,' Cassie hit back quickly. 'It's you that wants to delve into the Cassavetes family history.'

'You don't find this intriguing? Clearly the man we've just met is not Spiro. He's far too young.'

'That's because I'm Darius,' the voice behind them cut in. 'Spiro is my father.'

Loveday turned, a flush of embarrassment burning her cheeks. She felt like a child caught dipping her finger in the honey jar. 'I'm so sorry. I didn't realize you were there.'

'Apologies not necessary.' Darius Cassavetes waved a hand dismissing her fluster. The voice was low and seductive. She guessed that charming people came easily to this man.

'What's intriguing,' he smiled, 'is what you ladies are doing on board the *Moonflyer*.'

Cassie shot out her hand. 'Cassie Trevillick,' she said. 'Resplendent Yacht Interiors, Cornwall.' She pumped Darius's hand. 'This is my friend, Loveday Ross. She's the editor of *Cornish Folk* magazine.'

Darius raised an eyebrow and regarded them with a slow smile. 'Forgive me. I didn't realize I was in such illustrious company.'

'Your bosun, Mr Crawford, contacted me,' Cassie explained quickly. 'Emergency repair work was needed on some of the yacht's soft furnishings.'

'And I came along for the ride,' Loveday interrupted.

Darius lifted the cocktail that had been poured for him and saluted them before taking a sip. 'So you're interested in our family history, Miss Ross. What can I tell you?'

Now the subject had been raised, Loveday saw no reason to be coy. 'I understand the Cassavetes family have a particular interest in Cornwall?'

Darius was watching her, that slow smile still on his lips. The man was flirting with her. She would have to be careful.

'The interest is my father's,' he said.

'And yet it's you who is here.'

'My father arrives tomorrow. We sail around the Cornish coast and then onto the Med.' He smiled. 'Why don't you ladies join us. You would be very welcome and our private jet could fly you home from Crete.'

Cassie spluttered over the bubbles she was drinking and threw Loveday a *get us out of this* kind of look.

Darius's attention was still on Loveday. Had the man seriously expected her and Cassie to accept such an invitation? Judging by the expression in his glistening eyes, he had. And yet she didn't want to walk away from what could be a great professional opportunity.

She cleared her throat. 'Sadly Cassie and I have engagements that tie us up over the next few days but I would be able to come back to the yacht in the morning if you and your father could spare an hour for a quick interview.' She knew she was chancing her luck but she was still curious about that photo in the owner's stateroom.

Darius continued watching her with interest. 'You are very direct, Miss Ross.'

'I'm a journalist, Mr Cassavetes.' She waited. 'Should I bring a camera?'

The slow smile was back. 'Come for lunch,' he said. 'Both of you.'

Loveday ignored Cassie's frown. 'We'd love to,' she said.

Her friend's brow was still furrowed as the yacht's tender sped them back to shore. 'What makes you think that man doesn't intend kidnapping us?' She scowled.

'For his harem, you mean?' Loveday laughed. 'I don't think so. Where is your sense of adventure, Cassie? It'll be fun.'

Cassie's expression suggested otherwise. 'Didn't you see the way Darius looked at you? I've met men like him before and believe me they don't appreciate being crossed.'

The tender had arrived back at the slipway in Falmouth Harbour. Loveday reached forward and touched her friend's arm. 'I have no intention of crossing him, Cassie. I'll be too busy interviewing his father.'

* * *

LOVEDAY AND SAM dined on a fillet of megrim sole that evening, locally landed at Newlyn and sauteed in butter with a parsley sauce. It was served with new boiled potatoes and garden peas. A simple dish but one of Sam's favourites. Loveday waited until they had eaten before mentioning her afternoon with Cassie on the *Moonflyer*.

'I have to hand it to Cassie, she certainly gets around,' Sam said.

'And we've been invited back for lunch tomorrow, although it's part of an interview I'll be doing.'

'You're having lunch on the *Moonflyer*? You call that work?'

'Of course it's work,' Loveday said, reaching for her coffee. 'But I haven't told you the most interesting bit. Spiro Cassavetes, who owns the yacht, has a photo of Maya beside his bed.' She watched him for a reaction. It came quickly.

He sat up, staring at her. 'Cassavetes knows Maya? Has she ever mentioned him?'

'Not to me. And I'd be grateful if you didn't ask her. This has nothing to do with your case.'

'I'll be the judge of that,' Sam said. He was clearly still thinking about it.

Loveday wished she hadn't shared the information with him. Now she would have to speak to Maya first. She had hoped to run it past Tom before she approached Maya. She glanced at her watch. Maybe that was still possible. She uncurled herself from her chair. 'I'm going for a walk.'

'It's dark,' Sam protested.

But Loveday was already at the back door and grabbing her jacket from the hook. 'I won't go far,' she called back to him as she went out.

It was a still night and the seafront was deserted. She stood for a moment, breathing in the stillness and looking across the bay to where the lights of Penzance twinkled. She raised her phone, scrolling down her list of contacts, and tapped Tom's number.

'Loveday? Has something happened?' Her unexpected call had alarmed him.

'No, everything's fine, Tom,' she assured him. 'I know it's late but I need to run something past you. Do you know a man called Spiro Cassavetes?'

'Cassavetes?' he repeated. She was imagining his brow wrinkling. 'Everyone knows Spiro Cassavetes. What's this about?'

Loveday smiled. Everyone in Tom's circle perhaps, but out in the real world where the less wealthy like her resided, things were different.

'Does Maya know him? I mean would you have introduced them?'

The phone went silent and Loveday knew Tom was considering this. At last he said, 'I can't think of any way she would know him, unless there was a connection with Jamie. My son knew all sorts of people. I certainly never introduced either of them to him. Why are you asking?'

It was Loveday's turn to pause. She had intended to tell him about the photo by Spiro's bed but something told her to hold back. If the connection she suspected was right there was no telling what bag of tricks she might unleash. No, best to keep this to herself for now.

'Loveday?' Tom was still waiting for an answer. What on earth could she say?

'I'm sorry, Tom. I shouldn't have bothered you. I really only wanted a heads up as to what the man was like. I have an interview with him tomorrow and was considering how to approach it.'

'But you asked if Maya could have known him.'

Loveday had to think on her feet. She had to avoid lighting a touch paper that might set off a potential bonfire.

'It was a long shot. I thought it might be a way into the interview. With all your connections and the people Jamie might have known I wondered if Maya had mentioned Spiro.'

It was feeble as excuses went and Tom knew her better than to swallow this, but her fingers were crossed. It would have to do for now. She thanked Tom and ended the call.

'If you want to be alone I'll go back to the cottage,' the voice behind her said.

Loveday spun round and found herself gazing into Sam's dark eyes. She smiled. 'No, don't do that.' She linked her arm through his. 'Let's walk.'

A man in a jogging suit was walking a dog on the other side of the road and he waved to them.

Sam waved back. It had started to rain. He pulled up his collar. 'Were you planning to go far?'

Loveday gave him a teasing whack. 'You're such a wimp, Inspector Kitto. It's only a bit of rain.'

'I'll make a bargain with you.'

'Go on.' Loveday laughed.

'If we go back home now I'll make you a mug of hot chocolate.' He grinned down at her. 'And I won't ask Maya about Cassavetes, not unless it's obviously connected to the case.'

Loveday stretched up to kiss him. 'Thank you, Sam,' she said. 'Bring on the hot chocolate.'

CHAPTER 15

*C*assie was at the kitchen door as Sam left the cottage next morning. 'Just checking you can make your own way to Falmouth,' she said. Loveday could tell by the sparkle in her friend's eye that despite any concerns she might raise she was looking forward to meeting the great Spiro Cassavetes.

'No problem,' Loveday said. 'I'll see you on the slipway. Shall we say about noon?'

They watched Sam's Lexus crunch up the drive and turn right onto the seafront.

'I'm still not sure about this,' Cassie said. 'I hope you know what you're doing. I'm not forgetting the kind of scrapes you can get into.'

Loveday was viewing her meeting with Spiro Cassavetes on a more professional footing. She was already planning how to approach the situation. Interviewing people was her job, but this morning she was feeling nervous. She had already decided on playing it all by ear, but if she was to discover more about why that photograph was in that stateroom she would have to be discreet. Spiro Cassavetes was famous for avoiding the press, yet he must have agreed to this interview or Darius would surely have been in touch to cancel the event.

Cassie was waiting on the slipway when Loveday arrived in Falmouth later that morning. They travelled together on the tender out to the *Moonflyer*.

Although she could rely on quality photos from the camera in her phone Loveday had brought the magazine's camera and folding tripod. Apart from discovering what Maya's photo was doing in the private quarters of this posh yacht's owner, the interview had the potential to provide a great magazine feature and she didn't want to make any mistakes, not after she had persuaded Merrick to hold the front page.

It had been a cavalier suggestion to pull the magazine's intended features and replace them with the Cassavetes interview, but if it succeeded it would be a triumph for all of them.

Darius greeted them as they stepped on board the yacht. 'My father is looking forward to meeting you two ladies.' He smiled, extending his hand to Cassie and Loveday in turn to help them aboard.

They followed him into the salon where drinks had been poured. As they relaxed and sipped their drinks, Loveday glanced around. Through the sliding glass doors to the aft deck she could see a table set for lunch. It seemed they were to be given special treatment, or was lunch on board always this formal? She didn't hear the man's approach and looked up when Darius jumped to his feet. 'This is my father, Spiro Cassavetes,' he said. 'Father, these are the ladies I told you about last evening. This is Cassie.'

Spiro smiled and shook Cassie's hand.

'And Loveday,' Darius said. 'Cassie works on luxury

yachts and Loveday is the journalist who would like to interview you.'

The hand that took Loveday's was firm. She knew from her internet search that the man was 45, a self-made millionaire who grew up in poverty in Ano Mera, a village on the Greek island of Mykonos. He was one of five children, all of whom now worked in the family business.

She kept up the eye contact. 'Thank you for agreeing to this interview, sir.'

Cassavetes glanced across to his son. 'You have Darius to thank for that, not me.'

If Darius was embarrassed by his father's comment he certainly wasn't showing it. The smile was more dazzling than ever.

But it was the older man who'd caught Loveday's interest.

'You could have refused,' she said.

'Yes, I could have,' he agreed, nodding to the young woman who'd stepped forward to tell them their food was ready. 'I don't do many interviews, Miss Ross. My privacy is important to me. But Darius has persuaded me that since this is for a Cornish magazine, I should agree this one time.'

Loveday gave him what she hoped was her most charming smile. 'I promise not to let you down, Mr Cassavetes. There's a reason why our magazine is called *Cornish Folk*. We are exclusively about Cornwall and the people who live here.'

'But I don't live in Cornwall.'

'Perhaps not, but I understand that you have a love of our beautiful county. And you take every opportunity to call in here when it's possible.'

Cassavetes smiled. 'I can see Darius has been talking about me.'

'Only in the most glowing terms,' Loveday said.

Spiro nodded his approval as he led the others out of the salon.

Loveday took several shots of the Cassavetes men standing by the rail on the aft deck with the sun glinting on the water of the Carrick Roads behind them. She took a few more, framing her subjects with the background of the harbour and the ships. She was feeling pleased with herself. This might make an even better piece than she'd hoped.

Lunch was a pleasant affair although the lobster served to them was a bit rich for Loveday's lunchtime palate. But from the animated expression on Cassie's face she could see her friend was thoroughly enjoying the experience, especially when their host singled her out for praise.

'I admire a spirit of enterprise when I come across one and I see that in you, Cassie.' He smiled. 'If I may call you that.'

Cassie beamed back her approval.

'It was very clever of you to open a business such as yours here in Cornwall. I imagine there are many beautiful yachts here whose owners must require your expertise.'

'I studied textiles at college,' Cassie explained. 'It seemed like a sensible idea to merge that interest with my business head. Fortunately there are not too many other people providing my service here, so I'm successful.'

'Our bosun, Mr Crawford, tells me you've made some repairs to the soft furnishings in my stateroom. I have to admit I saw no evidence of your work. Which I suppose is exactly what you would wish.'

Loveday saw an opportunity to bring up the photo, but she had to do it now because she was running out of time.

'It was fascinating for me as Cassie's friend to have the chance to see how she works.'

'Loveday assisted me yesterday,' Cassie said quickly.

'I was also privileged to see more of your beautiful yacht,'

Loveday went on. 'I couldn't help noticing the photograph by your bed.' They were all looking at her and she hoped she hadn't overstepped the mark. 'The lady with the child. It's charming.'

She'd done it. She'd brought up the subject of the photo. It was up to him now. Under the table she had her fingers crossed in her lap.

Spiro Cassavetes' eyes flashed with anger. 'That photograph is private. I keep it locked in a drawer. Would you mind explaining how you saw it?'

The friendliness of only seconds ago had vanished. Everyone was looking at Loveday. She felt the colour rise in her cheeks. 'I'm so sorry,' she stammered. 'I didn't realize.'

'You didn't realize it was private?' Cassavetes' voice was rising. 'Surely the fact that the photo was in a locked drawer was a clue.'

'But it wasn't!' Loveday cried. 'It was on the bedside table.'

Cassavetes fumbled in his pocket and produced a little gold key. 'The drawer was locked,' he said. 'This is the only key.'

'The photo *was* on the table, sir,' Cassie cut in. 'I saw it too.'

'So how do you explain that I had to unlock that drawer to take out the photograph when I came on board last night?'

The explanation was simple as far as Loveday could see. Someone had a copy of the key. She glanced at Darius, but his bland expression offered no support.

Cassavetes was on his feet. 'Make sure the ladies get safely back ashore,' he said curtly as he turned on his heel and strutted away from them. The lunch party was clearly over.

'You must forgive my father,' Darius said. 'He can be temperamental. There's no need for you to rush off. Please stay and finish your lunch.'

Loveday and Cassie exchanged a look. 'Perhaps someone should make sure Mr Cassavetes is OK,' Loveday said.

'Our bosun, James, will do that. We've got used to my father's little eccentricities. I'm afraid he is not very sociable these days.'

Loveday frowned. If Darius knew that, why had he invited them for lunch? Why had he agreed on his father's behalf for this interview? Or maybe things had gone exactly as planned? Had Darius wanted them to witness such a scene? Did he think she would put this in her feature? She sat back. She knew a few tabloid journalists who would view the reclusive Cassavetes' behaviour as a scoop. She could visualize a front page splash: 'Exposing the real Cassavetes.'

'Why is that photo so important to your father?' Loveday asked.

Darius shrugged. 'I have absolutely no idea.'

'You've never seen it?'

'No.'

Cassie raised an eyebrow at her across the table as she put down her cutlery. All pretence of any appetite had gone.

'I'm afraid you have a rather different story for your magazine than what you must have been expecting,' Darius said. 'When will you be going to press with this?'

'The next edition of *Cornish Folk* will be in the shops by this weekend,' Loveday said crisply. She was aware of Cassie's sharp look. She had no intention of writing about any of this, but it was interesting that Darius expected her to. Had the whole thing been orchestrated to discredit Spiro? He'd certainly believed the little silver frame containing that picture of Maya and her mother had been securely locked in a drawer, but she knew it hadn't. Her hand closed over the mobile phone in her pocket. She had the picture to prove it.

* * *

LOVEDAY AND CASSIE sat as far away as they could from the crewman at the tiller as the tender sped them back to Falmouth Harbour. They didn't want any comments they made reported back to the yacht.

'You're not really going to put what just happened in the magazine, are you?' Cassie said.

'Of course not.'

Cassie blew out her cheeks and looked back at the yacht. Loveday followed her gaze. Darius was still there by the rail looking out after them. But another figure watched from the far side of the deck. It was the yacht's bosun, James Crawford.

She was remembering the previous day and how he had showed them around the yacht. He'd held back when they entered Spiro Cassavetes' private stateroom. The little silver photo frame had been by the bed then. It was the first thing Loveday had noticed. James Crawford *must* have seen it. He had been hovering around during lunch, so why hadn't he stepped forward to say so? He could have cleared the whole thing up.

She looked back to the yacht, but the bosun had gone. Darius was no longer there either.

'That was so weird,' Cassie said. 'I know the man has pots of money and everything but I felt really sorry for him.'

'Maybe that's what we were supposed to feel,' Loveday said quietly. 'I have an inkling somebody just tried to set us up.'

'Why would anyone want to do that?'

Loveday's brow creased. 'I don't know,' she said thoughtfully. 'That little repair job you did for them yesterday, Cassie. Was it advertised?'

'No. I had a phone call from the bosun. He said he'd done some research and found me.'

Loveday had a busy afternoon ahead. She'd acted spontaneously when Spiro agreed to the interview and had persuaded Merrick to pull the magazine's intended front page. Back at the office they would be waiting for her to arrive with the photos and new article ready to write up. It had been a significant issue to reorganize the magazine's cover page and the linked adverts involved in favour of Spiro's story. But an interview with the reclusive Greek millionaire had been too good an opportunity to ignore. Loveday sighed, imagining the scramble she and Merrick faced to reverse it all again. Slotting the original front page back into place would be easy. The problem would be moving the adds now that space had been made for them inside the magazine. Her head was buzzing.

CHAPTER 16

The murky weather was getting Maya down, but Sam had said the centre could soon be open again. Being encouraged to stay home with April Rose instead of returning to her workplace was supposed to be good for her, but as far as Maya was concerned it was having the opposite effect.

She looked up when she heard a car arriving at her gate and felt a jolt of pleasure when she saw it was Tom's red Audi. She watched him get out and wave, but her smile froze when he walked around the car to open the passenger door. The young woman who stepped out and glanced casually about her was stunning. A strand of long golden hair had fallen over her face and she tucked it back, laughing up at Tom as he offered his hand.

Maya took in the perfectly fitting white jeans and expensive-looking mulberry-coloured jacket. For a second the blue eyes narrowed as they spotted her at the window. The woman's smile came too late to be genuine.

'*Candice!*' Maya muttered under her breath. The tiniest jab of panic was beginning to rise inside her. He'd brought

Candice! And she was even more gorgeous than Maya had expected.

Tom didn't walk into the cottage as he usually did after a quick knock. He'd waited for Maya to admit them. Already everything was different.

'I thought it was time you two met.' He smiled at her as they came in.

What Candice bestowed was more of a twinkle than a smile and revealed gleaming white teeth. 'What a cute little cottage,' she said, glancing around the room. 'I'm dying to see the rest.'

'You might be disappointed,' Maya said in a tone that was sharper than she'd intended. 'There's not much more to see.'

She saw Tom's frown and looked away. What was she doing? This was the woman Tom loved. She didn't even know her and already she was judging.

April Rose's sudden squeal of excitement when she saw Tom cut through the embarrassing silence.

The little girl rattled the bars of her playpen, bouncing up and down to be lifted. 'And this young lady,' Tom said, scooping the baby up in his arms with obvious pride. 'This is my granddaughter, April Rose.'

Candice's mouth twitched. 'What a darling child,' she said. April Rose flicked a look in her direction but it was Tom's attention she wanted.

'I'll make some tea,' Maya said, trying not to notice how many toys littered the floor as she turned away. She wished Tom had warned her about the visit.

When she returned with three mugs on a tray she caught Candice looking around the room with critical eyes and felt a stab of irritation. She wasn't about to allow this woman's opinion to pour scorn on her home.

'It's great, isn't it,' Maya said, putting down the tray. 'Of course I haven't got everything quite right yet, but Tom has been such a help buying little pieces of furniture he thinks will fit.'

She nodded to the old oak bookcase. 'Remember when you arrived with that strapped to the roof of your car, Tom?' She didn't wait for a response, pointing. 'And the little milking stool over there. That was another of your brilliant finds.'

She flashed Candice a smile. 'Tom has such a good eye for antiques, but of course you'll know that,' she said, enjoying the woman's uncertain blink.

Across the room Tom looked uncomfortable. Had she overstepped the mark? Did he think she was being mischievous? A flicker of guilt was beginning to creep in.

Why was she behaving like this? She'd been determined not to like Candice from the first time Tom mentioned her. That was hardly fair. But the woman had looked around Maya's cottage with a definite sneer.

Maybe she deserved the benefit of the doubt. Candice worked on a fashion magazine. She would have been used to London life, the best hotels, with everything around her stylish and expensive. Why would she even be comfortable in an old cottage like hers?

Maya's wide smile included both of them. 'It's wonderful to see you. How long will you be staying in Cornwall?'

'It's a flying visit I'm afraid,' Tom said as April Rose began to wriggle in his arms. 'I wanted Candice to see a little of how we live down here.'

'And what's your opinion so far?' Maya asked.

But Candice had turned her attention to April Rose. 'I think the baby wants to go back in her playpen, darling,' she said, moving across the room to Tom's side.

None of them had heard the silver Lexus pull up behind Tom's car or saw Sam step out and come to the cottage door. Maya went to answer the knock.

'Sam! Come in. Tom's here.'

Sam stepped past her and into the front room. Maya saw the two men nod to each other. She also saw Candice's eyes widen with interest.

'Inspector Kitto here is investigating our murder.'

Candice looked surprised. 'Murder?'

'I told you about it, darling,' Tom said. 'That body Maya found in the heritage centre.'

'Ah.' Candice's eyebrow rose. 'The one that disappeared.' She turned a sympathetic look on Maya. 'That must have been simply awful for you on top of all the other weird stuff that was going on.'

Maya's eyes flew to Tom. Had he really discussed with this woman the things she'd told him in confidence?

He was looking decidedly uncomfortable. 'We're all on your side, Maya,' he ventured. 'We only want to help.'

'Of course we do, darling,' Candice cooed, stepping forward to touch Maya's arm. 'You're probably a little stressed. We all imagine things now and again. You mustn't feel bad about it.'

Maya was trying to control her anger. How dare this woman behave so condescendingly to her?

She pulled away, wheeling round accusingly to Tom.

Sam, sensing the imminent confrontation, intervened. 'Nobody has been imagining anything,' he said sharply.

They were all staring at him. He'd have to be careful. 'New information has come to light, but as this is an ongoing investigation I'm sure you'll understand this is not something I can share with you.'

'No, of course not,' Tom said. 'We wouldn't want to hamper your investigation.' He glanced at the clock. 'We should go. We just popped in so you two ladies could meet.'

'No wait!' Candice raised her arm. 'I have a better idea. Wasn't that a pub I saw in the village?'

'The Miners' Lamp, yes,' Tom said.

'Then why don't we all go there for lunch?' She swung round, giving Sam the full benefit of her exquisite blue eyes. 'Perhaps the inspector could also join us?'

'I don't think the inspector–' Tom began, but Sam interrupted him. 'No, it's a good idea. You two go ahead. If Maya agrees, we'll join you shortly.'

Candice's eyes sparkled with triumph as her gaze held Sam's for a second longer than was comfortable.

Maya waited for them to go before rounding on Sam. 'You're not really falling for that? Candice is up to something.'

The thought hadn't escaped him. He turned to the window from where he could see the pair walking to the pub. 'How long has he known her?'

Maya pulled a face. 'Not long. Oh Sam, I'm worried. I don't know what that woman's up to. I just wish Tom wasn't so…'

He turned. 'Never mind them. It's you I've come to see, Maya. I need your help. I know it's difficult having your friends believe you were imagining the mischievous stuff Morwenna was getting up to at the centre but that has to stay between us for the time being. I need you to trust me.'

Maya sighed. 'If that's what you want. She felt a shiver run down her spine. She was picturing the cloaked figure slumped in the rocking chair with her hood falling over her face, exposing one staring eye. 'Was she really dead when I found her, Sam, or was she play-acting to freak me out?'

Sam shrugged, but it was a possibility they had considered. If Morwenna had confronted Maya with such a vicious practical joke, how would she react? Would she strike out in rage? Could her anger at being persuaded she was losing her mind be so out of control that she could kill? Was this what Will was encouraging him to consider?

He looked away. 'All I can say is that Morwenna Chenoweth was certainly dead when we found her on the cliff path.'

Maya puffed out her cheeks. 'What was this Morwenna woman even doing at the centre?'

'According to her boyfriend she was writing a book and had persuaded him that it was easier for her to go to the centre at night to study when it was quiet rather than during the day when she was tied to her teaching job.' He shrugged. 'At least that's what we've been told.'

April Rose had toppled over in the playpen and snuggled herself into a position from where she could watch her mother. She looked contented. Maya smiled at her as she got to her feet and began walking around the room. 'I'm definitely not going mad then,' she said quietly.

Sam shook his head. 'You're not going mad.'

'And the centre?'

'I see no reason to keep it closed.'

'You mean we can open up again tomorrow?'

'You can.'

Maya's eyes sparkled. 'That's the best news I've heard in weeks.'

Twenty minutes later when April Rose had been changed and dressed and her ready-made jars of food put into her buggy, Sam and Maya set off with her for the pub.

Tom and Candice had managed to get the big table by the fire. He smiled when he saw them and got to his feet. Candice nodded. Sam thought she looked distracted. He glanced around the pub. Only a handful of tables were occupied. 'I'll get us some drinks,' he said after Maya had settled April Rose. 'Same again for you two?' He raised an eyebrow at Tom and Candice.

'I think we're fine,' Tom said.

Candice looked as though she would have liked another

glass of wine but she said nothing. Her eyes were on Sam's back as he walked to the bar.

April Rose was awake and had begun to grumble.

'She's hungry,' Maya said. 'I'll ask the staff to warm her jars.'

'I can do that.' Tom was on his feet. 'I'll get a jug of hot water.'

'I hadn't realized Tom could be so domesticated,' Candice said. She didn't sound impressed.

'April Rose is Tom's granddaughter,' Maya reminded her. 'Of course he wants to be involved.'

'Of course,' Candice repeated, but the corners of her mouth had drooped. She turned to Maya. 'You look a lot happier after your little chat with the inspector. Anything you want to share?'

'We can open the heritage centre again tomorrow.'

A flicker of interest registered with Candice. 'Does that mean the police have a suspect?'

Maya turned to pick up April Rose. Her question was perfectly reasonable, so why did it make her feel uneasy. 'I've no idea. They don't give much away.'

Candice's attention had strayed to the bar again and the three men standing there. The stranger next to Sam kept glancing to them over his shoulder. Or was it Candice's presence that was attracting him? April Rose was settling as Maya gently rocked her. 'Do you know that young man, Candice? I think he's got his eye on you.'

'He's no one I know. Ignore him.' Her troubled expression stretched into a smile as Sam returned with the orange juice Maya had requested and his own half pint.

Tom appeared behind him and put down the jug of hot water as he reached for the jars of food. 'Patience, my pet,' he said, putting one of them in to warm. 'Just a few more minutes.'

Maya followed Candice's gaze to the bar. The young man had gone.

The ploughman's selection they had ordered arrived and the men tucked into the plentiful selections of crusty bread, cheese, relish and ham.

Candice hardly touched her food.

'So how long are you down here for?' Sam asked.

'It's a flying visit,' Candice jumped in. 'We're heading back to London tomorrow.' She smiled at Tom. 'Aren't we, darling?'

Tom reached for his beer glass. 'Let's see how it goes,' he said.

Maya didn't know why Candice's barely concealed look of fury made her smile, but it had. She looked at Tom. 'Does that mean we might see you again before you leave?'

'Maybe.' He touched April Rose's cheek and she gave a happy chuckle. 'I think that's your answer,' he said.

* * *

CANDICE WASN'T LOOKING happy as she and Tom left the pub and walked to his car. 'You love it here, don't you?' she said.

Tom nodded.

'Is that why you're selling your business?'

'Partly, and partly because it feels like the right time to cut the ties.'

Candice stared at him. 'But your friends are in London. You have history there. You can't cut yourself off from all that.'

'I don't plan to, not completely. Why does it matter anyway?'

'Well of course it matters. I mean what on earth are you going to do with yourself? I hope the plan isn't to bury yourself down here in Cornwall.'

'I thought you liked Cornwall?'

Candice screwed up her face, imagining the scratches the prickly hedges they were now edging past could do to the beautiful Audi.

'I do,' she said. 'At least I do if we're talking about the civilized parts. This is like a jungle, and that creek down there...' Her nose wrinkled in distaste. 'All that green slime. It's disgusting. When you said you had a boat down here, Tom, I was expecting a marina.'

Tom smiled. 'Well you're in for a surprise, my darling. This is the real Cornwall and my cottage is just around the next bend.'

Candice blinked as the stone dwelling came into view.

'Welcome to Creek Cottage,' Tom said.

'This is it?' Candice's eyes were wide with disbelief. 'It's a hovel, Tom. You're not seriously expecting me to sleep here?'

But Tom's thoughts were still back at Maya's place. He was remembering her expression when she opened the door to them. He'd been hoping the two women would be friends. Maybe he had imagined the hostility. Maybe not.

The transition of moving his life from London to Cornwall might not turn out to be as easy as he'd expected.

CHAPTER 17

*L*oveday's training on the Glasgow tabloid newspaper earlier in her career had more than equipped her for working under stress. The plan had been to send the photos she'd taken on the yacht to the magazine's graphic designer, Mylor Ennis, to place on the waiting pages while Loveday typed up the feature on her laptop. She'd been up since dawn researching any scrap of information she could find on Spiro prior to the interview. Every snippet would have been checked out with the man himself before she included it. But everything had changed now. There would be no exclusive story for *Cornish Folk*. Waving to Cassie, Loveday got into her car. She wasn't looking forward to breaking this news to the others.

* * *

THE PROSPECT of an interview with the elusive Greek millionaire had been enough for them to hold up publication and pull out all the stops to feature it.

Since what would have been a major scoop had fallen

through, Loveday and her team would have to work fast to rearrange the magazine's layout if they were to meet that important print slot. The printer who produced *Cornish Folk* ran a busy independent company on the outskirts of Truro. Accommodating any delay could throw the rest of the company's busy schedule into chaos and they weren't about to do that. Merrick and Loveday knew running publication times down to the wire was taking an enormous chance but if things had gone to plan it would have been worth it. They hadn't expected it to backfire as it had. As it was, missing the print deadline meant there was a possibility that the new month's edition would never see the shops. It was a situation that had never before happened in the history of *Cornish Folk*.

Thankfully traffic on the A39 was surprisingly quiet, but Loveday's heart still pounded as she sped back to her office.

* * *

'I DON'T UNDERSTAND,' Keri said when Loveday rushed in and was firing up her computer. 'Why can't we just cobble together a front page story about Spiro anyway? There must be loads of cuttings and photos on line. The fact that his yacht is in Falmouth Bay is surely enough to justify using that.'

Loveday shook her head. 'It's not good enough. Dredging up a load of old stuff from the internet will hardly give us a respectable front page. We have standards for *Cornish Folk*, Keri. Our readers expect it.'

'I thought you might say that,' Keri sighed. 'So it's back to plan one and resurrecting our original front page?'

But Loveday's attention was on Merrick and his anxious look as he hurried towards them.

'Please tell me this isn't more trouble?' she said.

'It's worse than that,' Merrick said. 'The Gillings have just pulled the plug on our main feature.'

'What?' Loveday stared at him.

The article was to celebrate the success of Mo and Zak Gilling's surfing business. It was to be surrounded by a major advertising campaign. Losing the feature would leave them with two empty pages. At this late stage that was disaster.

Merrick's face was ashen. 'Zak rang me. Mo's parents are in hospital. They were involved in a car accident in France this morning.'

'Oh no!' Loveday's eyes were wide with shock. 'How awful. Will they be all right?'

Merrick bit his lip. 'It's not looking good. Mo and Zak are flying over there, but the bottom line is they don't want us to publish the article, not at the moment anyway. Zak says they need to focus on being there for Mo's parents. He doesn't feel the time is right for a magazine feature celebrating their business success.'

'We can't argue with that,' Loveday said. 'Is there anything we can do to help?'

'He says not. Frankly we have our own worries. What are we going to do, Loveday?'

'Well, we're not going to panic. Let's take this a step at a time.' The calmness in her voice surprised even her.

A GLANCE to the clock told her they had less than an hour to complete the layout changes if they were to make the print deadline. She scrolled through the files on her computer. The pages had been thrown out of sync, but that wasn't the worst of their problems. The advertisers who had paid for their space in the magazine would have to be contacted. None of those ads could now be used and alternative copy would have to be found to replace them.

Loveday was flashing through the emergency file of stories she kept, mentally working out which piece would fill which space. Merrick looked over her shoulder. 'Can we do this?'

'I haven't missed a deadline yet and I don't plan to start now,' Loveday said.

'Tell me what to do,' he said, watching her fingers fly over the keys.

'We need to build these inside pages,' Loveday said. 'Can you find some more stock pictures? And this story needs a headline. We can still use the original front page if we can move a couple of these ads around.'

'Keri, can you double check these articles for typos before they're finally placed on the page?'

'No problem,' Keri said, her eyes were already scrolling through the copy as it appeared on her screen.

It was a minute past 4.30 when they hurried out of the office, the precious new files safe in Loveday's bag.

Two minutes later they were in Merrick's BMW and heading out of town.

The print company boss, Andrew Benson, was tapping his watch as they rushed in. 'Cutting it a bit fine, aren't we?'

'Sorry, Andrew,' Merrick said, as Loveday handed over the files. 'We had a last-minute hitch, but we dealt with it.' No point explaining things the man didn't need to know. Their work was done. Benson and his team would take it from here. They would have the proofs by morning and once they'd been checked and verified the magazine would be back on track for delivery to shops by the weekend.

'I think we deserve a drink,' Merrick said as they left and went back to the car. 'I've passed the word for the rest of the team to join us.'

Loveday got in and sank her head back into the comfort of the BMW's expensive grey upholstery. She felt pleasantly exhausted. All she wanted now was to be with Sam in their cottage in Marazion, curled up before a crackling fire with a mug of steaming hot chocolate in her hand. But it was traditional for Merrick to take the team for a congratulatory drink once the magazine had been delivered to the printer. It was his way of thanking everyone for their dedication and effort in producing another great edition of *Cornish Folk*.

Loveday's colleagues were in high spirits when they joined them in the pub. 'Just orange juice for me,' she said as Merrick went to the bar.

Keri raised her eyebrow. 'Not even a teeny glass of wine?' She looked like she'd already enjoyed a few glasses.

'Not for me. I feel high enough as it is and I still have to drive home.'

'We'll give you a lift,' she offered. 'Ben's coming in to collect me. He said I couldn't be trusted to have only the one drink.' She waved her glass. 'I've no idea why.'

'You deserve to celebrate. You all do,' Merrick said, returning with a tray of drinks. He beamed a wide grin around the group. 'Well, we did it, folks.' His grin stretched wider. 'We did it!'

'You were all amazing,' Loveday chipped in. 'It's not the magazine we were expecting to produce, but it's a good one.'

She was still enjoying the warm feeling of achievement as she drove home to Marazion.

* * *

'I HAD LUNCH AT THE MINERS' Lamp today,' Sam said, after they'd had supper and were clearing the plates away. When Loveday didn't respond he continued, 'I was invited by a beautiful woman.'

He had her attention now. 'A beautiful woman, eh? Who was this?'

'Candice Chrichton-Smythe.'

'Ah.' Loveday nodded. 'Maya said Tom had turned up with her. Tell me more.'

'They were at Maya's place when I called in to see her this morning. Tom realized I wanted to speak to Maya on her own, but Candice was reluctant to leave. Eventually she suggested we all meet up at the pub for lunch.'

'And you agreed?'

'I was intrigued. It felt like a clumsy attempt on her part to find out what I had to say to Maya.'

'Why would she be interested in that?'

'That's what I wanted to find out.'

'And did you?'

He grinned at her. 'If you don't change the expression your face could stay like that.'

Loveday flicked a tea towel at him. They were stacking the supper things into the dishwasher.

'Well don't keep me waiting. Tell me.'

Sam laughed. 'Have you noticed Maya behaving differently lately?'

She looked up. 'How do you mean, differently?'

'Oh you know, strangely, acting out of character, that kind of thing.'

'Why do you ask?'

Sam reached up to take a whisky glass from the cupboard. 'You have a very annoying habit of answering a question with another question. Do all journalists do that or is it just an endearing characteristic of yours?'

'I'm sorry, Sam. I suppose I like to check around all the possibilities before I commit myself to an answer.'

'I'm not trying to trap you, Loveday. It's just something someone said about our victim.'

'OK, you've got my attention. What are we talking about?'

'It was something her boyfriend, Joss Teague said when Will and I interviewed him.'

'Yes?' Loveday said impatiently. 'Are you going to tell me or do I have to guess?'

Sam poured two fingers of malt whisky into his glass and held it up to the light examining it as though it was an old master painting. He walked with it to their little sitting room and settled before the fire. Loveday followed him.

'According to Teague, Morwenna was insatiably jealous of Maya,' Sam said. 'She was furious that Maya was successful in getting the job when she hadn't been. Morwenna thought the job should have been hers.'

'And?'

'Well apparently Morwenna used to sneak into the heritage centre at night, after everybody had gone, and move things about.'

Loveday frowned. 'How do you mean, move things about?'

'It was all mischief making really,' he said. 'She used to do whatever she could to undermine Maya. The intention was to make Maya's colleagues believe she wasn't coping with the job.'

'How did that help Morwenna?'

'I guess she was hoping Maya would be sacked.'

'You mean she thought she could step into her job?'

'Something like that.' Sam put down his glass. 'It goes without saying, everything I've just told you is confidential. I've put you in the picture so you don't try working this out for yourself or ask any questions that might unintentionally compromise our case.'

Loveday gave him an exaggerated salute. 'Yes sir,' she said. 'Am I allowed to ask if Maya is aware of all this?'

'She is now.'

'How did she take it?'

'She was shocked. She couldn't believe anyone would go to those lengths to discredit her.'

'At least it explains what Morwenna was doing at the heritage centre,' Loveday said.

Sam lifted his glass and took another sip. His brow furrowed. 'It doesn't explain why somebody killed her.'

'Or why Candice was so interested,' Loveday said.

Sam was recalling the scene in the pub. 'There was a bloke at the bar who made me curious. I'm not sure why he was there.'

'What do you mean?'

'Well he wasn't local and he wasn't a walker.' He paused. 'Put it like this, there was no way he had just spent the morning walking the cliff path.' He took another sip, savouring the whisky. 'I got the impression he and Candice knew each other.'

Loveday sat forward, her eyes widening. 'What made you think that?'

'I don't know. I suppose it seemed like they were watching each other, eyeing each other up.'

'He probably fancied her. Even you said she was quite a looker.'

'Maybe,' Sam said slowly. 'But it's not the impression I got. I felt they knew each other, but you're right, it was probably my imagination. You know what a suspicious mind I have.'

'Interesting though,' Loveday said. 'If this man and Candice were acquainted then why didn't they acknowledge each other?'

Sam pulled a face. 'Exactly what I was wondering.'

'I'll be in just after ten this morning to go through those proofs with you,' Loveday told Merrick when she rang him first thing.

'You don't have to do that. We'll manage,' he protested.

'I'll be there,' Loveday insisted. 'It's my fault we're in this situation. I was so certain of that Spiro Cassavetes interview making a sensational scoop for *Cornish Folk*.'

'And rightly so,' Merrick said. 'You know I was right behind changing the front page to make way for it. Losing the double page spread in that way was something no one could have predicted.'

'I'm still responsible,' Loveday insisted. 'I shouldn't have taken that time off. I feel terrible about the amount of work I've given everyone to move things back.'

'I can see I'm not going to persuade you differently,' Merrick said. 'But don't break your neck getting here. As long as we get the proofs agreed by lunchtime everything will be fine.'

'Thanks, Merrick. I'll be no later than an hour.' She ended the call and rang Maya.

'Hi,' Loveday said. 'How does it feel to be reopening the centre today?'

'I'm here now and I can't tell you how good it feels to be back.' She could hear the smile in her friend's voice. 'It's like I've been on some rollercoaster nightmare.'

'You need to put all that behind you now, Maya. None of what happened was your fault. That poor girl, Morwenna, had serious issues.'

'She didn't deserve to die though, did she?'

'No.'

'Sam told me about the things she did to discredit me. She must really have hated me.'

'I don't think she hated you. She just got things a bit out of proportion. What she did was hardly normal behaviour. At least you know you weren't responsible for all that stuff that was happening.'

Loveday could hear Maya sigh over the phone. 'It's such a relief to get all that cleared up.' She paused. 'Sam wasn't the only visitor I had yesterday. Tom turned up – with Candice.'

'Sam mentioned it. What was she like?'

'Snooty,' Maya said. 'But I was worse. I'm ashamed of how badly I behaved. Tom will think I'm a complete bitch.'

'Of course he won't. Tom thinks the world of you and little April Rose.'

'He did make me angry though. He told Candice about things I shared with him in confidence, things I said when I thought I was going mad.'

'But that's all cleared up now.'

'I know,' Maya said wearily. 'I was still annoyed with him.'

Loveday wondered if Maya was more than the tiniest bit jealous of Candice, but she knew enough to keep those thoughts to herself.

'Need a hand setting up this morning?' Loveday asked. 'I was going to drop by.'

'Maya laughed. 'You don't have to do that.'

'Too late, I'm nearly there. Better get that kettle on,' she said.

Loveday always felt a stab of pride as she approached the heritage centre. All the hard work for the interpretation boards was done by Maya, but she was proud of her own contribution.

Maya saw her as she got out of the car and waved. 'Just in time to help us move this display,' she called.

'If the coffee's on, it's a deal,' Loveday called back, nodding to Maya's young assistant, Sinead.

'I don't know what this thing's made of but it sure is heavy,' Maya said. 'We've been trying to push it into that corner where it won't take up so much space but people will still be able to read the information.'

'No problem,' Loveday said, walking towards them.

What happened next came too quickly for any of them to think about. Sinead had turned away as Loveday approached. The display towering over her slowly began to topple. Loveday let out a yell and sprinted forward, pushing Maya out of the way as the huge structure came crashing down.

Sinead rushed forward as the two women sprawled on the floor. 'Gosh, are you two all right? That thing could have killed you.' She touched Loveday's face. 'You're bleeding.'

Loveday raised her head. Her fingers went to her cheek and came away covered in blood from where her face had caught the side of a desk.

'You're injured.' Maya looked horrified. 'There's a first-aid kit in my office. Do you think you can stand?'

'Loveday struggled to her feet, waving aside her friend's concern. 'I'm sure it looks worse than it is,' she said, as Maya and Sinead supported her into the office.

When they looked back at the massive display board they saw it had split as it crashed to the floor and was lying in bits.

'How on earth did that happen?' Sinead said, her face full of concern. 'It couldn't have fallen on its own.' Her eyes went round the room. 'I can't understand it.'

Loveday was equally troubled. Out in the car park a vehicle was being driven off at speed. She jumped up to the window but only managed to catch sight of its tail lights as it sped away.

Maya pulled her back, pointing to a chair. 'Sit down, Loveday, and keep still,' she ordered, 'if you want me to stick this plaster in the right place.'

But Loveday's attention was still on the retreating car. 'Did you notice any other vehicles out there when you arrived this morning?'

Sinead shrugged and Maya shook her head. 'Walkers use our car park for access to the cliff path,' Maya said. 'It's not unusual to have a few vehicles out there. We don't really notice them.'

She stepped back, tilting her head at the Band-Aid she had just applied. 'Administering first aid is not my best skill, but it'll have to do. At least it stops the blood trickling down your face.'

Loveday touched the plaster. She wasn't looking forward to explaining the injury to Merrick and Keri when she got to the office. They already thought she was careless of her own safety. But she couldn't have stood back and allowed Maya to be crushed under that board.

Her mind kept returning to that image of it beginning to topple. Her attention had been focused on pushing Maya out of the way, but at the back of her mind she could visualize a dark shape moving away. Her head was all over the place, but surely she hadn't imagined it? Something wasn't right but she didn't want to frighten Maya.

She glanced out to the shattered display board. These things were built solid to be stable. It wouldn't have toppled, not without a little help, like someone pushing it from behind.

Her eye caught the camera high on the wall. 'Can we check the CCTV?' she asked.

'It's just here.' Maya turned away and flicked on a screen. 'But I don't know what you expect to see.' She replayed the video and they all stared at a blank screen. 'I don't understand. I set this myself. Where are the images?'

'They've been wiped,' Loveday said. 'We have to report this to the police, Maya.' She held out her phone. 'Like now!'

'You do it. You'll know what to say.'

Loveday was already walking off and tapping in Sam's number. 'I think you should come to the heritage centre, Sam.' She lowered her voice. 'I think somebody just tried to kill Maya.'

She heard his sharp intake of breath. 'Sinead's with her and she seems quite calm. I can't stay. I promised Merrick I'd help with the proofs. Is it all right if I go, Sam?'

He sounded hesitant. 'OK, you can go, but stay at the magazine office. We'll need a statement.'

Loveday felt guilty leaving her friend, but Maya had insisted she should get off to work, saying the police were on their way and she'd be fine.

In the car park Loveday glanced around her. Maya's little car was there, and another vehicle that probably belonged to Sinead. If the car she'd heard speeding away was being driven by whoever had pushed over the display board it must have been there when she arrived. Why hadn't she noticed it?

CHAPTER 19

*L*oveday's injured face raised a few concerned eyebrows as she walked into the magazine's editorial office. She put up a hand. 'Before anyone asks, it's only a scratch. I wasn't looking where I was going and I tripped.'

'If you say so,' Keri said, squinting suspiciously at Loveday's injury.

Merrick's expression was troubled as he strode towards them. 'That looks painful, Loveday. I can manage the proofs on my own. I think you should go home.'

She shook her head. 'I'm staying,' she said. 'It was my fault that we had to make all those changes yesterday. The least I can do is to help you check the proofs.'

Merrick's look was disapproving, but she knew she could get round him. 'We'll get through it in half the time if we work together,' she reasoned. He was still not looking convinced.

Loveday sighed. 'What if I agree to going straight home as soon as we finish?'

'I suppose that will have to do,' he said, still not happy but knowing further argument would be futile.

It was early afternoon before they'd finished checking and approving the proofs. It was a good feeling knowing they had once again produced a great magazine, despite the previous day's chaos. Loveday was in the staff car park and about to head home when Sam rang.

'How's Maya?' she asked before he had a chance to speak.

'Maya's fine. It's you I'm concerned about. You didn't say anything about getting injured.'

Loveday's hand went to her cheek. It felt painful. 'A slight graze. Hardly worth mentioning.'

'That's not how Maya described it. She told me how you leapt forward and pushed her out of the way when that display board fell.' He paused and she could sense his anger. 'You could have been killed.'

'What was I supposed to do, Sam? Stand by and watch my friend get crushed to death? Is that what you would have done?'

'I get paid to put my life in danger. You don't.'

Loveday sighed. 'It's a scratch. I'm fine.'

'We'll discuss it when you get home. How about supper at the Godolphin?'

The hotel was only a short walk along the seafront from their cottage but it was one of Loveday's favourite places to eat.

'That sounds like a special treat, Sam. What have I done to deserve it?'

'Absolutely nothing,' Sam said, but she could tell he was frowning as he ended the call.

* * *

SAM WAS ALREADY THERE when Loveday arrived. He was sitting at the table by the window, the one restaurant manager, Phil, always reserved for them. The tide was going out and the cobbled causeway to St Michael's Mount was gradually emerging from the dark water of the bay.

'I get the feeling you're spoiling me,' Loveday said, slipping off her grey wool coat. 'It's not some special date I've forgotten, is it?'

Sam reached out and touched her bruised cheek. 'The fact that you survived almost killing yourself makes this a special day.'

Loveday flushed. 'Stop fussing, Sam. Nothing bad happened.'

She ignored him shaking his head as she reached for the menu. 'I think I'll have the duck,' she said, running her eye down the list. When she looked up he was still shaking his head, but he was smiling now. He laid down the menu card. 'So tell me what you think about Maya? Was somebody really trying to kill her?'

Sam pursed his lips, still watching her. 'What made you think it was an attempt on Maya's life?'

'Well that board didn't fall by itself. Someone pushed it.'

'Did you see anyone?'

Loveday pulled a face. 'Sensed rather than saw,' she admitted. 'And then there was this car taking off at speed from the car park.'

She ignored his raised eyebrow. 'What about the CCTV? That had definitely been interfered with.'

'Maybe Maya made a mistake,' he said. 'She could have wrongly set the equipment. You know how much stress she's been under.'

Sam beckoned the waiter who'd been hovering uncertainly in the background and ordered their food.

'It wasn't an accident, Sam. You weren't there. I didn't imagine it.'

'I'm not questioning that the board toppled. That's a fact,' he said, splitting a bread roll the waiter had brought and spreading it with butter. 'But we have no evidence that it was done deliberately.'

'So you don't believe me.'

'I didn't say that.'

'But I thought…' Loveday frowned. 'So you're not dismissing it?'

Sam smiled. 'I'm not dismissing it, but you must trust me to do my job. If someone means Maya harm we'll catch them.'

Their food arrived and Loveday was thoughtful as she helped herself to vegetables. 'If somebody really was trying to kill Maya it puts a different slant on Morwenna's murder.'

'Does it?'

'You know it does. You and Will have been assuming the body had been placed in that chair for Maya to find. And the big mystery is why she was moved and who dumped her body behind that rock. Surely this changes everything?' Loveday put a forkful of duck into her mouth.

'I'm listening,' Sam said.

'I think you're indulging me. You know what I'm suggesting.'

Sam laid down his cutlery and fixed her with a warning look. 'You're thinking, what if Morwenna's murder was a mistake? What if the killer thought she was Maya?'

Loveday nodded. 'It would make sense that the killer would expect to find Maya at the centre. Anyone who knows her routine would know she's in the habit of checking the building out of hours. Finding a woman wandering about the place in that green cloak, they might easily assume she was Maya.'

'I trust you're not going to air that suggestion anywhere else, Loveday. We don't want worrying rumours circulating.'

'Of course not,' Loveday said. 'You know me better than that, Sam.' She swallowed, but she knew he agreed with her. Someone was trying to kill Maya.

* * *

THEY FINISHED the rest of the meal in silence. Loveday would definitely not have appreciated what was running through his mind. His sergeant's theory that Maya could have been involved with Morwenna's murder still concerned him. The two of them had visited the heritage centre earlier to check out that tumbling display board. It was unsettling that Will still had his doubts about Maya, but surely his suggestion that the board incident could have been orchestrated was crazy.

He'd asked Sam to consider the possibility that Maya had attached some kind of string and pulled on it at the appropriate moment so it came crashing down in front of her and Loveday. It would have been easy enough to get rid of the string. That thinking led to another possibility. Had Maya deliberately tried to kill Loveday?

The idea was ridiculous. Did it also follow that Will's suspicion of Maya was equally ridiculous? He certainly thought so, but while there was even the merest chance of any truth in that he had to keep an open mind. Loveday's insistence that he supported her over the danger to Maya just muddied the water.

CHAPTER 20

The cut Loveday had considered a minor annoyance the previous day had swollen into an angry black bruise. Attempts to disguise it with make-up only made it worse. She stared into the bathroom mirror in dismay. 'I look like a right bruiser,' she called through to Sam in the kitchen as she heard him pouring boiling water onto the coffee in the cafetiere.

He pushed a mug of black coffee in her direction when she came back. 'Not just a scratch then?' he said, giving her a sideways look.

She touched her cheek. 'It looks worse than it is,' she muttered.

'Don't go into the office today. Merrick will understand.'

'I have to go in,' she said. 'The chaos I caused having to change everything around when the Spiro interview fell through has affected everything.

'I can't risk falling behind. I have several articles and an advertising feature to write up for the next edition.'

She watched his eyebrow rise and conceded, 'I suppose I could do all that from home.'

'That's a much better idea,' Sam said, stuffing toast into his mouth as he snatched up his jacket and headed for the door. 'Call Merrick!'

Loveday sank into a chair, but then on impulse sprung up and ran after him. 'What about Maya?' she called as he turned back to her. 'Will she be OK?'

He dropped a kiss on her forehead. 'Don't worry about Maya. We'll be keeping an eye on her. I'll make sure the local patrol car makes regular calls at the centre.'

Loveday frowned after him as he got into his car and drove off. A police car making the odd appearance didn't sound like much protection to her but it was better than nothing. She knew Sam wasn't 100% convinced Maya needed protection.

Cassie emerged from her back door as Loveday was returning to her kitchen. Her jaw dropped as she caught sight of her friend's bruised face.

'Wow, that looks painful.' She sounded genuinely shocked. 'What have you done to yourself?'

Loveday attempted a smile and then wished she hadn't when it stung her face. 'It looks worse than it is.'

'Have you seen a doctor?' She half turned back to her house. 'I can get Adam to check you over.'

'No!' She touched Cassie's arm. 'I'm sure Adam has enough to do looking after his real patients. I'm fine.'

'Well I'm coming in and sticking the kettle on. I want to know why somebody punched you in the face – and why.'

'You'll be late for work,' Loveday reasoned. 'And nobody punched me in the face.'

'What then? What happened?' Cassie touched the cafetiere and found it was still hot. She refilled Loveday's mug.

'It was silly, really. An accident. I'd gone to see Maya at the centre yesterday and one of those great display things fell on top of me.' She touched her face. 'It's only a little cut. The bruise came up overnight.'

Cassie sat back in the kitchen chair and cocked her head at Loveday. 'For a woman of words that explanation falls remarkably short of the mark. Care to expand on it?'

She watched with a concerned frown as Loveday wrapped her hands around her mug. 'Take your time. I can wait, but I'm going nowhere until you tell me what really happened.' She narrowed her eyes. 'Does this have anything to do with Spiro Cassavetes?'

Loveday's head jerked up and she stared wide-eyed at Cassie. 'Why would you think that?'

Her friend shrugged. 'I don't know. He had that picture of Maya, and then there was the strange way he behaved, rushing off like that.'

It was something that had worried Loveday too, but she wasn't going to admit how the thought had kept her awake for most of the night. It made no sense that Spiro would want to harm Maya. But Cassie was still considering it.

'Spiro clearly didn't want to be asked any questions about that photo. Makes you wonder how far he would go to cover up any connection.'

Loveday bit her lip. A possibility was emerging that she didn't want to think about. 'What happened to me wasn't an accident, Cassie,' she said, looking up to meet her friend's eyes. 'Only I wasn't the target. Someone deliberately toppled that display board when Maya was standing under it. I saw it happening and shot forward to push her out of the way. The board crashed down and my face caught the corner of a desk as I tried to get out of the way.' She winced, touching her bruise.

'How do you know it was deliberate?' Cassie asked.

'I got the impression of a black shape moving away after it happened, but more importantly, the centre's CCTV was wiped clean. An unidentified car also took off at speed from the car park.'

Cassie blew out her cheeks, sinking back in her chair.

'There's more,' Loveday said.

'More? You've got me worried now, Loveday. What else's happened?'

Loveday raised a warning hand. 'What I'm going to tell you really must not go any further. I'm only telling you because you know Maya, and you saw how Spiro behaved on his yacht.'

Cassie nodded. 'You have my word.'

Loveday blinked. 'Sam and I suspect killing that woman at the heritage centre was a mistake.' She drew in a breath. 'It's possible the killer mistook her for Maya.'

Cassie eyes widened as she stared at her. 'But that's terrible. Is Maya aware of this?'

'Heavens no, but Sam has organized a police car to keep an eye on her.' She shook her head. 'I'm not confident that will make much difference if there really is a stalker out there ready to harm Maya.'

Cassie leaned across the table and took Loveday by the shoulders, forcing her to look her in the eye. 'You have to step away from this right now, Loveday. You've already put yourself in danger. This is Sam's responsibility and he's clearly doing what he can to protect Maya.'

'It's not enough though,' Loveday muttered to herself. Then louder: 'If anything happens to Maya I'll feel responsible.'

'That's nonsense,' Cassie said, her voice rising. 'If you wade in and get hurt, possibly more seriously next time, how does that help Maya?'

'It might save her life,' Loveday said.

'At the expense of you losing yours? That's hardly a result. You're not thinking this out.'

Loveday frowned at her. 'How do you mean?'

'Well what about all the other folk who care about Maya. What about Tom? Does he know what's been going on?'

Loveday glanced away, thinking. Cassie was right. Tom had to be brought up to date. He would understand her concern. A slow smile lit up her face. 'That's a great idea, Cassie. I'll go to see Tom. He'll know what to do.'

Cassie sent her a warning look. 'Just remember to keep Sam in the loop. Don't do anything he wouldn't approve of.'

'Would I ever do such a thing?' Loveday blinked.

* * *

Tom wasn't answering his mobile and Loveday hoped she was doing the right thing by dropping into his cottage unannounced. His little red Audi was parked at the bottom of the wooded path and looking as incongruous as ever in these rural surroundings. She was breathless by the time she'd negotiated the hilly terrain to his front door and was about to knock when she heard a raised voice through an open window.

'I told you to stay away,' the woman hissed. 'Do you think Tom's stupid?'

Loveday held her breath. What was this? She swallowed, listening.

'That's not a good idea,' the woman said. 'A jealous man is a violent one. Think about it!' There was a pause and then the woman snapped, 'Shit!' The call had ended.

Loveday shrank back into the greenery. She couldn't go barging in. She had to think. Was the woman Candice? Did what she'd just heard mean Candice was cheating on Tom? The blood was beginning to tingle through her veins. She didn't like this one bit.

She was still standing there, not sure what to do when a footstep from behind made her spin round. 'Tom!'

'Loveday! What are you doing here?'

She'd planned how this conversation would go but right now her mind was a blank. She saw the concern flash in Tom's eyes. He sprinted towards her.

'What's happened? Has something happened to Maya? April Rose?'

'No! They're both fine. Sam said you were back in Cornwall. I was passing and thought I'd drop by.'

It was a pretty feeble excuse and Loveday could tell from his expression that he didn't believe a word of it but he was too much of a gentleman to question it.

The cottage door opened and a young woman, a tumble of blonde hair framing her lovely face, fixed Loveday with a suspicious stare.

'This is Candice,' Tom said quickly.

Had there been a hint of embarrassment at the woman's prickly reaction? She'd been caught off guard and must be wondering if Loveday had heard any of her phone conversation.

'Candice, this is Maya's friend, Loveday.'

A smile flickered across the woman's face but suspicion still lingered in the watchful eyes. The hand she offered was limp. 'You're the policeman's friend,' she said.

'Partner,' Loveday corrected. 'Yes, Sam told me he and Maya joined you for lunch yesterday.'

'And April Rose,' Tom reminded as they all went into the cottage.

Loveday had had no reason to visit Tom in his cottage since April Rose was born. She was pleased to see it was no longer the derelict ruin she remembered. The immediate area around it had been landscaped and was obviously regularly tended.

Things had changed inside too. The previously dark hall had been brightened up with white walls and through an open door she could see the two rooms to the left had been knocked into one large lounge with an office area at the far end.

'Come into the kitchen,' Tom said. 'It's warmer there.'

To her surprise she was led past what had been the old kitchen. It now appeared to be a cosy snug, furnished traditionally with an old settle, paintings and antiques.

The adjoining room, where Loveday had once been imprisoned by the disturbed woman who'd later been revealed as Jamie's real mother, had become a cheerful flagstoned-floor kitchen with a green Aga in the corner. Gleaming copper utensils hung on the wall and a familiar old scratched oak table added to the cosiness.

'I can't believe what you've done with the place, Tom,' Loveday said, glancing appreciatively around her.

'I'm not sure Candice shares your enthusiasm,' he said, putting an arm around Candice's shoulder and giving her a squeeze. 'Too rural for you, my darling, isn't it?'

'It's all very quaint.' Candice sighed. 'And not exactly practical.'

'It looks practical enough to me,' Loveday said.

Candice's glare was cutting. Loveday decided this was one disagreement she would not pursue. But the woman was in no hurry to drop the subject. She shot Tom a glance. 'Tom develops a caveman persona when he comes here to Cornwall. I'm not sure it's healthy.'

Loveday wondered what Candice would consider 'healthy'. She had a sudden vision of Tom in a smart newly built house that overlooked a secluded beach. It would be an exclusive property, minimalist interior with gleaming white kitchen and a triple garage for his collection of luxury cars. That might suit Candice, but Tom would be like a fish out of water. Surely he would never put up with an existence like that? But love did funny things to people, and if Loveday's impression of Candice was right she was a lady used to getting her own way.

She knew Tom was watching her, no doubt curious about the real reason for her visit. But she couldn't share her concern for Maya's safety when Candice was here. She had the impression the woman wouldn't care two hoots if Maya was in danger.

She was about to make her excuses and leave when Tom turned to Candice. 'I think I've left my phone in the car, darling. Could you nip down and fetch it?'

Candice threw him a surprised look. She wasn't used to fetching and carrying for anyone. Loveday expected a spir-ited '*fetch it yourself*' retort. But Tom wasn't giving her the chance.

'Thanks, love,' he said. 'If it's not lying on the dashboard you might check between the seats. It sometimes slips down there.'

Candice didn't look pleased, but she went out anyway.

As soon as she'd gone Tom wheeled round to face Love-day. 'OK, we both know you didn't simply drop by.' His stare was unflinching. 'Why are you here, Loveday?'

There was no point in being evasive and besides, Candice could come back at any moment. 'Sam and I both think Maya is in danger.' She touched her bruised cheek. 'This was meant for her. One of those big display boards at the heritage centre collapsed. Maya was standing under it. I jumped to push her out of the way and caught my cheek on a desk.'

The shock she'd expected to see on Tom's face wasn't there.

He blinked. 'And that's it?'

'Not exactly.' She hesitated, not sure how much she

should share. His reaction was confusing. However, this was Tom and he had a right to be told.

But as she slowly described her and Sam's fear that Maya could have been the intended murder victim and not Morwenna, Tom's expression hadn't changed.

'Who else knows about this?' he asked sharply when she'd finished.

Loveday stared at him. She'd just told him Maya's life was in danger and he appeared more annoyed than concerned. 'Sam knows and I asked Cassie's advice. It was her who suggested I should contact you.'

He crossed the floor and squinted along the passage to the front door. 'We can't talk now. Candice will be back any minute. I'll ring you later when the coast is clear.'

'What?'

He held up a warning finger as the front door slammed and they heard Candice come in. Her eyes made a sweep of the room and stopped on Tom's phone which was sitting on the window ledge. She nodded at it and he pulled an apologetic expression. 'Sorry, love. I didn't see it there. I'm afraid I sent you on a wild goose chase.'

Candice did not look pleased.

Loveday had her own problems. She hoped her state of confusion over Tom's behaviour was not registering on her face.

Candice flashed Loveday a smile that was not sympathetic. 'Your poor face. That bruise looks so painful.'

'Would you believe I walked into a door?'

Candice held her gaze. 'I hope you've invited your friend to stay for lunch, Tom?'

'Yes, please stay,' he said quickly.

But Loveday shook her head. 'Sorry, this really was a flying visit. I hope you'll forgive me if I shoot off, but thanks for inviting me.'

'Maybe you can come back and stay longer next time?' Candice swung round. 'Tell her, Tom. She should come back.'

They were walking to the door. 'Loveday knows she's always welcome here,' Tom said.

Loveday glanced back to wave as she went down the path and saw Tom's eyes narrow at her. He was confirming that undertaking to ring her – when the coast was clear.

CHAPTER 21

*L*oveday's head was ringing with questions as she drove away from Karrek. Why had Tom behaved like that? It was almost as if he already knew Maya was in danger. And why had he not wanted Candice to hear their conversation? What was going on? She needed to clear her head.

Her mobile rang. It was Merrick.

'How did that article stand up?' Merrick had long since ditched any need for social niceties. 'Will it make a two-page spread?' he asked.

Loveday felt guilty. Merrick was assuming – as she had led him to believe – that she'd spent the morning writing it. How could she explain her visit to Tom?

The article he was referring to – an interview with a couple who had moved to Cornwall to set up a craft business – had been strong. There was no reason to believe it wouldn't make an excellent double-page spread, especially as she'd been so pleased with the photos.

'It'll be great, Merrick.' Her mind was flicking over the other things she had been planning to write. She had enough material in recorded interviews to fill several more pages.

'Working from home gives me such a good head start for the new edition, but we can go over this in detail when I see you.'

Was it enough to keep Merrick happy? She hated misleading him, but she knew he would understand when she was in a better position to explain things to him.

'I'm putting my foot down, Loveday. I don't want to see you in the office tomorrow. And there's no need to work from home. You're supposed to be having some time off.' He paused. 'I hear you have a black eye now.' There was more than a touch of mischief in his voice.

'It's a bruised cheek, actually,' Loveday corrected. 'But thanks for asking. It's improving. It certainly won't stop me coming in tomorrow.'

'You can be such a bossy woman.' Merrick sighed.

'Tell Keri I'll be joining her for that elevenses donut.'

He laughed. 'God's in his heaven, all's well with the world.'

'Something like that.' Loveday grinned.

She was already feeling more relaxed as she ended the call. She would have to work late that night to make up the time she'd lost, but she didn't mind. At least that was normal.

Tom's behaviour on the other hand was far from normal. She thought about contacting Sam, but what could she say? Tom had behaved strangely? She could already hear him suggesting she was imagining things.

Cassie would understand. After all, it had been her idea that she visit Tom in the first place.

She answered on the second ring. 'How did it go with Tom?' Cassie liked to get straight to the point.

'A bit odd really. That's why I'm calling you. Do you have a minute?'

'I was about to take a lunch break,' Cassie said. 'How far away from the marina are you?'

Loveday glanced at the dashboard clock. 'Fifteen minutes.'

'Come to the Boardwalk Café, I'll order you a pasty.'

'Thanks, Cassie.'

As she approached the marina, Loveday found herself scanning the boats off Falmouth Harbour. The Cassavetes' yacht was still there. They must have delayed that Mediterranean cruise Darius had invited her and Cassie to join him on.

She parked outside the café and went in. It was busy, but Cassie had found a table at the back. 'Thanks for meeting me like this, Cass. I know how busy you are.'

'It's fine. Refurbing *Mama Mia* is well ahead of schedule. I'm not due to hand the boat back to the owners until Saturday.'

'I thought weekends were strictly family times.'

'They are, but Adam's got his boat down here so we're going for a sail across the Carrick Roads and planning lunch at St Mawes.'

Loveday smiled. 'That'll be a treat for Sophie and Leo.'

Cassie nodded, looking up as a waitress appeared with two pasties on a tray.

'Those look good,' Loveday said, trying to sound enthusiastic although she wasn't feeling particularly hungry.

'I take it your meeting with Tom didn't go as well as we had hoped,' Cassie said, picking up her knife and slicing it through the steaming pasty.

'Not exactly. It was weird, Cassie. I thought I would have to calm him down, reassure him that the police were doing everything they could to protect Maya, but he didn't even look surprised.'

'You mean he already knew?'

'I'm not sure,' Loveday said. 'But he certainly wasn't keen to involve Candice, and that was strange too. They're supposed to be a couple after all.'

Cassie swallowed her mouthful of pasty before picking up her glass of mineral water and taking a sip. 'What did you think of Candice?'

'Aloof, superior, someone used to being in charge.' Loveday frowned. 'She has these frosty, suspicious blue eyes. I felt she was watching me the whole time I was there.'

'Not exactly a cosy couple then,' Cassie commented. She looked up as a thought struck her. 'What if Maya knows more about this than she's let on to you? Who else would she confide in?'

'Tom?' Loveday said. 'Which would explain why he appeared to be aware of it.' She pulled a face. 'But if both he and Maya believed her life was in danger why wouldn't they trust the police?'

'Maybe they're afraid to.'

'Or maybe they think they can deal with this themselves,' Loveday suggested.

Cassie sighed. 'None of this makes any sense. Why would anyone wish harm on a lovely girl like Maya?'

'What if there's something in Maya's past, something even she doesn't know about?' Loveday met her friend's stare.

'Like Spiro Cassavetes?' Cassie said.

Loveday's nod was slow. It was time they discovered the truth behind that photo in Spiro's stateroom.

* * *

Unknown to Loveday, at that moment Sam and Will were disembarking from a police launch to board the *Moonflyer*. 'We would like to speak to Mr Cassavetes,' they informed the surprised crew member who'd stepped up to meet them. Out of the corner of his eye, Sam thought he saw a figure on the far side of the deck draw back out of sight.

The crewman scanned their warrant cards and stood to attention as the two detectives looked around them. 'Would that be Mr Darius or Mr Spiro Cassavetes, sir?' he enquired.

'Spiro,' Sam said, turning sharply at the approach of another man.

'My father is resting,' the newcomer said, offering his hand. 'I'm Darius.' He smiled, revealing a row of dazzling white teeth. 'Can I help you?'

Loveday's description of Darius Cassavetes had been spot on – black curly hair framing a strong tanned face and challenging dark eyes. He moved with the assurance of someone completely in charge of his situation. 'Our guests will have tea.' The order was thrown to the deckhand. 'We'll have it in the lounge.' No *please* Sam noted. The man gave a little bow before moving smartly off.

'We are not your guests, sir,' Sam corrected stiffly. 'We are police officers conducting an investigation.'

'Investigation?' Darius repeated. 'How does that concern us?'

'That's what we're here to discover, sir. What's your connection to Cornwall?'

Darius's amused look went from one to the other. Sam knew it was intended to intimidate them. It wasn't working. He waited until a flash of irritation clouded the man's dark eyes.

'My father and I come to Cornwall regularly. It's a favourite place of ours.'

'That's not what I asked, sir. I was enquiring about the Cassavetes family connection with Cornwall.'

Darius gave a shrug. 'There is no family connection. I told you. This is a place we favour.'

'You've been here before then?' Will asked, responding to Sam's almost imperceptible nod.

A tray of tea arrived and was silently placed on a table.

'Isn't that what I said?'

Sam smiled. Darius's mask of control was slipping.

'What places do you visit when you go ashore?' Will asked.

'We go all over.'

'Not only the pretty coves and beaches then?' Sam cut in.

'I'm not quite sure what you're asking,' Darius said.

'Tell the officers about your passion for antiquities, Darius,' the voice said.

They all turned as an older man arrived. 'I'm Spiro Cassavetes,' the man said, a smile crinkling his pleasant round face. 'I understand you would like to speak to me.'

Sam introduced Will and himself.

'Father! I was told you were resting.'

'You were misled.' He turned to Darius. 'Why don't you tell the officers about your antiquities collection?'

Darius glanced away. 'I can't image any hobby of mine would be of interest to the police.'

'Antiquities?' Will enquired. 'You mean like standing stones?'

'No one *collects* standing stones.' Darius said coldly. 'I record these ancient sites.'

'Such modesty,' Spiro said, his eyes still on the man. 'He has the most amazing collection of antiquities.'

'Really?' Sam raised an eyebrow. 'That sounds impressive. I'm afraid my knowledge of old things doesn't stretch beyond antiques, which I presume is different from antiquities?'

'The two are worlds apart. Antiques are a hundred years old or older. Antiquities are historical objects from a time before the Middle Ages. They date back anywhere from the fifth to the fifteenth century.' He swept a superior look over the detectives. 'The culture of ancient times fascinates me.'

'It must surely be difficult to find such ancient things,' Sam commented.

'Some museums put artifacts up for auction as a way of securing funds for extensions and other improvements. Simply maintaining these places can be expensive.'

'I imagine acquiring artifacts doesn't come cheaply?'

'I only buy what I can afford.' He was giving Sam an irritated frown. 'Is there a point to all this?'

'Only in as much as I share your interest,' Sam lied. 'On a more modest level of course.'

The man narrowed his eyes at him.

'Presumably there will be private sales as well?' Will said.

'Occasionally.'

'Have you ever bought privately?'

'Rarely. It can be difficult to get a provenance.'

'So all the items in your collection have provenances?' Sam said. He'd been watching Spiro and saw the flicker of a smile. The man had wanted Darius to be questioned about this. But why?

Sam swung back to Darius. 'Cornwall is full of antiquities.' He waited until the man's eyes came up to meet his. 'Have you found anything from here for your collection?'

'I've taken nothing from here.' The sharp response came quickly, quick enough to maintain Sam's interest.

He followed Darius's cold stare out across the yacht's deck to the Carrick Roads and took in a slow breath. He would let this one simmer. But if Darius Cassavetes thought this was an end to the police interest in him he would have to think again.

Spiro, who had settled apart from the others at the bar, got to his feet. 'I have something to show you, Inspector,' he said. 'If you officers would follow me.'

Sam shot Will a questioning look and saw his slight shrug of response. Darius said nothing as he watched them leave.

They followed Spiro to the deck below and past the state-rooms where Sam imagined the well-heeled passengers would be accommodated.

'In here,' Spiro said, unlocking the door to a luxurious bedroom and stepping inside. 'Please take a seat.' He gestured to a pair of red velvet covered chairs separated by a low table.

Sam looked around him, his gaze taking in the vast bed with its brocade bolsters, an office area at the back of the room and an open door through which a vast marble bath with gleaming gold taps could be seen.

Spiro touched a pad of buttons by the bed and a cocktail cabinet slid out of the wall. 'Can I offer you gentlemen a drink?' he said.

The detectives accepted a couple of mineral waters. 'You wanted to show us something, Mr Cassavetes,' Sam said. He had no intention of appearing overawed by the luxurious surroundings.

Spiro unlocked a drawer on his bedside table and produced a framed photo. A gentle smile crossed his face as he glanced at it before turning it to Sam. 'This is my daughter,' he said.

CHAPTER 22

Sam stared at the photo of the curly haired child on the woman's knee. Was this what Loveday had found? Was this child Maya?

'Do you know who this child is?' Spiro asked, his eyes still affectionately on the photograph.

'You said the child is your daughter. I wasn't aware you had children, well apart from your son, Darius.'

Spiro's brow creased. 'Darius is my wife's son, not mine.'

'But he's taken your name,' Sam said.

'People can call themselves anything. Darius had his surname changed from Moralis to Cassavetes by deed poll. He did it because it suited him. It had nothing to do with me. I certainly did not sanction it, but what could I do? It would hardly have been in anyone's interest if I had caused a fuss. He is my wife's son after all.'

'What of your daughter?' Will said. 'That looks like an old photo.'

'It is. Maya is 24 now and with a child of her own.' He looked from one to the other with a sad smile. 'You see, I am not only a father but also a grandfather, yet I have never met either of my beautiful girls.'

The look the two detectives shared did not go unnoticed. 'You're right,' Spiro said. 'You're wondering how I have this information from what is otherwise an anonymous photograph. Well I've been doing my detective work too, or at least I've been employing someone to do it on my behalf.' He went back to the drawer in the bedside table and produced a plastic wallet of photographs, which he spread out on the table in front of them. Most of them were of Maya outside her cottage pushing April Rose in her buggy. Others appeared to have been taken inside the heritage centre.

Spiro smiled down at the pictures. 'Those wild green eyes, the curly hair, the cheeks flushed with roses. Maya is the image of her mother.'

To Sam and Will's surprise, the man's eyes filled with tears. 'My darling Cara. I loved her so much.'

Sam didn't know if Spiro's story had any relevance to their current case. He only knew he had to hear it. 'Tell us about Cara,' he said gently.

Spiro picked up the framed photo. His mouth curved into a distant smile as he sat on the bed gazing at it. 'We met 26 years ago. We were in love. Cara had taken a summer job as a housemaid at the Hotel Adamos on the Greek island of Mykonos. I was a waiter there, but I had ambition for greater things.

'I was the eldest of five children brought up in poverty in Ano Mera, a village in the centre of Mykonos. I wanted better for all of us, so when Voleta Stephanopoulos, the daughter of the man who owned the hotel, began to show an interest in me, I encouraged her.

'Voleta's family was rich and she was in love with me. She wanted us to get married.' He shook his head. 'How was I to know Cara was pregnant? I saw a way of getting myself and my family out of poverty.

'Cara and I talked about it. She said she completely understood. I believed her.

'We agreed this thing between us was a summer romance and like all good things it had to come to an end. At least that's what we said.' He swallowed. 'Cara hugged me that last day and said it was time to go our separate ways. She wished me and Voleta every happiness. That's the kind of sweet, lovely girl she was.' He dropped his head into his hands. 'I should never have let her go. I wouldn't have if I'd known about the baby.'

Sam waited, giving the man time to collect his emotions. When he spoke, his voice was quiet. 'What happened to Cara after that?'

'I never heard from her again, not until I received that photo soon after Voleta died.' He sighed. 'It wasn't a love match between Voleta and I. We both knew that. I was ambitious, greedy for success back then. Voleta's father, Theo, was my way to the top. The Stephanopoulos family was comfortably wealthy. They owned several hotels in Greece, but they were not forward thinking enough for my liking. I knew I could escalate the business to another level and eventually persuaded Theo to trust me. He did and together we built new luxury hotels in Italy, France, Monaco. They all prospered and the world was now our oyster. Shares in the company were my reward for our increasing success. Soon I owned more than half the business.'

Spiro's eyes were fixed on a spot on the far side of the room as his mind travelled back. 'I used Voleta as my way into the Stephanopoulos family. I know how cold and calculating that must sound – and it was. I'd given up the love of my life, my beautiful Cara, to marry Voleta. I had to make it work. I didn't share Voleta's all-encompassing love, but as the years passed I grew to care deeply for her. The fact that we were not blessed with children seemed to draw us closer. We had thirteen good years together. I was devastated when the cancer took her from me.'

He looked up. 'The photograph came out of the blue. I had no idea what it meant, or even if it was Cara who'd sent it. There was no accompanying letter of explanation, just the photo in an envelope with a Bodmin postmark. I didn't dare hope that this was my child – our child – but I had to find the truth, so I hired Pierre Danka, a private detective.

'The photograph had been taken on a beach. Further examination of it showed a row of shops in the background. One of them had a sign. St Ives Gifts! We concentrated our search there. Pierre discovered that Cara had given birth to a girl at the hospital in Truro – Maya Theresa O'Brien. She'd put *father unknown* on the birth certificate.' He paused. 'He also learned that Cara had been ill. She had mental health problems and struggled to care for Maya. The child was put up for adoption. She went to an Irish couple, Dermot and Molly Brookes.

'Giving up her child must have been terrible for Cara. I can't imagine how she lived after that, but somehow she did. Sending me this photograph must have been one of the last things she did before taking the overdose.'

Will sat with his head bowed and Sam could see how much he'd been affected by the man's story. He took a breath. 'I'm guessing you're still being kept up to date with Maya's life?'

Spiro nodded.

'Even though there was no actual confirmation that she was your daughter?'

'Ah, but I do have confirmation,' Spiro said, 'not that I needed it. It was Pierre who suggested collecting a DNA sample for a paternity test. He slipped into Maya's cottage when she was out and took some strands of hair from her hairbrush.'

Sam's eyebrow went up. 'Her cottage? So this happened recently?'

'About a month ago,' Spiro said. 'It's because I had asked Pierre to keep an eye on Maya that we discovered someone was trying to kill her.'

Sam shot Will a look. 'You know this?'

'Of course I do. Isn't that why you and your sergeant are here?' He got to his feet and crossed the room, picked up an elegant white phone and ordered a tray of coffee and sandwiches. 'Something tells me we have much to discuss,' he said.

Sam watched him, frowning, as the coffee was brought in by a young woman. They waited for her to pour it and hand round the cups before leaving.

'I suppose I should start by explaining how Darius came into my life,' Spiro said, dropping a cube of brown sugar into his cup. 'I kind of inherited him four years ago when I married his mother, Helena Moralis. It wasn't a love match either. Helena was a friend of my late wife and became a friend of mine too. I'd long ago given up any hope of love with a woman, but Helena and I liked each other and I needed a companion.' He smiled. 'My wife is like a gentle child. She hates the limelight. She doesn't mind at all when I jet off and sail all over the world to attend to my business interests. So long as I return to her and our home in Mykonos at the end of the trip she is content.

'Her son Darius is a different matter. He's greedy and wants his finger in every pie. He sees himself taking over my hotel empire when I die.'

'I take it that's not going to happen?' Sam said.

'I'd rather give it all away to charity than let him get his hands on it. He doesn't know that. He thinks he will inherit a bottomless pit of money to fund his collection of antiquities. Darius is fanatical about that – and so secretive.'

'That sounds like an expensive hobby. Doesn't Darius have his own means?'

'Darius has two casinos, one in Athens and another here in London.' He looked away. 'He has his own way of dealing with those who owe him money.'

'Such as?' Will asked.

'He gets his heavies to lean on his debtors. Once he has them where he wants them he uses them, makes them do his bidding.'

'His bidding?' Sam frowned.

Spiro shrugged. 'I have proof that he makes them steal things for him, antiques.'

'If you have proof why don't you go to the authorities?' Sam asked.

'I will, when the time is right. For now I am content to watch him and collect evidence against him.'

'Evidence of what exactly?' Will asked.

'Abduction, attempted murder.'

'Who has he attempted to murder?'

'My daughter, Maya.'

'Maya?' Sam's eyebrows shot up. 'But why?'

'Because he knows she is my daughter. Already he is suspecting she will benefit from my will when I die. He probably imagines I intend to split their inheritance between the two of them. Darius won't want that to happen. It puts Maya and my granddaughter in constant peril. That's why I have a bodyguard watching over them 24/7.'

'I think you need to get yourself a better bodyguard,' Sam said grimly. 'If my partner, Loveday, hadn't jumped in to stop a heavy display board crashing down on Maya, your daughter might already be dead.'

'You're talking about Miss Ross? Yes, I heard about that. I'm so sorry she was injured. Is she all right?'

'She took a whack on the face and is still shaken up.'

'Your Loveday is a very brave young woman,' Spiro said. 'I was shocked when that incident was reported back to me. It should never have been allowed to happen. That was the point of hiring a bodyguard. I lost no time in replacing that particular individual.'

'Who reported the incident back to you?' Will asked.

'Pierre, my private detective.'

Sam's head was whirring with a hundred questions. Was Darius behind the murder of Morwenna Chenoweth? Had he really ordered the attempt on Maya's life? Was he also behind the attempted theft of the St Piran carving? 'We need to take Darius in for questioning.'

'No! Please!' Spiro was on his feet. 'If you do that he will slither away like the snake he is and we will lose him. We must wait, give him enough rope to hang himself. He mustn't know that we are onto him, not yet.'

Sam shook his head, frowning. He wasn't sure about this, and yet it could make sense. But was this man right, or was his case against Darius built on assumptions?

'We're investigating a murder, sir, and from what you've told us your wife's son could be involved.' He hesitated, glancing across to Will's concerned face. 'But you're right. We don't have enough evidence to arrest him. Inviting him into the station for questioning right now could be counter-productive.'

'Thank you, Inspector.' Spiro's relief was clear. He handed Sam a card. 'This is my private mobile number. Not many people have it. Please ring me if I can help in any way.'

Sam took the card, meeting Spiro's eyes. 'If we have good reasons to question Darius then we will. You understand that, don't you, Mr Cassavetes?'

Spiro nodded.

Sam turned as he and Will reached the door of the state-room. 'Don't move your yacht out of Falmouth, sir.'

Spiro's face stretched into a grim smile. 'We're going nowhere.'

* * *

LOVEDAY'S HEAD was still buzzing after she left Cassie. Maybe she'd been looking at this from the wrong angle? There was clearly more to the relationship between Tom and Candice than a straight forward romance, not that romance was straight forward. Love had so many twists and turns it could stand a person on their head. What if their relationship was a cover for something else? But what? She needed to know more about Candice.

Loveday was remembering Tom's curious behaviour that morning and how he'd sent his girlfriend out on the pretext of fetching his phone from his car. What was she missing? He said he would contact her *when the coast was clear*. What did that mean? She was on her way back to the cottage in Marazion to write up those urgent magazine interviews, although she doubted how successful that would be when her head was all over the place. She needed to go back to the beginning. She knew nothing about the murder victim...that strange young woman in the green cloak that Maya had first seen in the church.

When she was at a crossroads like this Loveday's instinct was to sit down and sketch everything out logically. She had to clear the decks she thought as she turned into her drive and parked by the back door. Once inside she went in search of a notepad and pen and sat at the kitchen table with a strong coffee to hand.

She began to make a list.

*Morwenna Chenoweth – the young woman whose poor broken body had been found on the cliff path near the Carn Hendra Heritage Centre. Sam said she'd been a primary teacher in St Ives with a passion for Cornish antiquities.

*DARIUS CASSAVETES – Did he deserve a place on the list? She'd had a feeling it was no coincidence he'd invited Cassie onto the *Moonflyer*.

*SPIRO CASSAVETES – Why did he have that photo of Maya in his stateroom and then deny it? Why had he cancelled the interview he'd agreed to at the last minute? Had he really believed she'd been poking her nose into his private things, or was there another reason?

*TOM SCOBEY – Possibly Maya's best friend, and grandfather to her daughter, April Rose. He was suddenly being mysterious. He definitely knew more than he was saying.

*CANDICE CHRICHTON-SMYTHE – Tom's glamorous girl-friend. How was she involved?

*AND MAYA HERSELF. Why was someone trying to kill her? Was it connected to the heritage centre?

*WHO WAS the shadowy figure she thought she'd seen when the display crashed over at the centre? She wasn't even sure it had been a man. Anyone could dress in black.

* * *

LOVEDAY'S EYES scanned the list. Who was missing? The handsome face of the *Moonflyer* bosun, James Crawford, drifted into her mind. He surely was not involved, but he had invited Cassie onto the Cassavetes' yacht. Her gaze travelled down the list again. What connected all these people?

Three of them were linked to the *Moonflyer*.

All of them knew Maya except Candice, Darius and James Crawford.

Only Morwenna and Maya had an interest in Cornish antiquities – or did they? Antiquities were valuable commodities. People collected them. She was remembering the attempted theft of the St Piran carving and the attack on the unfortunate cleaner, Jess Tandy. Maybe she wasn't as innocent as she'd appeared. She hadn't wanted the police to be involved. Had her so-called attack been set up as a distraction to what was really going on?

She pushed her fingers through her hair and scanned the list again. Who else might be interested in antiques? Or was that the wrong question? Whoever was behind the planned theft of the St Piran carving had to be fanatical, ruthless, greedy.

Candice? Darius? She didn't know enough about either of them to rule them out.

The buzz of her mobile phone interrupted her musing. She found her jacket and rummaged in the pocket to retrieve it. 'Keri,' she said, punching the *accept* button as she sank back in her chair. 'Please don't tell me there's a problem.'

'No.' Keri laughed. 'You're such a pessimist, Loveday. There's no problem. It's just a catch-up call.' She paused. 'You're sounding a bit stressed. What's up?'

Loveday pushed her fingers back from her face again. She *was* stressed. She'd been on edge all day.

'Having trouble writing up the articles? I thought they were all straight forward.'

The articles! She hadn't even made a start on them and it was already... Her eyes went to the clock. God, it was four o'clock! She'd wasted almost the whole day and was no further forward in learning who was trying to harm Maya. She tried to keep the panic out of her voice. This was her job. People were depending on her doing it right.

'Everything's fine. I've had to deal with a few distractions along the way, that's all.'

'The price of working from home, eh?' Keri came back.

'Yes, that's it.' Loveday hoped her light tone was convincing. 'Any calls for me today?' she asked.

'Nothing that can't wait till the morning. I was only checking up on you. I'll let you get on,' Keri said. 'Don't work too hard.'

CHAPTER 23

*I*t was eight o'clock before Loveday heard Sam come in the back door. He'd rung earlier telling her not to cook, saying he'd pick up a takeaway. She'd had four solid hours of writing and had completed three of the five articles. It was time for a break.

'I called in on Tom today,' she said as he slipped off his jacket. 'He was behaving very oddly.' She took a bottle of Glenmorangie from the cupboard, poured a good measure into a glass and handed it to him.

Her glass of wine was already sitting on the low table by her chair in the small sitting room. 'Would you know anything about that?' she asked casually.

'In what way odd?' Sam asked, following her through.

'Put it this way, I don't think his relationship with the glamorous Candice is a love match made in heaven.'

'Shouldn't that be a marriage made in heaven?'

'No, far from it and that's my point. Tom might have us believe he's enamoured with this woman but I think it's an act.'

Sam put down his whisky and sank into his chair, stretching. 'What makes you say that?'

Loveday recounted her earlier meeting at Tom's cottage in Karrek, including how he'd sent Candice out for his phone.

'What were you doing there? I thought the point of not going into the office today was so you could work from home.'

'It was, but it didn't stop me being worried about Maya.'

'Maya's fine,' Sam said. 'Will and I called in to see her. You can be sure she is being well looked after.'

'Well looked after? I don't consider a patrol car driving past her place every couple of hours as being well looked after.'

'It's more. Trust me.'

Loveday narrowed her eyes at him. 'What are you not telling me? What's happened, Sam?'

'You know I can't share the details of a police investigation with you. Why can't you just trust me?'

'Because Maya is my friend and I care about her.'

'We all do, Loveday, which is why you have to leave this to us now.'

Loveday tilted her head to one side watching him. 'OK, then let's go back to the dead girl. The one whose body was on the clifftop, the one Maya saw at the heritage centre. You said her boyfriend mentioned something about a plan to steal the St Piran carving in the church. What was the dead girl's involvement in that?'

She sat back, wondering how much he would share.

'We're still investigating. Morwenna Chenoweth's boyfriend told us she was trying to protect the thing.'

'Because it's a precious Cornish antiquity?'

'Exactly,' Sam said.

'So are you looking for someone who collects antiquities?' Loveday asked.

'We are.'

'And do you know of anyone?'

Sam leaned over and reached for his glass. 'Can we change the subject? Now if you have any questions about fine old Scottish whisky, ask away.'

Loveday sighed. She wasn't going to get any more out of Sam tonight, but she might try one last thing. 'So what about Tom? You didn't say what you thought.'

'I think you're reading too much into how he was with you,' Sam said.

Loveday was 100% sure that wasn't the case. Tom had said he'd ring her when the coast was clear, but he hadn't rung and that was strange too. She got up and went to her desk to power up her computer. She didn't hear Sam get up and go into the kitchen, but she looked up smiling when he put a mug of steaming hot chocolate beside her and ruffled her hair. 'Don't stay up too long. I get lonely in bed without you beside me.'

'I promise,' she said as he kissed the top of her head.

It was past midnight when Loveday closed the computer and sat back stretching. She was exhausted but there was a kind of euphoria when her work went well. She set the alarm on her clock for 6am which would give her plenty of time to call in on Maya before her friend left for the heritage centre. She had questions to ask and hopefully Maya would have some of the answers.

* * *

LOVEDAY HAD SHOWERED and dressed and was tucking into a bowl of home-made muesli when Sam came into the kitchen.

'You're an early bird,' he said, planting a kiss on her head as he went to pour himself a mug of coffee.

'I've got a busy day. What about you?' She slid him a look, hoping for a hint of how his investigation was going, but he said nothing.

'I expect you'll be digging deeper into the attempt to steal the St Piran?' She waited, but Sam wasn't rising to the bait. She had another go. 'Isn't that where all this started? Morwenna Chenoweth tried to stop some thugs stealing it and got herself killed.' Her brow wrinkled as she went over in her head what she'd just said. 'But that can't be right, not if Morwenna died because she was mistaken for Maya.'

'We might have got it wrong,' Sam said. 'The two things may not be connected.'

Loveday stared at him. 'But Morwenna was in the heritage centre?'

Sam nodded. 'That's right but forensics confirmed she wasn't killed there. She may, however, have gone there to hide. We know she had a key.'

Loveday blinked. 'Wait a minute, Sam. Are you saying Maya's life is not in danger after all?' She touched the fading bruise on her cheek. 'I didn't imagine that display board crashing over. It was definitely done on purpose. And it was Maya who was being targeted.'

Sam's expression was grim and Loveday knew it signalled the conversation was ending. Under different circumstances she might have tried pursuing it further but she was seeing Maya herself soon. She watched Sam drain his coffee mug and reach for his jacket. 'What about your breakfast?'

'I'll grab a bacon butty in the police canteen,' he called over his shoulder as he went out.

Loveday followed him out minutes later. Leaving so early meant she missed the going to work traffic. She could probably be at Maya's cottage by 7.30. She rang ahead to tell her friend she wanted to catch her before she left for the centre. If Maya was surprised, she didn't show it. 'I'll put another croissant on to warm,' she said.

Her friend's kitchen was fragrant with an enticing aroma. 'Sorry about crashing in on you at this ungodly hour, Maya. I wanted to check you were OK before I headed off to work.' April Rose wriggled contentedly in her buggy and Loveday grinned down at her.

'The childminder will be here in a minute,' Maya said. 'Now what's all this wanting to check up on me business? I'm fine.'

Loveday sat down at the kitchen table and watched her friend take a tray of two delicious-smelling croissants from the oven. She poured them mugs of tea from a teapot.

'I wondered if you'd heard any more about that attempt to steal the St Piran carving?' Jumping to the heart of an issue, especially when time was short, often produced results.

'The church has ramped up security,' Maya said. 'I hear they have a rota of volunteers on duty every day now and there's an old guy who sits in overnight.'

Loveday raised an eyebrow. She was picturing a collection of geriatric helpers and wondered how effective they would be if they came up against a gang of determined thugs. 'Has anyone tried to steal the carving before?'

Maya shrugged. 'Not in my time, but it's so famous I don't know why anyone would take it. It's not as though they could ever sell it.'

'What if someone wanted it for a private collection?'

'I think it's unlikely. Such a collection would be priceless.'

'And yet someone did try to steal the thing,' Loveday said. She was racking her brain for anyone with the kind of wealth that would support a private collection of priceless antiquities. One person came to mind. She looked up.

'Have you ever heard of a man named Spiro Cassavetes?'

'No.' Maya shook her head. 'Should I have?'

Loveday swallowed. Now wasn't the time to share her suspicions. If Maya really was Spiro's daughter he clearly hadn't contacted her. If that was true it would need some gentle handling. 'Cassavetes is a Greek millionaire. He has a yacht called the *Moonflyer*. It's been moored off Falmouth for the past few days.'

Maya's eyes widened. 'Does Sam think it was this Spiro man who took the St Piran?'

'I've no idea. I'm just running through my mind who in Cornwall could afford a collection of antiquities.' She blinked. There was another possibility. Darius Cassavetes! She needed to do some serious research there.

'I saw Tom yesterday,' Loveday said.

'Really?' Maya looked away. 'Is Candice still at his place?'

'Yes, Tom introduced us.'

'What did you think of her?'

Loveday's brow wrinkled. 'I think she's an odd choice of girlfriend.'

Maya used a pinkie to flick flakes of croissant from her mouth. 'That's exactly what I thought. Did Sam tell you we had lunch with the pair of them at the Tinners' the other day?'

'He did.'

'I know he thought the same as me. Candice is beautiful and doesn't she know it, but she's so self-centred and arrogant. I really can't understand what Tom's doing with her.'

'Maybe he's smitten by her looks,' Loveday said. 'Once some men reach their forties they start yearning for their lost youth.' She paused, wondering if she should share how Tom had been with her the previous day. But that would involve explaining she was concerned for Maya's safety and she didn't want to worry her.

Maya was shaking her head. 'It's not that, I'm sure of it.'

A slow smile was creeping over Loveday's face. She had suspected it, but now she wondered again if it could be true. Was Maya in love with Tom?

'What do you know about Candice?'

'Practically nothing,' Maya said. 'Tom mentioned her for the first time only days ago and then he was bringing her here and presenting her as his girlfriend.'

'How did they meet?'

'Even that was odd. Now Tom has made the decision to move to Cornwall permanently he's been tying up his connections with London. I believe he's keeping on his flat, but his business has been more or less sold.'

'What about his yacht?'

'It's currently in the marina at St Katharine Docks. Somehow Candice got to know he was considering selling it. She approached him saying she was interested in buying it. They ended up having dinner and things progressed from there.'

Loveday blew out her cheeks. 'Candice can afford a £750,000 yacht?'

Maya shrugged. 'She didn't need to be able to afford it, did she? All she had to do was to give the impression she was interested.'

Loveday pulled a face. 'You think Tom was set up? But why? Surely he's not so easily taken in?'

'Normally I would have said not, but you've seen Candice. I imagine once she's set her sights on something, or someone, she gets what she wants. Tom is a rich man.'

'And he's not bad looking, either,' Loveday added. She hadn't missed the faraway look in Maya's eyes. Discovering more about Candice Chrichton-Smythe was now a priority. It was concerning her that Tom still hadn't rung. If she could distract Candice for a while it might give Tom a chance to contact her.

She took a breath. 'How do you fancy inviting Candice for lunch?'

Maya blinked at her in disbelief. 'You're not serious?'

'Yes, why not? If you could keep Candice busy for an hour or so I could speak to Tom. I got the feeling there was something he wanted to tell me but he couldn't while she was around.'

'What kind of something?'

'That's what I need to find out. You only need to spend an hour with the woman. You can do that.'

Maya pulled a face. 'What if she refuses to come?'

'She won't, not if you tell her it's Tom you want to talk about. Trust me. You know April Rose is safe with her child-minder. Take a long lunch break and invite Candice to join you for a pub a pub lunch. I'll do the rest.'

'I'm not sure about this. Do you really think it will help Tom?'

'It will, I'm sure of it. Just let me know where and when Candice is with you.'

*I*t was an hour later when Loveday was in the office and in front of her computer that Maya rang. 'It's done,' she said. 'I didn't think for a minute she would go for it, but she did. Candice is meeting me in Penzance. Tom is driving her there.'

'Perfect,' Loveday said. 'Don't forget to text me when she arrives.' The call ended and she sat back with a satisfied sigh.

Sitting across from her, Keri raised an eyebrow. 'Am I allowed to inquire what that was all about?'

'I'll tell you later when I know more myself.'

'Why do I get the feeling you're jumping in at the deep end again?'

Loveday smiled. 'Don't worry. I can swim. There is some-thing you can do for me though, Keri. Can you google a woman called Candice Chrichton-Smythe?'

'Who's she?'

'Tom Scobey's new lady friend. I want a printout of every scrap of information you can find.'

She had already started her own search on Darius Cassavetes. A series of images scrolled past of Darius at

various high-profile events. The man went to a lot of cocktail parties. He'd introduced himself to Cassie and herself
as Spiro's son, but according to what she was reading this
wasn't accurate. His mother was Spiro's current wife, the
former Helena Moralis, widow of failed entrepreneur,
Stephan Moralis, who hanged himself, leaving her and their
son penniless. Darius was no blood relation to Spiro
Cassavetes. As far as she could see he wasn't even a
stepson.

Loveday sat back as the images scrolled by. Spiro didn't
appear in many of them, but there was one face that did crop
up, the bosun on *Moonflyer*, handsome young Scotsman,
James Crawford. She examined the photograph in greater
detail. It was a reception in one of Spiro's hotels. It wasn't on
the yacht, so what was the bosun doing there?

'I've found all these,' Keri said, coming up behind Loveday
and placing a batch of pages on her desk. Loveday glanced
down at them. The top sheet was a photograph of Candice
directing a fashion shoot. Loveday skimmed through the
others. They didn't tell her anything she didn't already know
about the woman. She was about to push them aside and
return to her computer when something caught her eye. She
picked up the page. The caption told her the event was to
celebrate the thirtieth wedding anniversary of Candice's
parents, Eleanor and Charles Chrichton-Smythe at the
family home, Craigallen Castle, in the Scottish Borders. The
photo showed Candice and her brother, Freddie, toasting
their parents and surrounded by a party of guests. Loveday's
attention was drawn to a face on the edge of the group. She
zoomed in on it, blinking. The man was holding his champagne glass in front of his face as though trying to conceal
his identity. But there was no mistaking who it was. The
question was – what was Darius Cassavetes doing at
Candice's parents' family party?

Did these two know each other? Her brow creased. Of course they did.

Her eyes were moving over the faces and stopped when she recognized someone else. The man wasn't standing next to Darius, but he *was* looking in his direction.

James Crawford!

He'd been present at that hotel reception and now here he was again.

Was he more than just the bosun on Cassavetes' yacht? Was he Darius's right-hand man both on board the *Moonflyer* and off? It was interesting.

The buzz of her mobile phone signalled the arrival of a text message. It was from Maya. *She's here*, it told her. Loveday texted back a thumbs up. She was about to ring Tom when he beat her to it. 'I don't have much time. I've dropped Candice off in Penzance. She's having lunch with Maya. Can we meet up, Loveday? I need to speak to you.'

'There's a pub in Angarrack,' she said. 'Off the Hayle bypass–'

'I know it,' Tom cut her off. 'Come as soon as you can, I don't have much time.'

'I'm leaving now,' Loveday said.

'Don't forget you're interviewing a group of litter pickers on Hayle beach at 2pm,' Keri reminded, looking up as Loveday grabbed her bag.

'I'll be there,' Loveday called back as she left the office.

* * *

TOM WAS SITTING at a table away from the bar with an untouched pint in front of him. He'd been watching the door for her and jumped to his feet when he saw Loveday come in. She waved him down, touching his arm as she sat. 'What's this all about, Tom? What's happening?'

'I think I'm being set up for something and I don't know what, but it involves Candice. She watches everything I do. I can't have a private phone call without her lurking around one corner or another listening in.'

'What on earth is she up to, Tom?'

'I've no idea, but I'm sure it was no accident we met. I have a boat that I keep at St Katharine Docks, in London. The *Sea Witch*. She's a beautiful six-berth cruiser. I originally bought the boat for Jamie.' He looked away, swallowing.

It might have been two years since the tragedy of his son's murder but the hurt was still raw. Loveday understood completely. She had her own dark memories of finding Jamie's body.

Tom gave himself a physical shake before carrying on. 'I'd been working on the boat when Candice turned up. She said she was in the market to buy a boat and heard *Sea Witch* was for sale. I invited her on board to take a look around. She was very engaging and it wasn't only the boat she was interested in.' He sighed. 'She was irresistible. Any man would have been flattered by the attention of such a woman.'

He glanced at the clock. 'Anyway, it wasn't long before I realized something was wrong. Candice was asking too many questions. She was particularly interested in my life in Cornwall. I didn't tell her about Maya and April Rose and yet she seemed to know about them, or at least I suspected she did.

'The way she ended telephone calls and shut off her phone when I walked into the room was another thing that made me uneasy. She laughed it off saying I was imagining it and accused me of being jealous.'

'And were you?' Loveday asked.

Tom looked away. 'I suppose I was. I couldn't understand why she was being so secretive about these calls.' He reached for his pint and pulled it closer, but didn't drink from it. 'I knew she wasn't being honest with me and it hurt. I began to wonder if our meeting at St Katharine Docks back then hadn't been about any interest she had in buying my boat.' He shook his head. 'I began to suspect Candice had targeted me. I just had to figure out why.'

Loveday's eyes were glued to his. 'And did you?'

Tom swallowed. 'Not completely but I was sure it had something to do with Maya. Once her name had been mentioned Candice insisted on meeting her. I thought she wanted her and Maya to be friends, but she showed no interest. She was arrogant and condescending. All the charm she had lavished on me before had vanished.'

'Are we talking about the day you all had lunch at the Tinners? The day Sam was there?'

Tom nodded, his brow wrinkling as he remembered it. 'Something happened in the pub that day,' he said slowly. 'Something involving Candice. I'm sure Sam sensed it too.'

Loveday said nothing. She was recalling what Sam had said about a young man at the bar and his feeling that he and Candice knew each other. It crossed her mind this unknown man might be Darius, but she quickly discarded the thought. Tom had never met him, but he didn't fit his description. She opened her bag, took out the sheets from the printer and spread them on the table in front of Tom. 'Take a close look. Is there anyone here you recognize?'

Tom looked at her, screwing up his face. 'What's this?'

'You're not the only one to be suspicious of Candice,' she said, tapping the pages. 'This one in particular.' She slid the image of the Chrichton-Smythes' anniversary celebrations in front of him. 'Recognize anyone here?'

She watched Tom's eyes scan the page and saw him frown. He tapped his finger on the page. 'This one,' he said. 'This is the man who was in the Tinner's Lamp that day.'

Loveday didn't need to turn the page towards her to see

who he meant. The face Tom identified was James Crawford, bosun on the *Moonflyer*.

The fact that Darius and Crawford were in the picture was proof Candice knew both of them. But what had Crawford been doing in that pub? And why had Candice been annoyed to see him there?

'Can you remember if this man was in the pub before you arrived?' Loveday asked.

Tom nodded. 'He was, yes. Who is he?'

His stare widened as Loveday related what she knew about the man and his connection with the Cassavetes.

'So they all know each other?' he said slowly. 'I knew Candice was up to something.'

'We still don't know what's going on but I think Sam needs to know about this.' She was already feeling guilty she hadn't rung him as soon as she found the information online. He might accuse her of interfering but she'd risk it.

Tom was on his feet. 'I need to collect Candice. I don't want to leave her with Maya any longer than I have to.'

* * *

CANDICE LOOKED at Maya with a slow smile. 'I must admit I was surprised when you rang Tom and invited me to lunch, especially when he wasn't included in the invitation.'

Maya forced a smile. 'I felt we should get to know each other, just you and me.'

A waitress arrived at their table and Candice ordered drinks before dismissing the girl.

'What about your food order,' she said, pen poised over her notepad.

'Later,' Candice snapped, shooing her away.

The girl gave her a resentful look as she marched off and Candice turned her attention back to Maya.

'You were saying you wanted us to get to know each other.' She raised an eyebrow waiting for a response.

Maya moved uncomfortably in her chair. 'I suppose you think I'm overprotective of Tom.' The other woman narrowed her eyes. 'Tom isn't only April Rose's grandfather, you know, he's my best friend.'

'And I suppose you want to know if I'm worthy of him?'

'I want Tom to be happy.'

Their drinks arrived. Candice lifted her stemmed glass and took a long sip of wine. 'You don't have to worry about Tom. I take care of everything he needs.' She paused, fixing Maya with a steely blue stare. 'I get no complaints.'

Maya tried to ignore the shiver running down her spine. The Tom she knew would never allow himself to be controlled, and this woman was all about control. Surely he wouldn't be taken in by her? She was much younger than him. Was that it? Had he been seduced by the idea of a younger, beautiful woman falling in love with him? Would he be flattered, or would he see right through it? Candice had an agenda and at the moment it seemed like Tom was being led by the nose.

The pub was quiet and not many of the tables were occupied, but Maya felt the walls were closing in on her. She desperately wanted to get away from this woman, but unless she discovered more about her, Loveday wouldn't be the only one who was disappointed.

Candice was taking out her phone. 'I think we're done here.'

'But we haven't eaten yet,' Maya protested.

'I don't think we need lunch, do you?' Her thumb was moving over the keypad. 'I think it's time for Tom to collect me.'

Maya was on her feet. 'I have to nip out to the ladies.'

Candice nodded, her attention still on her phone.

The tables were separated by glass partitions and Maya could clearly see Candice's reflection. Candice was watching Maya walk away as she reached into her bag and glanced around her before shaking a powder into Maya's drink.

Maya blinked, unable to believe what had just happened. Was this woman attempting to poison her? Her hand shook as she reached for her phone and called Loveday.

'She what?' Loveday forced herself to stay calm. 'Are you sure?'

'She certainly put something in my drink.' Maya's voice was unsteady. 'What should I do?'

'Take a few deep breaths and try to stay calm. Tom should be arriving any minute to pick Candice up. It's important to behave normally. If you're right, she'll encourage you to finish your drink. You have to stall her, Maya. Pretend you have an important phone call to make when Tom arrives. Tell the two of them to get off while you deal with your call. Candice won't like it, but with Tom there she'll have to go along with the situation.'

Maya gave a shaky sigh. 'I don't believe this is happening.'

'Try to keep your nerve, Maya. I'm on my way. I'll hang back when I get there to make sure Tom and Candice have gone. Don't let the waiter take your drink away.'

Loveday slowed down as she neared the entrance to the pub. Tom's Audi was emerging from the pub entrance. Loveday ducked behind the wheel as they passed, and watched in the mirror until the vehicle was out of sight before pulling into the pub car park. She grabbed the bottle of water she always kept in the car and tipped the contents on the ground before stashing it in her bag and hurrying inside.

Maya's face lit up when she spotted Loveday. Her hands were shaking.

'Don't worry. She's gone,' Loveday said, unscrewing the

empty plastic bottle. 'Is this your drink?' Maya nodded as Loveday reached for the wine glass and dribbled the contents into her water bottle.

'You were right, Loveday. Candice did try to encourage me to drink the wine. I told her I'd no intention of leaving it. She tried to dawdle, hang around while I made my fake phone call. I could see how embarrassed Tom was about this. He told her it was a private call and they had to leave me to it.'

'You did brilliantly.' Loveday smiled. 'I need to get this wine back to Sam. He can have it analyzed.'

Calmer now, Maya was collecting her things when she saw Loveday suddenly dart behind a large potted plant. Candice was hurrying back to the table. Maya saw her glance at the empty glass as the flicker of a smile twitched at her mouth.

'I couldn't find my phone,' she said quickly, making a pretence of searching around for it. Then she fumbled in her pocket. 'Oh, look, it's here. How stupid of me.'

Maya couldn't see Candice's face as she hurried off, but she knew she was grinning.

Loveday stayed behind the plant until Maya gave her the thumbs up that Tom's car had left the car park.

'What was that about?' Maya asked.

'Candice came back to check you finished your drink. She probably now thinks her plan worked.' She smiled. 'She's in for a surprise.'

'Is he in?' Loveday demanded of the desk sergeant as she battered through the double doors into the police station.

The sergeant's hand was already on the phone.

'I have a young lady down here asking for you, Inspector,' he said, as Loveday paced impatiently in front of him.

'He wants you to go up. I'll get someone to take you.'

'No need,' Loveday said, waving a hand and taking the visitor ID lanyard he held out. 'I know the way.'

Sam looked up from his phone as Loveday walked in and he motioned her into a chair.

She took out the water bottle she'd filled with Maya's wine and sat it in front of him.

'What's this?' Sam said, eyeing the plastic bottle as he put the phone down.

'If we're right, this is what Candice tried to poison Maya with,' Loveday said.

He squinted at her. 'Is Maya all right?'

'She's fine, a bit shaken up. Fortunately she saw Candice

put the stuff into her wine so she didn't actually drink any of it.'

Sam put up his hands. 'OK, let's start from the beginning.'

'It's not as far-fetched as it sounds. Maya had invited Candice for lunch.'

'Maya and Candice had lunch together?'

Loveday let out an exasperated sigh. 'Do you want to hear about this or not?'

'Of course I do. Carry on.' He listened with a deepening frown while Loveday described how she'd persuaded Maya to get involved in her scheme to get Candice out of the way while she met Tom.

'You *do* know you were putting Maya's life in danger?'

'Well I do now, but neither of us was expecting Candice to attempt to poison her.'

Sam pursed his lips. 'We don't know yet that this is poison. I'll get the lab people to look at it.'

Loveday's mobile phone rang and she tutted, annoyed at the interruption. 'Yes!' she barked at the unknown caller. Her eyebrows crept up as the caller introduced himself. She shot Sam a look. 'Mr Cassavetes? How are you?' Loveday had Sam's full attention now. 'Dinner? Tonight?' She shrugged at Sam. 'The Pandora Inn? Yes, I know it.' She paused, listening. 'I'm not sure what my partner's plans are for this evening. I'll ring him.' She waited again while the caller spoke. 'Yes, 8pm,' she responded. 'Like I said, I'll ask him. Hopefully we'll be there.'

The call ended. Loveday stared at Sam. 'That was Darius Cassavetes. He's invited us to dinner.'

'I got that much,' Sam said, his brow wrinkling. 'What I don't know is why?'

'He said it was by way of an apology for wasting my time over the abandoned interview with his father.'

'Spiro is not his father,' Sam said.

Loveday's mind went back to her research into the man. 'Of course,' she said. 'He took the Cassavetes name when Spiro married his mother. But how did you know?'

'You're not the only one who checks up on things.'

'So Darius is a suspect for the Morwenna Chenoweth murder?'

'At this stage everyone is a suspect, including Candice.'

'What about James Crawford, the bosun on *Moonflyer*? They're all connected, you know.'

'Like I said, we have eyes on all of them, which is why I'm interested in what Darius is up to with his dinner invitation.'

* * *

SAM's brief encounter with Darius Cassavetes on board the *Moonflyer* had whetted his appetite to discover more. He had a rich man's hobby. Not many people could afford to collect antiquities – or would know where to find them, for Sam was certain Darius didn't wait for legitimate sales to crop up. He couldn't see the man competing against other bidders either.

* * *

AT HOME that evening Loveday was changing for their dinner date when she heard Sam's mobile ring.

'The lab results are in for Maya's wine,' he called to her.

Loveday came through to him, a hairbrush in her hand. 'Well?' she asked.

Sam's expression was grim. 'It was strychnine,' he said.

Her mouth dropped open. 'That woman tried to poison Maya with strychnine? But why?'

Sam shrugged. 'That's what we have to find out.'

'Where would she have got it?'

'It's a pesticide, a rat poison. It's not difficult to find online.'

Loveday shook her head in despair. 'Will she be arrested?'

'She'll be brought in for questioning, but right now we only have Maya's word Candice did this.'

'But the proof was right there. I brought it in to you.'

'I know, but you didn't actually see Candice put the strychnine in Maya's wine.'

'Well, no, but surely you have enough to be suspicious?'

'We need more than a suspicion,' he said, pulling a face as his phone rang again. 'It's DC Fox. I'll have to take it,' he said, hitting the *accept* button. 'Yes, Amanda?'

Loveday watched Sam's frown deepen as he listened. He looked up and met her stare.

She was instantly beside him. 'What is it? What's happened?'

'It's Maya,' he said. 'She's been in a car crash.'

Loveday's eyes flew wide as Sam put up his hand. 'Don't panic, she's fine,' he said quickly. 'Just cuts and grazes. Her car was run off the road, the one from Penzance to St Ives.'

'Is she badly hurt?'

'She hit a tree. According to A&E at Treliske, she's a bit shaken up. She has cuts and bruises but none serious enough to keep her in overnight.'

He turned back to his phone, putting it on speaker so Loveday could listen. 'What about this other vehicle, Amanda?' he asked. 'Did we get a number?'

'Do you want the good news or the bad?' Amanda said.

'Just get on with it,' Sam said.

'Miss Brookes' car had a dashcam fitted, so we've got the other vehicle's reg. Bad news is we've checked it and–'

'It's stolen,' Sam interrupted her.

'I'm afraid so.'

He hissed an expletive. 'Where is Miss Brookes now?'

'She should be home, sir. Her friend, Mr Scobey, collected her from A&E.'

'OK, thanks, Amanda. Keep me posted.'

'It wasn't an accident, was it,' Loveday said as Sam cancelled the call.

He shook his head.

'Oh, Sam,' Loveday said quietly. 'You have to take this seriously now. Somebody out there wants Maya dead.'

* * *

THE PANDORA INN's setting by the edge of Restronguet Creek was magical. Being an old, thatched cottage added to the romance of the place and made it a magnet for Cornwall's yachting fraternity.

From the window table Darius had booked, Loveday and Sam had an uninterrupted view of the boat landing and the diners who arrived by water. It occurred to her that placing them here had been deliberate. She imagined Darius liked to make an entrance.

A small tender was tying up at the far end of the pier and four people were scrambling out of it onto the decking amid much hilarity. Across the dark waters of the creek Loveday could see lights twinkling in the windows of the desirable properties opposite.

'I suppose you're going to tell me this place is haunted,' Sam said, raising his voice over the buzz of the diners around them. He was following her gaze across the flagstoned floor to the intimate nooks and cosy corners of the pub.

'I'm working on that one,' Loveday said. She was toying with the idea of writing a book about Cornwall's quirky old inns and pubs. All she knew about the place was that parts of it dated back to the thirteenth century. Following a few name changes, it became known as the Pandora Inn, after the HMS

Pandora, the naval ship sent to Tahiti to capture the muti-neers of Captain Bligh's *Bounty*.

'This looks like our man arriving,' Sam said, nodding to the activity at the far end of the pier.

Loveday recognized the tender from the *Moonflyer*. The man hopping off to secure it to the mooring was the yacht's bosun, James Crawford. 'A man of many talents,' Loveday murmured as Darius Cassavetes, in immaculate white jeans and what looked like a dark navy silk shirt and leather blouson jacket strode confidently towards the pub.

She saw him duck his head under a low beam as he gave them a wave and made his way to their table.

'I'm so glad you could come.' He smiled as they all shook hands and he sat down looking around him.

'What a wonderful place,' he said.

'The food's not bad either,' Loveday said as Darius hailed a waiter to order drinks. Although he was charming and animated in his small talk, it was clear to Loveday that it was Sam who held his interest.

The dinner invitation was no gesture of friendliness. Darius Cassavetes had an agenda and Loveday was intrigued to discover what it was. She smiled as she sipped her wine. The evening was going to be more fascinating than she'd imagined.

'I hope my father was able to help you with your enquiries,' Darius said.

Sam raised an eyebrow. 'Enquiries?'

'That poor murdered girl. I read about it. Isn't it why you wanted to speak to him?'

'If you're talking about the body found at Carn Hendra, we haven't said she'd been murdered.' He gave Darius a bright smile. Even Loveday could see the man was fishing.

'Why would you think your father would know anything about it?'

'I don't,' he said quickly. 'It's just that you were named in the newspaper article. I assumed visiting my father was part of the investigation.'

'It wasn't.'

The response was sharp, even for Sam. He hadn't mentioned his meeting with Spiro but Loveday guessed it would have been to discover more about the photograph of Maya and her mother she'd seen in the man's private state-room on the *Moonflyer*. Beyond that, she knew nothing. But why was Darius so keen to know?

'How's the antiquities collection coming along?' Sam said.

'I haven't added to it since last we spoke.'

'Isn't that why you're here in Cornwall?'

'No.' Darius fired the word back at him. His relaxed confidence was slipping. 'Why would you think that? I told you before. My father and I love coming to Cornwall.'

The lobsters they'd ordered arrived and Loveday saw Sam give his plate an appreciative look. Darius emptied his glass and ordered more wine. She hadn't known he collected antiquities. It was interesting.

'We have many fascinating old places of interest in Cornwall,' Loveday said. 'Although maybe not as many as you must surely have back home in Greece.'

'That's true,' Darius agreed. 'But history differs and there is room for all interests.'

Sam finished his mouthful of food. 'Loveday has an involvement in our Cornish history,' he said. 'Tell Mr Cassavetes about the Carn Hendra Heritage Centre.'

Loveday gave Darius a shy look. 'I don't think Mr Cassavetes would be interested in our little collection. It must be small fry compared to the antiquities he will own.'

'On the contrary,' Darius said. There was a flash of interest in the dark eyes, but the surprise was missing. So the man already knew about Loveday's connection to the heritage centre. Sam was intrigued to know more. He watched Darius's face as Loveday described how she'd gifted the land and her ongoing involvement in the work of the centre.

'It must have been difficult finding someone with the specific level of local knowledge to run the place,' Darius commented.

Loveday smiled. 'Not that difficult. The young woman who is our conservator has been involved in the project from the beginning. In fact, it was more or less her idea.'

'Really? I'd like to meet her.' He looked up and met Loveday's eye. 'Perhaps you could arrange it?'

Sam kept his expression bland. Darius's sudden interest in Maya had grabbed his attention. 'Was this why they had been invited to dinner? Were they about to be pumped about Maya? He didn't need to look at Loveday to know she was well aware of where this conversation appeared to be going.

'I'll speak to her,' she said.

'When you do, please let her know how impressed I am to hear about the lady's knowledge of local history.' He smiled. 'What's her name?'

'Maya Brookes.'

They both watched him for any sign of recognition at the name. There was none. Instead he asked if she had a local background.

Loveday avoided Sam's eyes. 'She was living in the area at the time of the centre's conception. I'm not sure about her background previous to that.'

'You were not involved in the interview procedure?'

Loveday blinked. 'I was on the interview panel, yes, but it was the candidates' professional qualifications that interested us. We didn't delve into their private lives.'

Darius nodded, but his eyes remained on her for a second longer than she felt comfortable with.

'What qualifications would a candidate need for such a post?'

Loveday considered the question before answering. She felt she was being drawn into giving details of Maya's background.

'Someone who had a good grounding in the area,' Loveday said. 'We were looking for candidates with a BA (Hons) Archaeology degree. Experience of curating at a museum was also desirable.'

Darius gave a thoughtful nod. 'The archaeology because of the nature of the landscape in the area,' he said.

'Exactly,' Loveday agreed. Maya had studied archaeology at York University and had written several books on Cornish standing stones. But Loveday would leave Darius to discover that for himself.

She looked up at him. 'Why don't you give Maya a ring yourself and arrange a visit to the heritage centre?' If he had been involved in the hit-and-run escapade that could have killed Maya he might give himself away.

But he was too clever for that. Darius's face broke into a smile. 'Sounds like an excellent idea.' He looked at his watch. The dinner they'd shared had been a leisurely thing and James Crawford was still waiting by the tender at the end of the pier.

'I'm afraid I have to go, but please feel free to stay and enjoy a brandy with your coffee.'

'Thank you,' Sam said. He had no intention of ordering any brandy when he had to drive back to Marazion.

They watched the man as he went to the bar and handed over his card. He didn't turn for a final wave as he headed for the door, ducking his head under the dark beam again as he left.

'He wanted to know about Maya, didn't he?' Loveday said, her eyes on Cassavetes' back as he strode along the pier.

She could see Crawford at the far end squaring his shoulders ready to greet his boss as he approached.

'Yup,' Sam said, getting to his feet. 'And now he has a legitimate reason to meet up with her.'

'We should have asked him if he knew Candice,' Loveday suggested.

'Maybe that's a question for Candice,' Sam said.

'Will she have been picked up yet?'

'No, I'll be going to see her myself in the morning. I want her to feel she's safe for a little longer.'

Loveday rang Tom as they left the restaurant. 'How is Maya?' she asked the instant he picked up the call.

'She's resting comfortably now. The doctor prescribed something to help her sleep. I'm staying with her and April Rose at the cottage tonight to keep an eye on them.'

Loveday sighed into the phone. 'That's such a relief, Tom. Tell Maya I've been asking after her. I'll ring again in the morning.'

'Is she OK?' Sam asked, as Loveday got into the car beside him.

She nodded. 'Tom's staying with them tonight. Any more news about who rammed her car?'

'Not so far.'

She slid him a look, but his handsome profile gave nothing away. She wondered how much he would share with her if there had been any more news.

CHAPTER 26

Sam beckoned for Will and Amanda to join him as he strode into the CID suite next morning. 'OK, Amanda, tell me more about the Maya Brookes accident.'

'The vehicle responsible was abandoned in a lane close to the incident site. It had been torched.'

'Have we checked the dashcam footage?'

Amanda Fox nodded. 'We have. It shows the other car approaching, but no clear image of who was driving it. Sorry, boss.'

She'd turned to leave when Sam's mobile rang. He had intended bringing Candice in himself but the call changed his mind. 'We need to speak to Candice Chrichton-Smythe. She might not be happy about accepting our invitation, but that's too bad. You should find her at Tom Scobey's cottage.'

'Has something else happened, sir?'

'There's been a burglary at Fenwick Church. Somebody's pinched the St Piran carving.' He gestured to DS Will Tregellis to follow him out.

The Truro traffic had eased off a lot since Sam had driven

into the city half an hour earlier, but it was still busy enough to slow them up.

'Is this carving a valuable thing then?' Will asked.

'Historians might say it's priceless.'

'A priceless antiquity, eh.' Will gave a slow smile. 'Who do we know who collects antiquities?'

'Darius Cassavetes,' Sam said grimly, wondering if the man really was shameless enough to have robbed the church straight from having dinner with him and Loveday. He suspected the answer might be yes.

The Rev Sara Corey was waiting for them in the church. 'I wasn't sure if I should report the theft to the police station or ring the mobile number you gave me.'

'Ringing me was the right thing to do,' Sam assured her. 'When did you notice the carving was missing?'

'About 7am, after I discovered poor Mr Nelson, our security officer lying unconscious in the churchyard. He was coming to when I arrived. He had a severe headache but had no idea what had happened to him. I couldn't see any blood or bruises but I called for an ambulance anyway to be on the safe side.

'I stayed with him until the paramedics arrived and took him off to hospital for a proper check-up.' She smiled. 'Poor Walter, he wasn't exactly pleased about going to hospital.'

Sam nodded. Someone would have to interview the man. He punched Amanda's number into his phone and instructed her to visit the hospital after she had delivered Candice Chrichton-Smythe to the station.

'OK, vicar, let's see the damage,' he said, turning with her to the small chapel where the carving had been.

'It was right here,' Sara said. 'We were talking about it just the other day.'

Sam asked Sara to stay back. 'The thief may have left

DNA evidence. Our forensic officers will need to examine the site,' he explained.

'They haven't left much damage,' Will commented. 'Whoever did this knew what they were doing.'

Sam nodded. The St Piran had been mounted on a wooden plinth. The whole thing had been unscrewed from the wall. He turned to the vicar. 'You mentioned before about seeing some people taking a special interest in the carving? Could you describe them to our e-fit specialist?'

'Yes of course, I'll do anything I can to help.' An expression of concern crossed her face. 'I heard about poor Maya. Is there any news from the hospital?'

'She's at home still feeling a bit shocked but I'm told she's making a slow recovery.'

He looked down at her. 'You look pretty shattered yourself.'

Sara Corey gave him a weak smile. 'It's the thought of someone breaking into our church in the dead of night and stealing from us. It makes me feel personally violated.'

'You said it was about 7am when you came down to the church. Do you normally open it so early?'

'No, our cleaner Jess does that. She arrives about 8am and works for two hours. I came to the church to collect some notes I'd left in the vestibule. I like to work on my sermon as and when I have time and I needed the notes.

'I didn't actually come into the church until after Walter went off in the ambulance.'

'Was the door open?' Sam asked.

Sara nodded. 'It was. I felt wary about coming in but I had to do it. I had to investigate. I was worried the intruders would have caused havoc. Fortunately they hadn't. It's bad enough they stole the carving.' She frowned at Sam. 'Why would anyone do that? There are many more valuable treasures in our church, yet they took the St Piran.'

'That's what we have to find out,' Sam said.

Sara sighed. 'Would it be all right if I put the kettle on? I think we could all do with a cup of tea.'

'Sounds like a good idea,' Sam said, turning as Will joined him. He'd been arranging to get the forensic team down to the church.

'What d'you think, sir?' he asked. 'Is it a professional job?'

'It didn't need to be professional,' Sam said. 'Anybody with a screwdriver could have done it. But they would have needed transport. Somebody in this village must have seen something. Let's get a door to door organized.'

'Also, we need Les Maynard and his box of tricks down here for a couple of e-fits.'

'We have a witness who can identify our raiders?' Will raised an eyebrow.

'Sadly no, but the vicar here, did notice a few suspicious-looking people taking a special interest in the carving over recent days.' He grimaced at the narrowing of Will's eyes.

'All right, I know it's clutching at straws but at the moment it's all we have.'

Sam's mobile buzzed. 'Yes, Amanda. What've you got for us?'

'Not a lot, boss. The security officer looks like he'll be fine. All he remembers though is having a cloth put over his mouth and a woozy feeling before he passed out.'

'What was he doing out in the churchyard? He must have heard something that took him out there.'

'He said he heard a noise and went out to investigate. He heard voices, so there must have been more than one of them. Two, possibly three men, he thinks, but he couldn't swear to it.'

'Did he leave the church door open when he went outside?'

'Yes he did,' Amanda said. 'The place was wide open. Our friends didn't even have to break in.'

'What about the lovely Miss Chrichton-Smythe? Did she give you much trouble?'

'Nothing I couldn't handle, sir,' Amanda said. 'Although I suspect the lady isn't exactly happy about accepting our hospitality at the nick.'

'I don't suppose she is,' Sam said, knowing Candice would already have been busy on her phone summoning a solicitor.

'Was Miss Brookes badly hurt, sir?' Will asked, changing the subject as they walked around the churchyard.

'More shock and bruises than any serious injury. She was lucky.'

'Was she?'

Sam gave him a sharp look. 'You don't sound convinced. Surely you're not still thinking these attempts on Maya's life are a set-up?'

'I'm trying to keep an open mind. But think about it, sir. That display board poor Loveday took the brunt of. It could easily have been orchestrated. How do we know Maya hadn't attached a string and yanked on it as they passed? I'm not saying she wanted to hurt Loveday. Maybe Maya hadn't expected her to jump in to save her.'

'And the strychnine in her glass?'

'She could have done it herself. No one but her actually saw Candice do anything.'

'And running her off the road? We have that dashcam footage, remember.'

Will shrugged. 'It could all have been pre-arranged.' He met Sam's eyes. 'And we only have Maya's word for it that she fled the heritage centre after finding Morwenna Chenoweth. Who's to say the two women didn't walk out on the cliffs together? Maya could have bashed the poor girl's brains in with the stone we found.'

Sam's face creased into a frown. 'Everything you've said is assumption, Will.'

'It is, sir. But so is assuming Maya is completely innocent of all these things. I think we should keep an open mind.'

'Of course we do, and we will,' Sam said, drawing in a deep breath. He was imagining what Loveday would say if she'd heard this conversation. But he knew Will was right. He didn't believe for a minute Maya was guilty of any of this, but they had to consider it.

CHAPTER 27

*L*oveday had just arrived at the magazine office when Maya rang. 'The village is crawling with police. What's going on, Loveday?'

'Maya! I was about to call Tom to ask how you are after yesterday. We were all quite worried about you.'

Loveday could hear the sigh in her friend's voice.

'I wasn't injured, you know, just felt a bit shocked.'

'Tom was concerned enough to stay overnight with you and April Rose.'

Maya laughed. 'He's been brilliant. I feel such a fraud being spoiled like this. What I'm not enjoying is Tom insisting I don't go into work today. I'm beginning to feel like a prisoner in my own home.'

'Tom really cares about you, Maya. You should trust him.'

'Of course I do, but how much will he trust me when he learns I've been accusing his girlfriend of trying to poison me?' She paused. 'Has Sam arrested her yet?'

'I don't know about arrest, but I think they'll be talking to her down at the police station.'

'Will that have anything to do with all this police activity in the village?'

'I shouldn't think so,' Loveday said. 'There's been a burglary at the church.'

'Burglary! Gosh, is Sara all right? Maybe I should ring her?'

Loveday nodded at the phone. 'That's a good idea. And the call's better coming from you.' She knew Sam wouldn't appreciate her contacting the vicar. He would see it as interference.

It was five minutes before Maya got back to her. 'You'll never guess,' she said. 'The carving of St Piran has been stolen.'

'Has it now.' Loveday was thoughtful.

'I can tell by your voice you know something, Loveday. What is it? Do you know who stole it?'

Loveday pulled a face as she remembered the previous evening's dinner with Darius Cassavetes. She might have no inside knowledge about the theft, but she could take a wild guess at who might be behind it.

* * *

THE E-FITS the Rev Sara had helped create had come through by the time Sam and Will arrived back at the station. Sam scrolled through the images. If they were lucky they had a 70% chance of an e-fit looking something like its intended subject. This was one of those times. 'Get Joss Teague down here, Will.' He felt like punching the air. 'And Tom Scobey too.'

'Scobey is already here. He followed Candice in.'

'I need to speak to him,' Sam said.

It took only five minutes to locate Tom in the station canteen.

'How well do you know Candice, Tom?' Sam asked.

'I know I don't trust her. I've heard a whisper she's to be questioned about an attempted murder.' He screwed up his face. 'Is that right, Sam? Did Candice try to kill someone?'

Sam evaded the question as he passed his phone across the desk. 'These are three e-fits we received today. Do you recognize any of these people?'

Tom picked up the phone. 'It's Candice,' he said, nodding.

'What about the other two?'

Tom studied the faces. 'I've never seen this man before. But this one...' He pointed to the younger of the two men. 'I've seen him at the Miners' Lamp.' He looked up. 'You must remember, Sam. He was there the day we all had lunch at the pub.'

Sam did remember, but he needed Tom's independent confirmation.

'You still haven't told me about Candice. What's she done?'

'I'm sorry, Tom. I can't discuss it. We haven't interviewed her yet.'

But Tom persisted. 'She had lunch with Maya yesterday. Has it anything to do with that?'

Sam wasn't quick enough to hide his reaction.

Tom's eyes widened. 'It was Maya she tried to kill!' He slapped a hand to his forehead. 'This is all my fault. I should never have brought Candice here.'

'You can't blame yourself. Maya is safe and Candice won't be trying anything else. Leave this to us now, we'll deal with it.' Sam's tone was uncompromising.

Tom sucked in a deep breath. 'Does Maya know Candice tried to kill her?'

Sam nodded. 'You should get back to your cottage. We'll contact you there if anything changes.'

Tom nodded wearily and his shoulders slumped as he turned and walked from the room.

Will waited for Tom to leave before going into Sam's office. 'Do you want me to sit in on the interview with Candice, boss?'

'No, let her stew for now. I want this man brought in.' His finger tapped the e-fit image that resembled James Crawford. 'And where's Joss Teague? We need him to see these e-fits.'

'You know Candice is screaming for a lawyer?'

'I would expect no less.'

'He, or she, is bound to insist their client knows nothing about poisoning Maya. I can see us being accused of setting the whole thing up,' Will said.

Sam was aware they had no concrete evidence. Loveday had brought a water bottle containing wine slaked with strychnine. He had no doubt Candice had poured the poison into Maya's wine glass as she had said, but knowing wasn't proof. He sighed. He knew they would have to release Candice.

He got up and went to the window, staring down to the street. Tom was bound to want the woman out of his cottage ASAP. He might even be tempted to throw her belongings out. There might be evidence in those things. Knowing DC Amanda Fox, she wouldn't have given Candice time to dispose of anything when she brought her in. If there was any physical evidence against her it would still be in Tom's cottage. He called for Amanda.

She hurried in, grabbing a pen and notebook as she left her desk.

'I want you to go back to the place where you picked up the Chrichton-Smythe woman.' Sam was already reaching for his phone. 'I'll tell Tom Scobey to expect you.'

'What exactly are you asking me to do?'

Sam smiled. 'You're going to be an observer, DC Fox.'

'*How* ow did the date go last night?' Keri asked as Loveday walked into the office.

'Date?'

'You said you and Sam were going out for dinner.'

'Oh that. Yes, it was good.'

Keri raised an eyebrow. She recognized when her boss was shutting down a conversation. It was the look of distraction that did it. Loveday was deep into her own thoughts.

Unknown to Keri, Loveday was going over the details of everything Darius had said about his love of antiquities. Had the purpose of last night's dinner been to provide him with an alibi for the theft of the St Piran? But if he had been responsible for that he wouldn't have done it himself. His lackeys would have been working on his behalf. She wondered how much a man would have to pay to buy a burglary.

A picture of James Crawford flashed into her mind. He certainly looked loyal to Darius, but would that stretch to stealing for him?

She frowned, wondering how Candice fitted into all this.

Maybe she didn't. Her attempt to poison Maya may have had nothing to do with the theft. But no, it was too much of a coincidence. Then there was the newspaper photo of Darius and James at Candice's parents' anniversary. The three of them knew each other, but was it more than that?

She was wondering if Candice had been romantically involved with one of them. Loveday couldn't see the ambitious Candice setting her sights on a bosun. Her interest would be with the man who gave the orders, not the one who obeyed them. Darius was handsome, dashing even – and rich.

She sat up. Was that it? Candice and Darius? Had she become involved with Tom Scobey and come to Cornwall with him while working under instructions from Darius? But why?

Loveday's mind went back again to the previous evening at the Pandora Inn. Darius had been engaging company. His fascination with antiquities had interested her although it had left her wondering how legitimate his collection actually was. And now the St Piran carving had been stolen. Was that a coincidence? She didn't like coincidences, but more importantly, neither did Sam. If Darius's possible involvement in the theft had occurred to her she knew Sam would also be considering it.

'Loveday.' Keri's voice brought her back into the room. 'It's a call for you. He won't give his name.'

Loveday blinked, clearing her head. 'It's fine. I'll take it.' She reached for the landline as the call was transferred.

'Loveday Ross,' she said crisply. 'How can I help you?'

The voice was rich and attractive. The accent Greek. 'Good morning, Miss Ross,' the man said. 'It's Spiro Cassavetes. Can we meet?'

* * *

THE SOLICITOR who turned up at the station to represent Candice could have stepped straight out of Savile Row. Charles Reece-Campbell was immaculate in a pin-striped charcoal suit and stiff-collared white shirt. He was fingering the knot in his pink silk tie as Sam and Will approached. 'I would like to see my client, Miss Chrichton-Smythe,' he demanded, his arrogant blue eyes moving from one to the other. 'And I don't appreciate being kept waiting.'

He was exactly what Sam had been expecting – self-important, pompous and irritatingly arrogant. Sam smiled. 'I didn't catch your name.'

'Charles Reece-Campbell. I've been retained by the Chrichton-Smythe family to represent their daughter.' He tapped at his watch. 'And we're wasting time.'

Sam turned to Will. 'Have Miss Chrichton-Smythe brought to one of the interview rooms, Sergeant,' he said. 'Her lawyer's here.'

He felt the man's resentful stare burn into his back as he strode away. Charles Reece-Campbell didn't like being dismissed.

They hadn't yet interviewed Candice. If there was anything incriminating in the personal belongings she'd been forced to leave at the cottage she would be getting anxious. Sam and Will were waiting to hear back from Amanda when the call came.

Sam put his phone on hands free so they could both listen.

'Mr Scobey was clearing out Miss Chrichton-Smythe's things when I got here,' Amanda said. 'So I did as I was instructed. I observed.'

'We don't need the drama, DC Fox,' Sam said crisply. 'Just tell us what happened.'

Amanda took a deep breath. 'Mr Scobey was putting the lady's things into a black bag. In doing so a cosmetic bag happened to fall and the contents spilled out.' She paused. 'There were a couple of interesting little bags of white powder amongst the things.'

'Powder? Candice was taking drugs?' Sam whistled.

'And that's not all,' Amanda said. 'There was a mobile phone hidden in a very expensive-looking trainer.'

'Did Tom touch it?' Sam asked sharply.

'Don't worry, sir. I had a spare pair of nitrile gloves in my bag and Mr Scobey put them on before lifting it out. We were both wondering why she needed two phones.'

A slow smile crossed Sam's face. 'Well done, DC Fox,' he said.

Will frowned. 'Surely we can't use any of this as evidence when we didn't have a warrant to search Candice's things?'

'But we didn't search them. DC Fox merely observed Mr Scobey clearing out Candice's property.'

'That's right, sir,' Amanda said. 'Under the circumstances, Mr Scobey was very concerned when he found these items and since Candice is a person of interest to us, he will be bringing them into the station. I'll follow him in.'

A smile flickered across Will's face. 'Very clever, sir. So we can, if necessary, use this evidence against her?'

Sam nodded. 'I'm sure her solicitor will insist the evidence was planted by a bitter ex-lover. He'll be trying to build up a case against Tom, but since he was wearing gloves when he found the phone his prints won't be on it.' He frowned. 'I'm not sure how it helps us find Morwenna Chenoweth's killer, unless of course Candice did it.'

'Is that likely?' Will asked.

'I've no idea, but the lady has questions to answer.'

* * *

THE LOOK CANDICE gave the detectives as they entered the room was pure venom.

Reece-Campbell's expression, however, was smug. 'If you have evidence against my client produce it now. If not, we will be walking out of here.'

Sam's face gave nothing away. Although Candice's phone and the suspected drugs Tom found were on their way to the station, they had not yet been examined or logged as evidence, so the woman *would* be released. But that would be a temporary situation for she would soon be back in custody.

There was one more thing to do and if they could pull it off Candice would be going nowhere. James Crawford had been brought in and Joss Teague had arrived at the station. A third person would also view the ID parade they'd set up.

The door to the interview room opened and a PC entered and passed a note to Sam. He glanced at the paper. It told him the identity parade was ready. He whispered a response to the officer and turned to Candice. 'We need your co-operation with one more thing, Miss Chrichton-Smythe.'

Candice threw a furious look to her solicitor, but his glare was fixed on Sam.

'We'd like you to take part in an identity parade,' Sam said.

'What identity parade?' Reece-Campbell demanded. 'There's been no mention of any identity parade.'

'It's only just been arranged,' Sam said as he and Will got to their feet. 'If you would follow the officer, please.'

They all moved into the corridor at the same moment James Crawford emerged from another room flanked by two officers. Sam held his breath. The meeting of the two people had been purposely set up to log their reactions. Even though the man had been a guest at Candice's parents' party it was not proof the two knew each other. Not even Reece-Campbell could have denied the shocked glance that flashed between Candice and James in the corridor. Sam hid a satisfied smile. They definitely knew each other!

It hadn't been easy to find women who looked enough like Candice to take part in a line-up. Most of those who agreed worked at the station.

Candice glanced along the line with a sneer of disgust. 'Is this a joke? None of these people look remotely like me.'

'Choose where you want to stand in the line, please,' Sam said.

'I'm not standing anywhere.' The woman shot her solicitor a look. 'I'd like to leave now, please.'

'This is a fiasco,' Reece-Campbell complained. He swung round to face Sam. 'I want to make it clear my client is only doing this because she wants to co-operate with you.'

Candice stared at him. 'You mean I have to do this?'

Reece-Campbell nodded, an irritated frown crossing his face. 'Let's just get this done.'

Candice pushed into the line, forcing the women on either side to shuffle sideways. She glared defiantly at the glass screen in front of them.

'Bring him in,' Will ordered from the other side of the screen. A door opened and Joss Teague walked in, his eyes on the line of women.

'Take your time. There's no hurry,' Will said. 'Take a good look at each woman and tell us if you see the one who was in the churchyard that night.'

Joss frowned, studying each woman in turn. His gaze briefly flickered over Candice before he moved on. He shook his head. 'I'm sorry, I can't be sure,' he said. 'I don't really recognize any of these women.'

Will tried not to give a disappointed sigh. 'Thank you anyway, sir. We appreciate your cooperation.'

Reece-Campbell looked up as the detectives walked back.

He sensed rather than saw their reaction and smiled. 'My client and I will be leaving now,' he said briskly.

'Not quite yet, Mr Campbell,' Sam said, deliberately misusing the man's double-barrelled surname. 'If you could return to the interview room and be patient for a moment or two longer.'

The Rev Sara Corey had also been brought in, but on Sam's instructions her presence had been kept from the others. On his nod Will went to fetch her.

'If you would come this way please, vicar,' Will said, moving with her to the viewing area.

She looked concerned.

He smiled. 'Don't worry. It's a one-way screen. The people on the other side can't see us. Take a good look at each person and let us know if you can see the woman in the church that day.'

Sara Corey took a deep breath and swallowed. She walked up and down the line and nodded to Candice. 'It's her. She's the one I saw.'

'You're sure?' Will asked.

Sara nodded. 'I'm positive.'

Will conducted her back to the room where she'd been kept separate from the others and went back to Sam, giving him the thumbs up.

Pleased the vicar had identified Candice, Sam was curious to see if she could also identify James Crawford.

A line of young men shuffled awkwardly into place. None of them had been under any obligation to take part in this but some clearly relished it more than others. Crawford had slotted himself in second from the end of the line before Sara was brought back.

'We do the same as before,' Will said. 'Go up and down the line looking at each man. Take your time. If you recognize the person you saw in the church then point to him.'

Sara nodded and did as instructed. 'That's him. Second from the end,' she said.

'Sure?'

'Absolutely no doubt.'

'Thank you,' Sam said, joining them. 'We'll get a car to take you home.'

As Sara left the building, escorted by a young female PC, Will Tregellis fetched Joss Teague.

Sam narrowed his eyes, studying the man's face as he scanned the line-up for any sign he recognized the bosun. It was interesting he hadn't identified Candice, especially as he had previously stated he would recognize the couple from the churchyard if he saw them again.

He waited, watching as Joss scratched his head. 'The one in the middle looks familiar, but I'm not sure.'

'You can have a second look if it will help,' Will said.

Joss's shoulders rose in a shrug. 'Sorry, I just don't know.'

They thanked him and watched him leave as the volunteers dispersed.

'What are you thinking, boss?' Will asked.

Sam pursed his lips. 'I'm wondering why our Mr Teague is lying,' he said.

CHAPTER 29

The Heron Inn was close enough to Truro city centre to be convenient and far enough from it to ensure Loveday's meeting with Spiro Cassavetes was unlikely to raise any interested eyebrows.

She had dismissed her initial annoyance with the man after he abandoned their interview. That was in the past and Loveday had never been in favour of holding grudges. She had no idea why Spiro had asked for this meeting but the anticipation was causing an edgy flutter in her stomach as she pulled into the pub's tiny, awkwardly shaped car park.

She got out of the Clio, pausing for a moment to look out over the water. A mist had settled and she had to strain her eyes to make out the movement of birds in the heronry on the other side. The pub's location, overlooking the spectacular view where the Truro, Tresillian and Fal rivers met, made it a popular tourist attraction, but today the place was quiet.

Spiro must have been watching for her. He got to his feet as she entered and held out his hand. 'I wasn't sure you would come. I have many apologies to make to you.'

Loveday flapped her hand, dismissing his concern. 'All forgotten.' She smiled, taking her seat opposite him.

A bottle of expensive red wine and two glasses sat on the table. Spiro poured them both a drink.

'Inspector Kitto will have told you about our conversation,' he said.

Loveday frowned. 'Actually, no, he hasn't told me.'

'Ah, I thought he would have mentioned it.'

'I know you met, but not the details. He doesn't discuss cases he's working on, not if he can help it. Admittedly those paths do sometimes cross if I know the people he needs to interview.'

'Does that include Maya Brookes?'

Loveday raised her eyes to meet his.

'My daughter,' he said quietly. 'But then I think you already know.'

'Maya is my friend.'

'That's why I wanted to meet you today. I need your help, Miss Ross.'

'Please call me Loveday. How can I help?'

'Advice really.' He looked away, biting his lip. 'How would Maya react if I told her I was her father?'

Loveday blew out her cheeks. 'I doubt if even she could tell you that. Maya has been through so much over these past two years. She's still pretty fragile emotionally.'

'I know about her partner, Jamie, being murdered,' Spiro said quietly. 'I also know how much she's come to depend on the support of Jamie's father, Tom Scobey. He's been a good friend to her.'

Loveday wondered, not for the first time, if Maya regarded Tom as more than a friend. 'Do you know Tom?' she asked.

Spiro took his time responding to the question. 'Only slightly. Tom and I share the same passion for boats. And before you ask, the answer is no, he doesn't know Maya is my daughter.'

Loveday sat back, frowning. 'Have you held back sharing that with Tom because you know about his involvement with Candice?'

Spiro threw his head back. 'Ah, Candice. Not a young woman to be trusted. We've been keeping an eye on her.' He paused, his expression cold. 'I know she tried to harm my daughter. I also know how concerned you have been for Maya's safety, but let me offer you some reassurance. Nothing bad will happen to my daughter while my people are watching over her.'

'Really?' Loveday was having difficulty taking all this in. 'Who are these people? Does Maya know she's being watched?'

'I employ the best people I can find. Maya doesn't even know they're there. They are keeping her safe and that's what's important.'

'Where were your minders when Candice almost poisoned Maya?'

'They were there and saw everything. They would have intervened had it been necessary, but you and Maya herself were already taking care of everything.'

'And when she was almost killed at the heritage centre by that display board?'

Spiro pulled a face. 'My man was too slow in intervening. He no longer works for me.' He smiled. 'He did however tell me what you did. You were very brave to hurl yourself forward to take the blow yourself and save Maya.'

Loveday waved his praise aside. 'What about the car accident? You didn't manage to prevent that.'

'Sadly not. My people are not invincible but they were there and intervened when they realised what the rogue driver was up to. They all but forced him off the road. If they hadn't done then Maya could have been involved in a head on collision. Thankfully my daughter saw the incident developing and had the presence of mind to take the action she did thus avoiding serious injury.'

Loveday reached for her glass. What she was hearing made sense. 'Tell me more about how I can help you.'

Spiro looked out across the water, his eyes tracing the progress of a yacht making its way upstream. 'I suppose what I'm really asking for,' he said, 'is for your help in telling Maya about me.'

'You want me to tell Maya you're her father?'

'I thought perhaps we could tell her together.'

Loveday shook her head. 'No, not like that. It would be too much of a shock. We don't know Maya will even want to meet you.'

Spiro's expression was startled. 'But I am her father.'

'Maya doesn't know that. Try putting yourself in her shoes for a moment.' Loveday's voice was gentle. 'She's still trying to deal with why Candice attempted to kill her.'

'So what do you suggest?'

'I'm thinking about it. Give me a minute.' Loveday pushed her fingers through her long dark hair as she mulled over the situation. 'We also have April Rose to consider.'

'I know,' Spiro said.

'We must approach this with caution. I don't want to see Maya hurt.'

Spiro's eyes filled with concern. 'Neither do I. If I thought for a moment she would be damaged by discovering who she is I would step back.'

'I know you wouldn't intentionally hurt her, but you're hardly an ordinary man.'

Spiro frowned. 'You mean because I am wealthy?'

Loveday was aware she was tiptoeing around the issue. 'Maya had a very simple upbringing. I'm not sure how she would cope with not only discovering a father she didn't know existed, but…well you are an extremely high-profile man.'

'That might be true now, but it wasn't always so. I also had a simple upbringing. I know what it is to struggle. Our family was poor, which is why I wanted to do more with my life. I may be wealthy now, but every last drachma I have was earned by my own efforts.' He turned his frown on Loveday. 'Are you telling me my daughter would not understand what it means to fight for what she wants in life? I know how she has struggled. I know she suffered over losing her Jamie.' He met Loveday's eyes. 'I don't imagine she was trusted to run your heritage centre out of pity. She got the job because she was capable and passionate about what she does.'

He was right. Maybe Maya was more like her father than Loveday realized. A slow smile crept across her face. 'We could go to the centre this afternoon,' she said.

Spiro's eyes twinkled with excitement. 'I could invite Maya to have dinner with me.'

'One step at a time,' Loveday said, glancing at her watch. 'This will be a lot for Maya to take in. Things might not go as you'd hoped. You must be prepared for that.'

'You think Maya will not accept me as her father?' The thought clearly shocked him. 'That will be up to her,' Loveday said, her voice still gentle. 'But I definitely don't think it a good idea to spring it on her.' She was thinking. 'Perhaps it would be better coming from someone she knows and trusts.'

'Like you?'

'I was thinking more of Tom Scobey. He knows both of you.'

'As I said, Tom and I are acquaintances.'

'Then it's a conversation you need to have first.'

They had risen from their table and were walking

together to the car park. It had filled since Loveday arrived. She frowned at the sight of the tight space she had to reverse out of. 'I hate this car park,' she said.

Spiro smiled. 'Let me drive out first and give you more room.'

She wasn't about to argue.

He flicked his key at the black sporty number parked next to her old Clio.

She put a hand on his arm as he was about to climb into his car. 'You know who is behind this business of trying to kill Maya, don't you?'

Spiro put his hand on top of hers and gave it a little pat. 'I'm afraid I do,' he said sadly.

'I HOPE it's being noted how co-operative my client has been,' Charles Reece-Campbell said stiffly as he slipped his notes into his black leather briefcase and snapped it closed.

Sam ignored his remarks. 'We will need to speak to your client again. Please make sure she does not leave Cornwall.'

'Be very careful, Inspector,' Reece-Campbell warned. 'This is bordering on harassment. If you insist on pursuing my client your career could come to an unpleasant end.'

Sam stared at him from under a rucked brow. 'Are you threatening me?' He took a step closer, towering over the man.

Will put a warning hand on his boss's sleeve. 'Leave it, Sam,' he muttered under his breath.

Sam didn't consider himself violent but punching this man would be so satisfying. He took a deep breath, narrowing his eyes. 'Your client is waiting,' he said stiffly.

The solicitor adjusted his tie, his face scarlet with indignation, but he made no further comment as he marched from the room.

'Insufferable twat,' Will hissed.

Sam stared after the man as he left the room. 'You should have let me flatten him.'

Will grinned back. 'You'll than me later.'

'Let's hope I can keep my temper in check when we get them both back in here.'

'What about Teague? Do we let him go?' Will asked, as he and Sam walked back to the CID suite.

'Not yet, I'd like another chat with him. Get someone to take him a coffee.'

There was no buzz about the place as they walked in. He could see detectives on the phones and others reading through reports. They were busy enough, but nothing was happening. It was time to stir things up. He made a loud rap on a desk. 'Gather round, people. We need some brain-storming.'

He strode through the room, stopping at the whiteboard. It was filling up with photos and information. The focus was the Carn Hendra Heritage Centre and the picture of the dead woman, Morwenna Chenoweth, and Joss Teague. It had been linked to Fenwick Church and the St Piran carving. Lines had been drawn from this to photos of the vicar, the Rev Sara Corey, Candice Chrichton-Smythe and James Crawford. The e-fit image of a third person had yet to be identified.

There was also a photo of the elegant *Moonflyer* yacht and links to Spiro Cassavetes and Darius Cassavetes.

Sam tapped the pictures of Morwenna Chenoweth and Joss Teague. 'There's a chance this man could identify the two people he saw when he and Morwenna were in the churchyard. On evidence supplied by the vicar, the Rev Corey, e-fit images were created of three people whose interest in the St Piran carving made her curious. That carving was later stolen during a raid at the church. Today the Reverend Corey positively identified Candice Chrichton-Smythe and James Crawford as a couple she saw examining the carving. Although this pair deny knowing each other, it was clear from the look that passed between them in our corridor they were no strangers to each other.

'Yet Joss Teague…' He pointed to the man's picture again. 'Joss Teague did not identify them in a parade.'

'You think he was lying, sir?' DC Amanda Fox chipped in.

'I do,' Sam said. 'What I don't know is why.'

Amanda screwed up her face, staring at the information wall. 'Maybe he and Morwenna had planned to steal the carving themselves. If he knows, or suspects, that this pair have the St Piran he could be trying to keep on their good side to get another shot himself at snatching the thing.'

DC Malcolm Carter tilted his head at the wall. 'Could Candice and James be related? They do look alike.'

Sam's gaze swept from the bosun to Candice. The blue eyes were the same and the blonde hair. Why hadn't he noticed this before? 'Get yourself online, Malcolm. Dig out a photo of the Chrichton-Smythe family. Let's see exactly who these people are.'

CHAPTER 30

Sam made a grab for the phone when it rang. The caller said, 'Tom Scobey is downstairs, sir. He's asking for you.'

'Bring him up,' Sam said, beckoning Will to follow him into his office. A seed of excitement was beginning to swell inside him. He was looking forward to Candice's reaction when she was presented with the mobile phone Tom had found hidden in her trainers. The substance discovered in plastic bags had yet to be analyzed, but it wasn't looking good for Candice.

Minutes later Tom was escorted to Sam's office, where he now sat looking around him.

'I thought it would have been bigger,' he said.

'Not for a lowly detective inspector.' Sam grinned. 'How are you, Tom?'

'Feeling pretty stupid if I'm honest. I can't believe I was taken in by her.' He pulled on the plastic gloves he'd been given and put a bag containing a mobile phone and two packets of a white powder on the desk. 'I think this is what you want.'

Will stretched his fingers into his own protective gloves before he removed the mobile phone and began to scroll through the call list and messages. 'It's mostly text messages,' he said. 'As far as I can see there's only two recipients. There's a Freddie.'

'That'll be her brother Freddie,' Tom said. 'I've never met him.'

'And the other?' Sam asked.

Will looked up. 'The other name is Zeus. Most of the texts and a few calls are to him.' He frowned. 'Probably a code name. Maybe Zeus is her dealer?'

'I doubt it,' Sam said. A tingle of interest flickered inside him. 'Zeus was a Greek god.' He was already thinking they needed to have another word with Darius Cassavetes.

'You might want to see this, sir.' DC Malcolm Carter had put his head round the door. 'Something interesting on the computer.'

Sam got to his feet. 'Come with us, Tom,' he said, following Malcom back to his desk.

'What are we looking at?' he asked, watching as the detective scrolled through the images of boats in a marina.

'That's St Katharine Docks,' Tom said, pointing at the screen. 'Look! There's my boat, the *Sea Witch*. I don't understand. What's…' The words died on his lips as the next images were revealed. 'It's Candice!'

'And look who's with her,' Sam said, shaking his head.

'It's the man we saw in the Miner's Lamp.' Tom's face crumpled into a confused frown. 'I don't understand. What's going on?'

'The man in the picture is James Crawford, bosun on the Cassavetes' yacht.' A smile was spreading across Sam's face. 'Let the two of them deny they know each other now.' He turned to Will. 'We need Mr Crawford back at the station. Bring Candice in again, too.'

'Her solicitor won't be happy,' Will quipped.

Sam was still smiling. 'I don't imagine he will,' he said.

'Can I sit in on Candice's interview?' Tom asked hopefully.

'I'm afraid not, but you can still help us,' Sam said. 'Come back to my office. I want to know every scrap of information you have about Candice. Does she have a key to your cottage?' he asked, as they walked into the office.

'Thankfully no,' Tom said, taking a seat. 'She'd have the place stripped by now if she had access to it and I have some valuable things there.'

'So where would she go?'

Tom shrugged. 'I wasn't aware she knew anyone in Cornwall.'

* * *

SPIRO FOLLOWED Loveday into the heritage centre car park and pulled up alongside her, pausing when he got out of his car to look around him. It was a distraction tactic in an attempt to calm the alarming way his pulse was racing. It wasn't working. He was about to meet his daughter face to face and he had no idea how he – or she – would react.

Loveday flashed him a concerned look. 'Are you sure you want to do this?'

Spiro nodded, taking a deep breath. He knew Loveday's concern was for Maya and not him. That was as it should be. She was trusting him to handle this meeting with all the care and consideration he could muster. He wasn't going to let anyone down.

'I'd like to meet my daughter, now,' he said.

'And we do this as agreed? You give Maya no clue who you really are, at least not yet.'

Spiro's eyes were already on the reception desk they

could see through the impressive glass frontage. Maya was there, a phone to her ear. She looked up as they approached, lifting her hand to wave when she saw Loveday.

She could see Spiro was shaking as he stepped into the building.

'I've brought someone to meet you, Maya,' Loveday said, turning to him. 'This is Spiro Cassavetes. He's interested in our work here.'

Maya raised an eyebrow as she took the hand he offered. 'You're a student of Cornish history? And I'm guessing you're not even Cornish.'

'I was born in Greece,' Spiro said, trying not to stare at her. This was his daughter, his beautiful daughter and she was right here in front of him. He was fighting to control how much he was trembling. He couldn't spoil things, not now. He swallowed. 'We Greeks are very proud of our heritage, just as you are of yours.' He inclined his head at her. 'Have you ever been to Greece, Miss Brookes?'

'I haven't,' Maya said. 'But it's on my bucket list. I'm sure my daughter, April Rose, would love it too.'

Spiro's heart gave a little lurch at the mention of April Rose's name. It felt so strange knowing he not only had a daughter, but a granddaughter too. How would they feel when they were told who he was? Would they resent him? He couldn't bear that.

'Would you like to have a look around the centre?' Maya was giving him a questioning smile.

'There's nothing I would like more, but only if you can spare the time.'

The look he gave Loveday told her it was fine to leave him, and seeing the two of them together she was happy to agree. The time might not be right for Spiro to reveal who he was but it would come. She gave Maya a wave. 'I'll get off now. Ring me tonight. We'll have a proper catch-up.'

'I will,' Maya called after her.

* * *

SAM STUDIED James Crawford as he was put into an interview room. His edgy pacing of the floor gave away how nervous he was, as well he might. The man had a lot to explain.

Candice's anger at being arrested surpassed any nerves she might be feeling. 'I'm saying nothing until my solicitor arrives,' she muttered as she flounced into the room. She jabbed a finger at the two-way mirror. 'And don't think I don't know you're watching me. Big mistake. My solicitor will be making a complaint.'

'Not happy, is she?' Will remarked as he stood with Sam.

'Has Mr Reece-Campbell been informed of his client's arrest?'

'A message was left with his office.'

'Fine,' Sam said. 'Let's start with James Crawford. I have a feeling he could be more co-operative.'

The man spun round as the detectives entered. 'Why have I been brought here?' he demanded. 'I co-operated with your identity parade. I can't take any more time off work.'

'Sit down,' Sam said as Will went through the preliminaries. 'I won't waste your time or ours, so for the tape, I repeat, what is your name?'

A red flush was beginning to creep up the man's neck. 'You know my name.'

'Please don't mess us about. State your name.'

The man fidgeted, avoiding Sam's eyes. 'You know, don't you?'

'What do we know?'

'That I work for the Cassavetes family. You saw me last

night when I brought Mr Darius to meet you at the Pandora Inn. I'm James Crawford.'

'You know Candice Chrichton-Smythe,' Sam said.

Crawford nodded. 'She's a lovely woman. Yes, I know her.'

'Tell me about the St Piran carving, James.'

The man's brow wrinkled into a frown. 'Tell you what? I don't even know what that is.'

'I think you do. I think you stole it.'

'What? No! That had nothing to do with me.'

'Really? Then why are you getting so excited?'

'I'm not.'

'You and Candice have been seen in Fenwick Church studying the carving.' Sam shook his head, tutting. 'Candice Chrichton-Smythe and the bosun on a Greek yacht interested in Cornish history. Who would have thought it?'

'OK, so we were in the church. Since when was that a crime?'

'Since when were you interested in ancient Cornish saints?' Sam watched the man's growing discomfort. 'Maybe you've started a collection. Is that it? Are you and your friend, Candice, collectors of historic artifacts?' He paused, cocking his head. 'Or maybe not you. Is it a different friend who collects this stuff and you two were doing him a favour? Is that how it was, James? Were you casing the church for him, checking out the lie of the land?'

Sam could see James's mind working. He was wondering if this was a way out of his troubles. If he confessed to a lesser crime would the more serious one go away?

'Who is he, James? Who wanted the carving?'

'I don't know,' the bosun insisted. 'We were never told. Rufus organized the whole thing.' He looked up. 'I don't know what all the fuss is about, it's only an old carving. It's not as if it's worth anything.'

Sam's interested expression never changed. 'How did you get involved in this, James?'

The man swallowed, glancing away.

'Was it Candice? Did you steal the carving for her?'

'No!' The word exploded from his mouth. 'Candice wasn't involved!'

'But you're friends?' Will cut in.

'Not really, it's Candice's brother, Freddie, who's a mate. We both play rugby. He told me his sister was coming to Cornwall and asked me to keep an eye on her.'

'And you did that by getting her involved in a burglary in a church,' Sam said. 'Or was it her idea?'

James Crawford's head jerked up. 'Candice had nothing to do with this. It was all my idea. I offered to do it.'

'Who were you doing it for?'

'Rufus. I told you, it was Rufus who was in charge. I like to play the tables. I owed him money. He said he would wipe the debt if I did what he asked.'

'So you owed Rufus money?'

Crawford gave a miserable nod. 'I had a bad run of luck. It happens.'

Sam and Will exchanged a look. 'Are you telling us this was a gambling debt?'

'£5,000. The casino wanted it back.'

'What casino?' Sam asked.

'The Castle Casino, Rufus North's place in Edinburgh.'

'Are you saying it was Rufus's idea to steal the St Piran carving?'

James blinked. 'Didn't I say that?'

'So this Rufus collects antiquities? Is that what you're telling us?'

'I don't know. Maybe.'

'Or maybe the carving was being taken for someone else?'

James Crawford folded his arms. 'I've told you all I know. Speak to Rufus. Ask him why he wanted to steal the thing.'

Sam leaned back in his seat, studying the man's face. 'Tell me about this Rufus.'

Crawford gave an exasperated sigh. 'All I know is that his name is Rufus North. I don't know him. It was Alex Scott, the manager of the casino, who was threatening me over the debt. Rufus is the real boss but I only met the guy twice.'

'Twice?'

The bosun lifted his head and stared at Sam. 'Yes, twice. You did know about the first time when we had to abort it?'

'Go on,' Sam said.

'Nothing much to tell. We were there in the churchyard ready to jemmy the door open when this mad female reared up at us from behind one of the headstones.' He ran a hand over his head. 'Jeez. I almost freaked out. That place is creepy enough anyway without any ghosts leering up at you.'

'But she wasn't a ghost?'

'I don't know what the hell she was. Rufus didn't wait to find out. He brought one of the heavy spanners down on her head and she kind of crumpled at his feet. We were panicking by then.'

'Panicking?'

James looked up, swallowing. 'Before her, there was another woman, an older one. She'd come into the church-yard and was trying to unlock the door when she heard us. Rufus pushed her and she fell on the steps. She must have struck her head because she didn't get up again. She wasn't moving. We thought she was dead.'

He sucked in a shaky breath. 'Hardly surprising we were spooked when this banshee woman sprang at us.' He licked his lips. 'Rufus told to me to help pick her up and carry her to my van. We were about to throw her in the back when she came to and took off like a bat out of hell. Rufus let out a torrent of expletives and tore after her.'

He paused, eyes wide, remembering.

'What happened then?' Sam prompted.

'I grabbed the tools I'd brought and chucked them in the van and I went back to the pub.'

'The pub?'

'The one across the road where I work.' Crawford sighed. 'Don't look so innocent, you knew I had a job there. It was part of the scam. Rufus wanted someone in the village who could keep an eye on things.'

'But you're bosun on the *Moonflyer*,' Sam said. 'You're Darius Cassavetes' right-hand man.'

'I think you've misjudged my importance. Anyway, I was due some time off. The pub had been advertising for a live-in barman. I got the job.'

'But you were also still working for Darius. You brought him to the Pandora Inn in the tender from the yacht.'

'I packed in the pub job.' He raised his hands in a gesture that said *'Why not? I didn't need it anymore.'*

Sam threw Will a look to take over the questioning. He did.

'What were you and Candice doing in Fenwick Church?'

The unexpected probe seemed to throw him.

'Candice had nothing to do with this, I told you.'

The man's sudden edginess was interesting.

'You were seen together,' Will said. 'Our informant told us you were showing a lot of interest in the St Piran carving.'

'You make it sound sinister. Candice had come down to visit me. When I came off duty we wandered across the road to have a look at the church.' He sighed. 'Well, let's face it, there's not much else to do in the village.'

Sam pursed his lips as he slowly got to his feet. The man

was irritating him now. It was Candice they needed to interview.

Crawford pulled a face. 'Well? I've told you the truth. Can I go now?'

'Go?' Sam stared at the man. 'Of course you can't go. You've just confessed to attempted burglary at a church, possibly even assaulting an innocent old lady and another younger woman.

'We haven't even got to the second more successful burglary yet.

'You'll be charged, Mr Crawford, so you will be enjoying our hospitality for a while longer.'

'But I thought if I told you...if I confessed? You said I would be fine.'

Sam turned to Will. 'Did I say that, Sergeant Tregellis? Did I tell Mr Crawford he would be free to go if he told us everything?'

Will shook his head. 'I certainly never heard that. No, sir, you didn't.'

'I want a solicitor,' James Crawford demanded. 'I'm not saying another thing until I have a solicitor.' He was still protesting loudly as the officers led him away.

'Do we have a duty solicitor available?' Sam asked, watching as the man was taken to a cell.

'I'm on it, sir,' Will said, as they both turned back to the CID suite.

'That little scrote's got some cheek. Did he really believe he was going to walk away from this?'

Sam blew out his cheeks. 'That's exactly what he was expecting. He thinks this was a prank. I really don't believe he considers he's done anything wrong.'

'Maybe that's why he didn't have the family solicitor, the very lovely Charles Reece-Campbell in there with him.'

'Perhaps,' Sam said thoughtfully. 'Let's see if anyone else

rides in to his aid. In the meantime we need to find this Rufus North.'

'Are we thinking he might be our killer?'

'Well if what James Crawford said is true and North chased after Morwenna, he could either have killed her or been the last person to see her alive.'

'If she could identify him as the thief who stole the carving then maybe he felt he needed to silence her. We need to find this man.'

It was an hour before duty solicitor, Brian Pascow, arrived and was given interview time with James Crawford.

Sam's look was stern. They had Crawford back in the interview room. 'You have already described what happened during the first failed attempt to steal the St Piran carving from Fenwick Church and we have your version of the assaults on two women, Jess Tandy and Morwenna Chenoweth, whose dead body was later found on the clifftop at Carn Hendra.'

James Crawford's eyes flew open. 'Murder! I had nothing to do with any murder.'

Sam ignored the man's protest. 'You were going to tell us about the second attempt to steal the St Piran carving.'

Crawford glanced to the solicitor and he nodded. 'Just tell the officers the truth, Mr Crawford.'

Sam could see the man was shaken now. He was in deep water and he knew it. He waited, allowing the tension in the room to grow until James Crawford's head jerked up.

His stare was defiant. 'I didn't sign up for any violence. I want that to be clear. What happened to those two women before had nothing to do with me.' He looked from Sam to Will but got no reaction. He gave a nervous little cough.

'I thought Rufus would have given up on stealing that thing, but he hadn't. He'd been keeping an eye on the church and knew they had employed an old boy as a security man.

We'd watched him come out and wander around the church with a torch. Rufus produced a hankie soaked in chloroform. He grabbed the old man and held the hankie to his face until he sank like a stone to the ground.'

He looked around him and shrugged. 'The church door was open and we didn't even have to jemmy it to get in. Rufus went directly to the carving and I followed. We both started to unscrew it from the wall. When it came free, Rufus carried it off, leaving me to tidy up and hurry after him.'

Will frowned. 'What about the old boy you knocked out?'

'I didn't knock him out,' James Crawford cut in angrily. 'Rufus did that.'

'Did you actually check you hadn't killed him?' Sam asked.

The man looked away. 'He was still breathing when we left.'

'So, what are you saying? You simply stepped over him and took off?' Will shook his head.

'I'm not proud of myself. You asked what happened and I've told you.' He looked at Sam. 'What happens now?'

'You'll be charged,' Sam said wearily, getting up from his chair and instructing the uniformed officer outside to escort the man to the cells.

CHAPTER 31

*T*his better be good, Detective Inspector Kitto, otherwise I will be advising my client to file a complaint for harassment.' Charles Reece-Campbell glared at Sam.

Sam ignored the solicitor's remarks. He was focused on the woman. 'We've been having a chat with your friend, James Crawford,' he said, deliberately taking his time. The challenge was still there in the woman's flinty blue eyes. He wondered if she had hurried back to Tom Scobey's cottage and broken in, panicking to retrieve the drugs and her second phone when she'd been released from custody earlier. She would have been disappointed. No point in keeping her in the dark.

Sam's eyes were still locked into hers. 'Who is Zeus?'

'Zeus?' Candice's voice faltered. 'I don't know any Zeus.'

But it was too late. That split second's loss of composure said it all.

'Why have you been making so many calls to him?'

Candice's angry eyes bored into him.

'You've been going through my things?' She flashed the

solicitor a look of fury. 'They need a search warrant for that, don't they?'

'We have not been searching your belongings, Miss Chrichton-Smythe. I believe Mr Scobey was packing your bags. He tells us you are no longer welcome at his place.' Sam watched her gasp. 'He brought the phone to us. He also brought a quantity of white powder he found in your things, which is currently being tested for drugs.'

Charles Reece-Campbell leaned in, placing a warning hand on hers. 'That's enough. Don't say any more,' he instructed.

But Sam's questions didn't stop.

'Zeus,' he said, turning to Will. 'Wasn't he a Greek god?'

Will nodded. 'Definitely a Greek god.'

A flush was creeping up Candice's neck, turning her cheeks an uncomfortable-looking shade of fuchsia.

'How many Greek men do you know, Candice?'

Reece-Campbell made another attempt to intervene, but Candice was already shaking her head. 'I don't know any Greek men,' she insisted.

Sam opened the brown folder he'd brought with him and slid out a photo of Eleanor and Charles Chrichton-Smythes' anniversary celebrations. He tapped a face amongst the guests. 'Who's this, Candice?'

She glanced at the photo. 'I don't know. A friend of my parents probably.'

Sam nodded. 'We wondered about that, which is why we emailed this photo to our colleagues up in the Borders and asked them to check it out with your parents, and guess what?' He paused. 'They said the man was a friend of yours. It was you who invited Darius Cassavetes to the party. His stepfather's yacht is still anchored off Falmouth.' He pointed to another face. 'And this is his bosun, James Crawford.' He tilted his head, examining the photo. 'A handsome young man, don't you think? You must have been so angry when he brought a member of his crew to your parents' party? Or maybe you were jealous? Was that it, Candice? Were you jealous?'

She leapt from her chair, flying at Sam. 'Darius loves me,' she yelled. 'He loves me!'

Reece-Campbell jumped to his feet and lunged after her. 'Sit down, Candice,' he ordered, grabbing her arm and forcing her back into her chair.

'My client is distressed. She needs to take a break.'

'She'll have to wait,' Sam said. He had no intention of letting either of this pair squirm out of what had just been admitted. Candice and Darius. There it was. Confirmation. Until now he had only suspected this connection. Now it had been admitted. Fascinating though to see how touchy she was at any hint of a relationship between Darius and his bosun. Sam had thrown the notion into the mix to get a reaction and boy did he get a reaction. He hadn't really considered Darius might be gay. But why not? James Crawford certainly appeared to be devoted to Darius. Was this the link they'd been seeking?

Sam lifted his head and locked eyes with Candice. 'Did you help James Crawford to steal the St Piran carving?'

'What?' She looked confused. 'What are you talking about?'

Sam shrugged. 'Darius collects antiquities. James does what Darius tells him. Can you see where I'm going with this?'

Candice's head began to shake. 'No! Darius had nothing to with it.'

'Two men were involved with that theft. Your friend James Crawford was one of them.'

'No!'

'People do what Darius tells them. You know that's true,

Candice.'

'No!' But her voice was beginning to crack.

'What did he tell you to do, Candice?'

She was tearful now. 'Nothing.'

'Did he tell you to poison Maya?'

'Don't answer that!' Reece-Campbell's hand was on Candice's sleeve.

The woman was shaking. 'He didn't tell me to do it. Darius had nothing to do with it.'

'Enough, Candice,' her solicitor said sharply. 'I don't want you to say any more.'

'So it was your idea?' Sam persisted.

Candice nodded.

'For the tape, please,' Sam said. 'Can you answer for the tape?'

'OK!' she yelled. 'It was me, OK? I put the poison in her drink. She was ruining everything.'

Reece-Campbell's hands went up in despair.

'How do you mean?'

'With Tom. She was trying to take Tom off me. Nobody does that.'

Sam was aware of Will's glance. He guessed his sergeant was as confused as he felt. He wasn't sure where this was going either.

'You said Darius loves you. Are you in love with him?'

She nodded miserably.

'How did you two meet?'

'A bunch of friends chartered the *Moonflyer* last year and invited me along. Darius joined them on the cruise. He and I clicked instantly.' She swallowed hard and a tear trickled down her cheek.

'If you loved Darius, what were you doing with Tom?'

Her shoulders rose in a shrug. 'Why not? They say a bit of competition does nobody any harm.'

Sam sat back blinking. 'Are you saying you got together with Tom Scobey to make Darius jealous?'

She nodded. 'It started out as a bit of fun and then Tom's little friend got involved. She was trying to take Tom away from me. How would it have looked to Darius if a little mouse like her could do that?'

Sam shook his head. 'You tried to kill Maya Brookes to make Darius pay more attention to you?'

'If you put it that way, I suppose so. Yes.'

Charging Candice with attempted murder wasn't as satisfying as Sam had expected.

James Crawford was being charged for his part in the theft of the carving and they were confident it was only a matter of time before the other man involved was also locked up. He sighed. This had started out as a murder investigation with the discovery of Morwenna Chenoweth's body. They were no further forward with that.

Maybe the visit they were about to pay Darius Cassavetes might throw more light on things.

* * *

LOVEDAY HAD CHOSEN the tearoom at the Royal Cornwall Museum to meet Tom because it was only a short walk from the magazine office. He was frowning. 'Are you sure about this?' he asked.

Loveday nodded as she watched him from across the table. 'Absolutely 100%. Spiro Cassavetes is Maya's father. He's willing to produce DNA proof if necessary, but there's no doubt.'

She swallowed. 'I took him along to meet her today. Of course she doesn't know who he is. I introduced him as an interested student of Cornish history, which is what we had agreed beforehand.'

She reached across the table and touched his hand, her eyes sparkling. 'They really got on well, Tom. I think this is going to work out.'

Tom glanced out at the passing traffic. 'I'll have to speak to Spiro first,' he said slowly.

Loveday nodded. 'Spiro knows that. He's waiting to hear from you.' She bit her lip. 'In fact, he's here. I brought him with me. He's waiting outside in reception.'

Tom sprang to his feet. 'Spiro is here?' He was already striding from the room.

Loveday stared after him. She'd done this all wrong. She should have taken things more slowly. Telling Tom about Spiro must have been a shock for him too. She put her head in her hands. She shouldn't have brought Spiro here.

Loveday had no idea how long she'd sat at the table, chastising herself, when a familiar voice made her look up. 'We have a guest,' Tom said. 'Mr Cassavetes is joining us.'

Loveday blinked, her unsure gaze travelling from one man to the other. 'Is this all right?'

Spiro smiled down at her. 'It's more than all right, my dear, and I owe it all to you.' He held out his hand and she took it. 'Tom and I have many things to talk about now.'

'And Maya…?' She glanced to Tom.

He nodded. 'Once Spiro and I have talked we will go together to see Maya.'

'Please be careful how you break the news,' Loveday urged. 'I have no idea how she will react to learning she has a father.'

Tom's smile included both of them. 'Maya and April Rose now have someone else who loves them. They will be happy about that. I'll make sure of it.'

Loveday glanced back as she left the tearoom. The two men were talking like old friends. She swallowed, a prick of tears in her eyes. Everything was going to be all right.

CHAPTER 32

*M*aya rang later as Loveday was leaving the office.

'Something very strange has happened,' she said. 'How well do you know Spiro Cassavetes?'

Loveday's heart gave a lurch. Was this it? Did Maya now know Spiro was her father? She hesitated. 'I don't know him that well.' Her voice faltered. 'Why?'

'A note has been pushed through my door and I'm not sure what to make of it.'

'A note?' It wasn't what she'd been expecting.

'Yes, but it doesn't make any sense. Can I read it to you?'

'Go ahead,' Loveday said, frowning.

Maya gave a little cough. 'It says:

Maya,

Something terrible has happened and I need your help.

Someone is trying to kill me!

I fear it is one of my friends.

You are the only one I can trust now, my dear. Can you come to Fenwick Quoit as soon as you can? I will explain everything.

Don't show this note to anyone. Come alone.

244

Your friend,
Spiro Cassavetes.'

Loveday was trying not to gasp. What was going on?

'What do you think, Loveday? Should I go?'

'Definitely not.' Loveday's mind was racing. If this was about someone making another attempt on her friend's life they were getting desperate.

And they knew about Spiro's meeting with Maya! How could they know about that? This had to be Darius's work. He was the one who'd be waiting for Maya at the quoit, not Spiro.

'I think I should I go,' Maya said. 'The poor man sounds really desperate.'

'Absolutely not. Leave this to me, Maya.'

'But it's me he wants to meet,' Maya insisted. 'He was a nice man, Loveday. I liked him. If he's in trouble I need to help him.'

'I don't believe Spiro wrote the note.'

'In that case we need to tell Sam.'

'I will. I'll ring him,' Loveday promised.

'You're not thinking of going in my place?' There was panic in Maya's voice.

'Trust me. I know what I'm doing,' Loveday said. 'I'm not daft enough to wander into any danger.' She was in her car now. 'I need to go, Maya. I'll keep in touch.' She ended the call.

Her finger hovered over Sam's number. But if she told him about this she knew he would insist she stayed out of it. That would definitely be the sensible thing to do, but she felt responsible. Maybe if she hadn't announced so publicly on the *Moonflyer* how she'd found that photo by Spiro's bed then none of this would be happening. She laid down the phone. She would ring Sam later.

The mist was lying in patches as Loveday drove along the

winding coastal road. She was watching for the house on the hill. It was a landmark for a layby where she could leave the car before taking the footpath that wound up onto the moor. She remembered the last time she was here. Cassie had been in discovery mode then and had persuaded Loveday to join her quest to reach the quoit. That day there had been a couple of other vehicles parked nearby, but tonight it was only Loveday's car. Had Darius found another parking place? Was he already here waiting up at the quoit for Maya?

The thought set her anger growing, overriding any sense of the danger she might be walking into.

But now, alone on the moor with Darius somewhere out in the mist, her confidence was beginning to abandon her. She'd turned her mobile phone to silent and jumped when it vibrated in her pocket. It was Sam. 'Maya rang me. What the hell do you think you are doing, Loveday?' He wasn't sounding impressed.

'If you've spoken to Maya then you know what I'm doing,' she hissed into the phone. 'I'm trying to end this thing.'

'Well you can turn around and come back right now. And it's not a request. It's an order,' Sam stormed. 'So help me, Loveday, I'll have you arrested for obstruction.'

She could hear he was trying to control his anger. 'We're dealing with this now.'

'Really?' Loveday let out a sigh as she sank down onto a giant boulder by the side of the path. 'So why aren't you here?'

'We're on our way. Just get yourself out of there, Loveday. What you're doing is dangerous.'

'I was trying to help Maya,' she said. The mist was getting thicker and she wasn't all that confident she could find her way back down to the road.

The bullet zipped past her arm as she stood up.

'What was that?' Sam said abruptly. 'Loveday! Are you all right?'

Loveday's heart was beating out of her chest. She'd thrown herself to the ground as the sound of the shot resounded around her. Now, her face buried in the heather, she was fumbling for the phone that had flown from her hand as she'd hit the ground.

Somewhere amongst the heather she could hear Sam's panicked voice calling out for her.

'Loveday! Loveday! What's happened?'

Her hand touched the phone and closed over it as another shot rang out. Loveday crawled behind the boulder. She was trying to rationalize what was happening. Was someone firing a gun into the mist not knowing she was there? Or was it Darius trying to kill her?

Her voice shook as she whispered into the phone, 'Somebody's shooting at me.'

'Shit,' Sam cursed. 'Can you see them?'

'No, and there's not much cover here, unless the shooter is up by the quoit.'

'We're not far away. Is it a man?'

'I think so.'

'Try to work out where he is and get yourself behind him.'

'I'm not sure my commando training covered that.'

'Just don't stand up and make yourself a target.' He was trying to sound calm but she could hear the urgency in his voice.

It didn't make her feel a lot better. She wondered how long she could stay hidden behind her rock. What if the mist lifted? She'd be a sitting duck, a sitting duck flat on her stomach being poked by bracken and prickly heather. Why did she put herself in positions like this? If she had merely stopped Maya from coming here it would have been enough, but no, she had to catch the bad guy herself. The best she could hope for now would be to stay safely hidden until Sam and the cavalry turned up. But what then? She'd ruined everything. Sam would probably want nothing to do with her ever again.

She could feel the hot tears burning her cheeks. How stupid was this? Tears wouldn't save her now. She had to get out of here. Loveday lifted her head and listened. She could hear nothing. Perhaps Darius had decided she'd managed to escape and was now in her car speeding away from the moors.

Had he given up and left? She struggled up into a crouching position and peered into the mist. She swallowed, it was definitely thinning. Her rock wouldn't protect her much longer. Loveday estimated she was about fifteen minutes from the road. If she was going to make a dash for it she should do it now. She began to move down the hill. The mist was definitely lifting and there was no cover further on, but it was dark now. She squinted ahead, concentrating on moving one step at a time.

She sensed rather than heard the bracken behind her crunch under a heavy foot fall. She shrank back, gasping as the dark shape loomed above and the gun pointed directly at her. Loveday squeezed her eyes tight waiting for the explosion, but none came, only an irritated expletive.

'You're not the Brookes woman. It's her who should be here. Where is she?' her stalker demanded.

Loveday opened her eyes. The man had stepped back. She had to think quickly. 'I'm writing a book and researching Cornwall's standing stones. I was on my way up to the quoit when the fog set in.' She screwed up her face. He knew exactly who she was. He'd shared a meal with her and Sam the previous night. Should she admit she knew this was him? The gun had freaked her out.

He was staying in the shadows. 'It's not safe for young

women to be out on the hill by themselves. You should be more careful.'

'Well, yes. I can see that now,' Loveday said, edging away.

She could feel him move closer. 'Where is she? Where is Maya?' His voice was muffled.

'It was you who sent the note. Spiro has nothing to do with this, has he?'

'And you're not researching any standing stones,' he retorted.

Loveday's courage was returning. 'Why are you trying to kill Maya?'

'She should be here, not you.' He sounded angry. 'Why did you come? You've messed everything up. You shouldn't have come. You do know I have to kill you now?'

She was imagining him raising the gun, pointing it at her. She squared her shoulders. 'Why are you doing this, Darius? Maya has never harmed you.' She was straining her eyes trying to work out which of the looming shapes was him.

'You knew how trusting she was. You knew she would believe the note came from Spiro.'

'I wasn't sure she'd met Spiro. I had to find out.'

'Is that why you brought a gun?' Loveday's tone was bitter.

'She knows he's her father now, doesn't she?'

Loveday sucked in her breath trying to keep control of her anger. 'It's the inheritance, isn't it? This is all about greed…your greed.'

The man stepped closer. She could feel the gun pointed at her. She had to keep him talking until help arrived.

But how? She tried something. 'Did you know an ancient carving was stolen from Fenwick Church? You collect antiquities, don't you?'

'You're on a fishing trip. You want me to admit I stole the St Piran?'

'I didn't say it was the St Piran.'

'And I didn't say I knew anything about the theft.' He was so close now she could hear him breathing. 'You're taunting me,' he snarled. 'That's not a good idea right now.'

She'd been expecting a retort like that. She would have to be more careful. She swallowed, trying to work out exactly where he was, when she heard the rustling. Someone else was out there.

'Whose there?' the gunman yelled. Silence. 'I know you're there. Step forward where I can see you!'

More rustling and the shape of a man stepped out of the dark. 'Don't shoot,' he shouted. 'My name is Tom Scobey. I'm a friend of Spiro's.'

Loveday stood stock still. 'Tom?' she gasped, her voice muffled. 'What are you doing here?'

'Don't worry, Sam's on his way.'

She could feel him moving closer.

'Be careful, Tom. He has a gun,' she whispered.

'And I wouldn't think twice about using it, so stay right where you are.'

The voice sounded close. It sent a shiver down Loveday's spine. Where was the Greek accent? She'd made a huge mistake. It wasn't Darius.

'The police are on the way,' Tom called out. 'Don't make this any worse. Throw the gun down.'

'Shut up,' the gunman yelled.

Loveday could hear his breath coming in quick bursts. He was going to run! She had to keep him there until Sam came or this thing would never end.

'He wants to kill Maya, Tom. He wants to stop her inheriting the family's fortune.'

'What?' Tom exploded. 'This is about money?'

There was a rustle of twigs as Tom rushed forward. She heard the gun go off.

'Tom! Tom! Are you all right?' Her scream was drowned out by the tramp of running feet as chaos erupted around them.

'Loveday? Where are you?' It was Sam's voice.

The light from the police torches revealed two men struggling on the ground.

'It's Tom,' Loveday called to Sam. 'Be careful. The other man has a gun.'

Two burly uniformed officers had waded in and were yanking the struggling pair apart. She could see Sam stoop to pick up the gun with gloved hands and slip it into a plastic bag. He handed it over to DC Amanda Fox behind him before turning to hold his arms wide for Loveday.

She went into them, burying her face in his shoulder as he stroked her hair. 'You crazy, stubborn woman,' he said, his voice trembling. 'You could have been killed.'

'I'm so sorry, Sam,' she whispered.

Tom was getting to his feet and brushing himself down. 'What kept you?' He grinned at Sam who was looking over Loveday's shoulder at the gunman.

'So we meet again, Mr Teague,' he said.

'What?' Loveday turned to peer into the dark. 'You know who this is?'

The man was being yanked to his feet by two police officers.

'You could say we're old acquaintances,' Sam said.

Loveday stared at him open mouthed. 'So who is this?'

'This, my darling, is Joss Teague. Morwenna Chenoweth's boyfriend.'

CHAPTER 33

*F*ollowing the uneven track back to the cars by torchlight wasn't easy and Joss Teague, hand-cuffed between two uniformed officers, repeatedly stumbled.

'Are you going to tell me who he is?' Loveday hissed, lowering her voice as she and Sam brought up the rear of the group.

'No, I am not,' Sam said firmly.

'That's not fair. I've spent the best part of an hour with this man pointing a gun at me. I should at least know who he is.'

'She's got a point.' Tom smiled over his shoulder as he followed DC Amanda Fox's confident step along the rough path to the road.

'She's not getting off the hook as easily as that,' Sam said, trying to disguise how the relief of finding Loveday safe had taken the edge off his anger. 'You still have a lot of explaining to do, young lady. This should have been left to us.'

The ringing of his mobile saved Loveday from any further reprimand. 'Yes, Will,' Sam said, glancing at the digital caller display.

'Good news, boss. We've found Rufus North. He's being brought to the station as we speak.'

'Great.' Sam sighed into the phone.

'You've not heard the best bit. We've also recovered the St Piran carving. It was in the lock-up where North had been hiding out.' He paused for effect. 'How did you get on?'

'Success here too, Will. We've got our man.'

'Anyone we know?'

'I'll tell you when we get back to the station,' he said, ending the call.

He turned to Loveday. 'Give DC Fox your car keys. Loveday. I'll drive you back to Marazion.'

'There's really no need,' she had begun to protest, but the trauma of the last terrifying hour was taking its effect. Her knees were trembling.

'It's not an option, Loveday. Amanda will follow us in your car then she can come back to Truro with me.'

Loveday sat in the Lexus watching in the mirror as Amanda Fox got into her Clio. She glanced at Sam's stern profile. 'I'm sorry,' she said quietly. 'I know you're angry with me, but it was the only way to flush this guy out.'

'You could have been killed.'

'But I wasn't.'

He glanced sideways at her as he pulled out behind the marked police car with their prisoner, Joss Teague, hand-cuffed in the back. 'We'll talk about this later,' he said.

Loveday was too tired to argue. She let her head sink back into the soft grey leather of the Lexus and closed her eyes.

Sam had wanted to enjoy the relief that Loveday was safe for a bit longer, but his anger that she had once again put herself in danger was overriding every other emotion. She'd promised never to get involved in his cases again, yet here she was, right in the middle of it. He knew she would try to justify her actions because Maya was a friend and she was helping her, but still…

He sighed. Poor Loveday. She'd looked all in when they'd arrived back at the cottage. He had rung ahead and asked Cassie to keep an eye on her and was pleased to find her waiting in the drive for their arrival.

He was aware of Amanda watching him as they drove back to Truro. Loveday was safely in Cassie's care now and he was free to turn his attention back to the current situation, but his mind kept returning to that dark moor and the gun in Teague's hand. It could all have had a very different outcome. The man had pursued Maya. It didn't appear he had any qualms about killing her. It was just good luck Loveday hadn't died back there.

Teague had presented himself as meek mannered and innocent. Now Sam was doubting his whole story. Had he killed Morwenna?

* * *

'Let's have Rufus North in first,' he told Will when he arrived back at the station. 'We'll leave Teague to stew for a while.'

The two arrests had sent a buzz of anticipation through the incident room and the place was alive with excitement as Sam and Will strode through the room.

'OK, Will, brief me about Rufus North,' Sam said, perching on a corner of his desk.

'We circulated a photo of Rufus so the troops had all been looking out for him. A patrol officer spotted him going into a lock-up in an industrial estate at the back of Falmouth. He'd been holed up in there.'

'And we've recovered the carving?'

Will nodded. 'It was in the lock-up, in the boot of North's

car, wrapped in newspaper. He could hardly deny his involvement after that.'

Sam gave a grim smile. 'Let's have a chat with Mr North,' he said.

* * *

Rufus North shot an anxious look to Sam and Will as they entered the interview room. 'None of this is my fault,' he insisted when the preliminaries had been done. 'I was heading for bankruptcy and on the point of losing my business. He said he could save me. I knew I was being stitched up but what choice did I have? I had to take a chance.'

'Who are we talking about?' Sam asked.

'Cassavetes, Darius Cassavetes. He's wanted to take over my business for months. He offered to bail me out in return for 50% of the company.'

'And you agreed to this?'

Rufus gave a defeated nod.

Sam frowned. 'I don't understand. Where does the theft of the St Piran carving come into this?'

'That was Darius's little surprise. As part of the deal I had to – how shall I put it? – remove the thing from the church's collection to his personal collection. His man, Crawford, was to provide the transport, and source the tools.'

'Darius suggested using Crawford?' Sam's eyebrow went up.

Rufus nodded. 'Mr Crawford likes to play the tables, unfortunately he does not have a winner's luck. Darius paid his debts but there was a price.'

'The carving,' Sam said.

'Exactly.' He sighed. 'We would have been better off without him. We had to abandon the first attempt because he panicked so much. He was convinced we were being watched and that the spirits of the bodies in the churchyard had come back to haunt us.

'He was still wittering on about ghosts when suddenly she was there, rushing past us on the path.'

'You saw a ghost?' Will's eyebrow went up in disbelief.

Rufus gave an irritated scowl. 'She wasn't a ghost, believe me, but she'd seen us so I had to stop her.'

'Like you stopped the other old woman,' Will said coldly.

Rufus pulled a face. 'She had no business being there in the middle of the night. She saw us. I had to stop her. But I didn't hit her, I only gave her a bit of a push and she fell. It wasn't my fault she knocked herself out when her head hit the path.

'After that the church put a security man in there. I almost ditched the whole thing but then I remembered the hold Darius had over me, so we dealt with the security guy and got on with it.'

Sam put up his hand. 'Slow down, Rufus. We'll talk about your attack on the security officer in good time. I want to know what happened when you took after the woman.'

'I didn't kill her if that's what you're going to suggest,' Rufus snapped. 'I don't kill people.'

'Really?' Sam threw Will a look. 'And you expect us to believe you?'

'It's the truth!'

Sam folded his arms. 'Convince us.'

Rupert's glance travelled from one detective to the other. He sighed. 'OK, I'll tell you.' He took a deep breath and swallowed. They waited.

'I'd been staking out the church since the previous weekend. I needed to know if the carving was wired. It wasn't.' He gave a little laugh. 'But then who in their right mind would want to steal the thing anyway? I never could understand why Darius wanted it. The thing didn't even look all that special. As far as I was concerned it could have been done yesterday and made to look old. We all know how artworks can be aged. Unless you were an expert it would be easy to be fooled.' He allowed himself an indulgent smile. 'The young woman I followed...I'd seen her hanging around the church before. She would sit at the back in those weird clothes attracting curious stares. I had to find out why she was spying on us, so I followed her out of the village to the heritage centre.

'I saw her stop, take a key from her pocket and open the big double glass doors. She went in, leaving the door ajar. I followed and hid behind one of those big display boards. I was intrigued about what she was up to.

'...And then *he* arrived.'

'He?' Sam screwed up his face. 'Who are we talking about?'

'The man who came in. I didn't know who he was, but the girl did. He went towards her with this big grin on his face. They embraced and then she began to move.' Rufus swallowed. 'She was swaying, gyrating like a stripper. She unbuttoned her cloak and let it fall to the floor. Her long red skirt was next. She unhooked it and stepped out of it, still swaying provocatively as she moved in front of the man. Then she put up her arms and he slid off her top.'

Rufus swallowed again, blinking. 'Well who wouldn't watch? It was a free show. And then the man said, *"You're such a wicked woman, Morwenna Chenoweth."*'

A look shot between the detectives. 'You definitely heard him call the woman Morwenna Chenoweth?' Sam said.

Rufus nodded. 'It was like some sensual hypnotic scene happening right there in front of me. The sex was slow and lingering. I was mesmerized. I hadn't been expecting that.' He shrugged. 'Maybe I should have turned away and left them to it, but I didn't. I couldn't drag my eyes away from them. It was like I was part of it, matching the couple's passion until at last it was over and they had collapsed, breathless, still clinging to each other.'

Rufus closed his eyes, the memory of the couple's passion still had the power to disturb him.

Sam raised an eyebrow. 'All I'm hearing, Rufus, is that you're a peeping Tom. Is there a point to all this?'

'There is, just let me finish. Like I said, I was watching them. They were on the floor, their arms wrapped around each other. I desperately wanted to stand up and stretch, but I couldn't move, not until they did.

'Then I heard the man say they should go. He was worried somebody would come and find them there.

'But Morwenna was laughing. "*Don't you see, Joss?*" she said. "*That's the fun of it. Somebody* is *coming. Maya's coming. She checks the centre's security every Sunday about this time. I've followed her.*"

'The Joss one scrambled up and frantically began pulling on his clothes. He told Morwenna to stop fooling about and said they had to leave right away.

'But she didn't want to, she said there was something she had to do. He told her they were leaving. He bundled up her clothes and threw them at her, telling her to get dressed. She said she would, but after he'd left. She said he needed to trust her and that she had one last thing to do after which no one would want to employ sweet little Maya.

'Joss pleaded with her that she'd done enough to discredit the woman but Morwenna wasn't having any of it. She was giggling as she shooed him away.'

He paused, licking his lips.

'What happened then?' Will asked.

'I heard a car coming into the car park. A young woman got out and stared at the open door. She looked concerned as she came in.

'Part of the building had been laid out like an old cottage kitchen with a rocking chair by a black range. Morwenna was in the chair, but she was slumped to the side, like she was playing dead. The young woman saw her and let out a scream before taking off faster than a scared rabbit.

'When she'd gone, Morwenna stood up, giggling. She stretched and I heard her say, "*Job done.*"'

Rufus shook his head. 'I couldn't believe what I'd just witnessed. The woman had staged a death scene so convincing that it sent shivers down my spine. This wasn't merely mischief, it was cold, calculated cruelty. I needed to get out of there.'

'What about Morwenna? Did you see her leave?' Sam asked.

Rufus shook his head. 'I didn't. I don't know what happened with Joss either. I was more interested in making myself scarce before the coppers arrived.

'I made my way back to the village. It all looked amazingly quiet. I checked out the church. There was no sign of Crawford. It was like our attempt to steal the St Piran had never happened. I'd hired a car using a false driving licence and had parked it by the travellers' hostel. I went there and stripped off my wet things then sat back in the dark wondering what to do next. What I really needed was a hot meal and some dry clothes. I'd been using the lock-up where you lot found me as a base. I picked up a takeaway and went there to change my clothes. I had to work out a better plan to steal the bloody carving.'

CHAPTER 34

Sam and Will watched Rufus North march off flanked by two uniformed officers before they went to join Joss Teague in the other interview room.

'We meet again, Mr Teague,' Sam said, tossing a thick brown file onto the table between them before taking his seat.

'Not my idea,' Teague said, his mouth curving into a sneer. 'I wouldn't have shot the silly cow, but maybe I should have.'

'Watch your tongue, mister.' Will was out of his seat, fists clenched.

Sam waved him down.

Teague grinned. 'You need to watch that temper, detective. It could get you into trouble.'

Both officers glared at him. 'Why wouldn't you have shot the young woman?' Sam asked.

'Because I'm not a freaking maniac.'

'So why did you have a gun?' Sam came back.

Teague sighed. 'I wasn't there to kill anybody. I was supposed to hmm, how shall I put it? I was supposed to

260

persuade her to go with me.' He shrugged. 'But it wasn't her, was it? It was the other…' He flashed a look to Will. 'The other *woman*.'

Sam stared at him. 'What happened to Morwenna, Joss?'

The detective's unexpected change of tack had him flinching. 'Morwenna?'

'Yes, Morwenna. Wasn't she your girlfriend?'

'Yes, I told you before.'

'Ah, but what you said before, was the last time you saw Morwenna in the churchyard at Fenwick?'

'That's right,' Teague said, but there was a new defensive attitude in his body language. The cockiness was slipping.

Sam pursed his lips and tilted his head, watching the man.

Will folded his arms.

Teague moved uneasily in his chair.

'You see, the trouble with that, Joss, is we have a witness who tells a completely different story,' Sam said.

'Your witness is a bleeding liar then.'

But Sam was into his stride. 'This witness tells us Morwenna didn't die in the churchyard. In fact she was fit enough to race away to the heritage centre,' he said. 'This witness says he saw you join her there and watched from the darkness as the pair of you copulated on the floor. He also saw you and your girlfriend stage the ridiculous death scene for Maya Brookes.'

'I had nothing to do with that,' Teague snapped. 'It was all Morwenna.'

'So you admit you were there with Morwenna,' Will cut in. 'She didn't die in the churchyard after all, did she?'

The colour was draining from Joss Teague's face.

'Was her behaviour too much for you, Joss?' Sam goaded. 'Did you argue with her? Did you follow her out to the cliff path and kill her?'

'No! I didn't kill her! I didn't.' Beads of sweat were glistening on Teague's forehead and he swiped angrily at them.

'What if I said your DNA was all over the site where we found Morwenna's body? We found the stone you used to bludgeon her to death.'

'You're lying!'

Sam shook his head. He knew he'd been stretching the truth. The killer had left DNA. All they had to do now was to match it to Teague. 'Why did you have to kill her, Joss? What harm had she ever done to you?'

Joss Teague hung his head. Sam and Will strained to hear the mumbled words. 'It shouldn't have happened. We had a plan. It would have worked if Morwenna hadn't freaked out.'

Sam flashed Will a look. 'What plan?'

'We had to make it look like the girl, Maya, had killed Morwenna. We had to throw her cloak onto the rocks and then she was to disappear.'

'Who told you to do this, Joss?'

Teague flicked his tongue over his dry lips.

'Who told you, Joss?' Sam repeated.

Joss hesitated, his eyes travelling around the room like a trapped animal. He swallowed. 'Darius. It was Darius.'

'What went wrong?'

'Nothing. I've been helping him. Darius discovered his stepfather, Spiro, had a daughter he'd never met. He was planning to cut Darius out and leave his fortune to her. That was all wrong. We couldn't let this happen.'

'So you've been trying to kill Maya?' Sam said.

Teague shrugged. 'It had to be done.'

'What happened with Morwenna?'

Teague wrapped his arms around his head and screwed his eyes tight shut. 'Morwenna was stupid. She'd found out about Darius and me and she was spitting mad.'

'Darius and you?' Will questioned. 'You mean you're in a relationship?'

Joss slid Sam an amused look. 'Your mate isn't very quick to catch on. Darius and I are crazy about each other. We've been together for years, ever since I was in the antiques business in London. I'd keep an eye out and tip him the wink when special things came into the auction house and he would buy them.'

'So how did Morwenna blot her copy book?' Will asked.

'I suppose it was my fault. I made the mistake of confiding my real identity to her. They say there's no fury like a woman scorned, well that was her. When she discovered Darius and I were together she was raging. She threatened to go to the newspapers. She said they would pay her if she told the world who I really was and that it was my testimony that sent the London drug barons, Abel and Aaron Caplan to prison.'

He looked up, eyes sparking fire. 'If the Caplan brothers ever find me, I'm a dead man. Morwenna shouldn't have threatened me. She shouldn't have done that.'

Sam lowered his brow, trying not to scowl as he watched the man. 'It was you who pushed over the display board at the centre. Wasn't it?'

Joss gave him a blank stare.

'There's no point denying it. Your DNA was all over the place.'

'Of course it was. I used to meet Morwenna there.'

'What if I told you we found your DNA on the board you tried to push over onto Maya?' Sam said. It wasn't true but it might be enough to rattle the truth out of him.

'It wasn't mine.' Joss's nose wrinkled in a sneer as he held up his hands. 'I wore gloves.'

'So you did push the board over?'

'No, err no. You're confusing me.'

'What about that hit-and-run last night?' Sam put up a hand. 'And before you make any excuses I have to tell you the victim had a dashcam operating at the time.'

'I know nothing about any hit-and-run.'

Sam sat back in his chair, shaking his head. 'You have such a knack for getting yourself into trouble. You've murdered one woman and attempted to kill another. Do you really think Darius Cassavetes will stand by you?'

'Darius and I love each other. He won't let me down.'

Will gave an incredulous laugh. 'I hate to burst your bubble, but Darius is only loyal to himself. He uses people.'

'That's rubbish.' Joss spat out the words.

'It's true I'm afraid. Haven't you noticed how close he is to James Crawford? And what about Candice Chrichton-Smythe? She was also willing to kill Maya for him.'

'I don't believe you.'

Sam gave a sad smile. 'Police officers boarded the *Moon-flyer* earlier today to arrest the man. He's here in custody at this very moment. Do you really believe he won't throw you to the wolves to save his own skin?'

'Stop it!' Joss Teague yelled. 'You're trying to trick me.'

'You trusted the wrong man, Joss.' Sam got to his feet. 'You will be charged with murder and attempted murder. Who knows, you might even get to share a cell with your Darius.'

Sam and Will stood in the corridor looking on as Joss Teague was led away. Sam swallowed. They'd found Morwenna's killer. Loveday's friend was safe now.

CHAPTER 35

'*M*aya rang after you brought me home,' Loveday said, stretching as Sam climbed into bed beside her. 'Tom was with her. He told her what happened out on the moor. She was horrified.'

'As well she might be,' Sam said, turning over so his back was to her.

'Am I still in your bad books?' she said sheepishly, sliding her arms around him. 'I'm sorry, Sam. I shouldn't have gone off there on my own. I thought I could handle it.'

He turned to face her, anger blazing in his eyes. 'He had a gun, Loveday. He had a bloody gun!'

Loveday sighed. 'Yes, I wasn't expecting that. I shouldn't have gone there on my own, but I did try ringing you. It's not my fault if there was no reception out there on the moor.' She reached out, stroking his hair. 'Am I forgiven?'

'No.'

'Really?' she coaxed, pulling his head down to kiss him.

* * *

LOVEDAY EMERGED from the shower next morning with a spring in her step. Sam was already up and dressed and there was a delicious aroma of freshly brewed coffee coming from the kitchen. She pulled on her white towelling robe and went to join him.

'Do you think Spiro will be upset because you've arrested Darius?' she asked, pinching the slice of toast he had just buttered from his hand and taking a bite.

'Get your own,' he said, snatching it back, but he was grinning.

'Well, do you?' she persisted.

'Considering the man has been trying to kill Spiro's daughter, I doubt it very much,' Sam said.

'When will you interview Darius?'

'This morning.'

'He won't like having spent a night in the cells.'

Sam smiled. 'No, he won't, will he.'

Loveday's phone rang and she padded through to the bedroom to fetch it. 'Maya. You're an early bird,' Sam heard her say.

It was a few minutes before she returned to the kitchen. She looked thoughtful.

'Is Maya all right?' Sam asked.

Loveday nodded. 'She was just calling to make sure I was OK after yesterday's drama. Tom stayed with her last night.' She paused. 'Apparently Spiro has invited himself over this morning.'

* * *

THERE WAS an air of celebration about the incident room as Sam walked in almost two hours later. Clearly the team felt Darius Cassavetes was their man and they'd got him locked up in a cell. Sam wouldn't be flying any flags until the man admitted attempting to kill Maya and stealing the St Piran.

'Mr Cassavetes doesn't like our hospitality,' Will said as he and Sam strode to the interview room where Darius waited. 'He's been pacing the cell all night and firing off threats. Apparently we'll all be facing the sack when news of his wrongful arrest is made public.'

'That strikes fear into my heart,' Sam said with a contemptuous grin. 'Let's go talk to him.'

'This is an outrage,' Darius Cassavetes spat out the words at the two detectives as they walked in. 'You will regret this.'

'I'm sorry.' Sam smiled at the man. 'Were you not comfortable last night?'

'Why have I been brought here?' Darius demanded.

Sam and Will exchanged a glance. Sam was spoilt for choice where to begin. He took a breath. 'Tell us about Candice.'

Darius's brow wrinkled into a confused frown. It wasn't the question he had been expecting. 'I don't know any Candice.'

Sam pursed his lips and shook his head. 'Wrong answer, Darius, or should we address you as Zeus?' His smile was slow now. 'Dear Candice. I can understand why you would be attracted to her, but she's not the brightest button in the box, is she?' He paused, savouring what he was about to say. 'We have her secret phone, the one you gave her, the one you used to persuade her to have a relationship with Tom Scobey. Was it your idea to call yourself Zeus?'

'I didn't suggest any relationship with Scobey and I have no idea who this Zeus is. I suspect I am being set up for something I know nothing about.'

'But you do know about this, Darius. You used Candice to get you closer to your stepfather's daughter, Maya Brookes. Candice tried to poison her. What would you say if I told you she said that was your idea too?' It wasn't true but Sam hoped it might flush out what was.

Darius moved his hands in a gesture of helplessness. 'Candice doesn't take kindly to being scorned. She wanted me to love her and I didn't, so now she hates me. She'll say anything.' He looked at Sam. 'Candice has an exceptional capacity for turning her affections on and off. She's quick to seek revenge. She can be like a snake spitting venom if she takes against you.'

'You were cruel to her,' Sam said. 'You let her believe you had feelings for her when all the time you were in another relationship, a gay relationship.'

Darius stared at him. 'That's ridiculous.'

'Joss Teague doesn't think it's ridiculous. He thinks you love him, which is why he has been trying to kill Spiro's daughter on your instructions.'

Darius's slow smile revealed a row of gleaming white teeth. 'I feel you will have a job proving it, Inspector Kitto. Joss is too impetuous for his own good.'

'What about Rufus North? Is he also impetuous?'

Darius shrugged. 'I've never heard of this person.'

'According to Rufus, he owed you a lot of money. He settled the debt by stealing an old carving of the Cornish saint, St Piran.' Sam raised an eyebrow. 'Was it to be another item for your collection of antiquities?'

Darius threw his arms wide. 'I have no idea what you are talking about.'

'What about James Crawford? Wasn't he Rufus North's partner in crime? After all, they worked together to steal the carving for you.'

'So many people itching to give evidence against you. They can't all be lying.'

'Well they *are* lying.' Darius swallowed hard. 'High-profile men like me make enemies.'

Sam tilted his head, watching Cassavetes. 'Do you know where the carving is now, Darius?' He waited, smiling. 'We have it, so all your efforts to steal the St Piran have been pointless.'

'The what?' Darius's handsome face screwed into a frown. 'I have no idea what you are talking about.'

'Really?' Sam shook his head. 'Perhaps it will help to clear your mind when I tell you we have already spoken to your friend James Crawford.' He sat back, watching the man's expression harden.

'James Crawford is the bosun on my stepfather's yacht. He is not my friend.'

'Mr Crawford also claims he is in a gay relationship with you.'

'The man is a fantasist.'

'He has also admitted his part in stealing the St Piran carving from the church in Fenwick.' Sam looked up, locking eyes with Cassavetes. 'It was stolen on your orders, wasn't it?'

'I told you. Mr Crawford is a fantasist. He's lying to you.'

'Such a carving would be a desirable addition to your collection of antiquities, though, would it not?' Sam said.

Cassavetes jumped to his feet. 'That's enough! I'm drawing a line under this right now. I demand to see my solicitor.'

Will Tregellis sprang up, ready to push Cassavetes back into his seat, but Sam held him back.

'Sit down, Mr Cassavetes.' Sam's jaw tightened as glared at the man. 'No line is being drawn under this investigation, and certainly not by you. However, you are entitled to see a solicitor and you will be permitted to contact one.'

Sam could feel the man's hostile eyes boring into his back as he and Will left the room.

'What do you think, sir?' Will asked as they made their way back to the incident room.

'I think Cassavetes is about to walk. The accusations against him might be piling up but we don't have any actual evidence.'

Will sighed. 'He's a clever devil all right. What do we do now, sir?'

'Apart from praying, you mean?' Sam said grimly. 'I'm not sure.'

CHAPTER 36

'*H*ow are you placed for a lunchtime drink?' Loveday asked when Sam picked up the phone.

'I'm not sure I can manage that today. We're waiting for Cassavetes' lawyer to arrive.'

'You don't sound as if things are going well.'

'They're not.'

'Take an hour off to clear your head, Sam. I'm sure it will do you good.'

'Maybe.' Sam sighed. 'Where do you want to meet?'

'The usual place, about one o'clock?'

'OK, I'll see you there.'

'No, wait! I haven't told you the best bit. It's Maya who wants to meet up with us. She says she has some news. She's asked her childminder to look after April Rose for a couple of hours while we meet. What's the betting Spiro has told her she's his daughter?'

Despite the gloomy cloud he felt he was under, Sam couldn't help smiling. 'Are we to suppose this will be good news?'

'Well, Maya sounded very happy. She's bringing Tom and Spiro with her.'

'I'll look forward to it then.'

'Me too.' She smiled at the phone, hesitating for a second. He could hear the catch in her voice. 'You know I love you very much, Detective Inspector Sam Kitto.'

'Do you?' he said, his smile stretching wider.

'You're supposed to reciprocate.'

He laughed. 'Ditto.'

* * *

SAM SPOTTED the four of them immediately he entered the pub. They'd found a big table in the corner. Loveday waved, calling him across. Spiro got to his feet and offered his hand in greeting. 'It's good to see you again, Inspector.'

Sam's attention went to the champagne bottle and glasses on the table. 'What are we celebrating?'

Maya beamed at Spiro. 'I've just been told I have a father.'

Spiro reached out to take her hand. 'I've been so worried about how you would react to this news. I know it's a lot for you to take in and I know you will need time to get used to it.' He took a breath. '...To get used to me. But I can be patient.'

'I was only little when my mum died,' Maya said, her voice quiet. 'I don't remember much about her. What I do remember is someone kind, who put her arms around me and made me feel safe. I think she was my mother.'

'I'm sure it was,' Spiro said, swallowing back his emotion. 'Oh my, Λουλούδι μου.' He laughed, dropping in a Greek term of endearment for his child. 'We have so much to share. I am so looking forward to telling you more about her and the lovely person she was.'

'That would be wonderful,' Maya said, her voice choking with emotion.

Spiro cleared his own throat. 'I think we should pour this champagne before it evaporates. Would you do the honours, Tom?'

'I'd be glad to,' Tom said, getting to his feet and filling the glasses. Loveday and Sam also stood, joining Tom in a toast. 'To Maya and Spiro,' he said.

'Maya and Spiro, fathers and daughters,' Sam said.

Loveday hoped no one noticed the tear she brushed away as she sipped her champagne. She leaned across to Sam. 'I told you this would clear your head.'

'You were right,' Sam said, but his eye was on the clock.

Spiro was watching him but waited until he caught his eye. 'I think it may not be easy for a policeman to relax when you have a major investigation taking place. How is it going, Inspector Kitto? I understand you have my stepson in custody.'

'Indeed we do,' Sam said. 'But as you say, it's an ongoing investigation and I'm afraid I can't really talk about it.'

'No, of course you can't. I completely understand. But if I know Darius he will have covered his back. I would be very surprised if you have any actual evidence against him.'

Sam spread his hands. 'Like I said–'

'Forgive me,' Spiro cut in. 'I don't speak up to interfere, but maybe I can help.'

He leaned forward and took Maya's hand. 'I'm sorry, my dear. What I'm about to say will shock you, but I only did it because I was concerned for your safety.'

'You've got me worried now,' Maya said. 'What have you done?'

'I've had a security officer keeping an eye on you.'

Maya's eyes widened. 'You've been having me followed?'

'Forgive me, Maya, but you are my daughter. I had to protect you.'

'Spiro is right, Maya,' Loveday said. 'You were in danger. We were all looking out for you.'

Maya put her hands to her head. 'I'm having trouble taking this in. You really had a security man looking out for me?'

'I did,' Spiro said. 'You and April Rose are very precious to me.'

'Thank you.' Maya's voice shook. She looked around the table, her gaze lingering on Tom. 'All of you. Thank you so much.'

Loveday didn't miss the special look that passed from Maya to Tom.

Spiro addressed Sam. 'What I was trying to say in my clumsy way is that I may be able to help you.'

'Help me?' Sam queried.

Spiro nodded. 'Perhaps we could step outside for a moment?' He looked at the faces around the table. 'I know this must seem very rude but could I ask you to excuse us for a few minutes?'

'So long as you come straight back,' Maya said.

'What I have to tell Inspector Kitto will only take a few minutes,' Spiro assured. 'We will be back.'

'There's a lane at the back of the pub. We can talk there,' Sam said, leading the way.

'Sorry about the cat and mouse stuff,' Spiro said when they had stepped outside. 'It's best if the others don't get involved in this.'

'You said you could help our investigation.'

Spiro nodded. 'That's right. You see, not only did I have a security man watching over Maya, but I also had a surveillance expert tailing Darius. So if it's evidence you need, Inspector, I have it.'

Sam was instantly alert. 'What kind of evidence are we talking about?'

'If I employ someone I make sure he is the best. The surveillance people I use have the most sophisticated up-to-date equipment. They can tape a conversation even when it's happening a long way off. And of course, they can follow someone without the subject ever knowing they are there.'

Sam was aware of the surveillance methods the force's security officers deployed, but he was still surprised at what he was hearing. 'I'm impressed,' he said.

'You will be when you've listened to the tapes. All this material is at your disposal, Inspector Kitto.

'My stepson will hardly be able to deny what he's done when he is presented with this evidence.'

Sam's head came up and he met Spiro's eyes. 'You're sure you want to do this? The charges could be attempted murder and theft of an ancient relic from a church. These are serious offences, Spiro. Your stepson could go to prison for a long time.'

Spiro nodded. 'He tried to kill my little girl. I can't allow him to get away with that.'

'No, you can't,' Sam said, putting a hand on Spiro's shoulder as they went back to the others.

IT WAS the middle of the afternoon before Darius's solicitor arrived from London. He was a dapper little man with a bald patch, and a chin that wobbled when he talked. Anything further from the glamorous, arrogant brief Sam had been expecting he couldn't imagine. 'Jeremy Fairbairn,' the man said, coming forward with his hand outstretched to shake. 'I represent Darius Cassavetes. Can I please see my client?'

Sam nodded to a uniformed officer. 'Could you take Mr Fairbairn through.'

The two detectives went back to the incident room. Will wasn't enjoying the wait. He checked his watch again. It was almost four o'clock. 'They've had an hour, sir. Shouldn't we go in now?'

Sam had been studying the material and video links Spiro had emailed to him. 'Have a look at this first,' he said.

Will came to stand beside him. He blew out his cheeks when he saw what was on the screen. 'This is dynamite, boss. Where did it come from?'

'A trusted source,' Sam said, getting to his feet. The excitement now surging through him might not be strictly professional but it was putting a smile on his face. 'Let's see what Mr Cassavetes has to say for himself now.'

Regardless of the evidence presented against him in the interview room, Darius still vigorously protested his innocence. But his resistance was cracking. It was just taking time. Even the little lawyer seemed to be losing heart. It was after an hour of more rigorous questioning from Sam and Will that Darius eventually gave in and accepted his lawyer's advice to plead guilty.

Sam was still at his desk, allowing the euphoria of the day's success to sweep over him, when Loveday rang. 'Well?' she said. 'Did you get your man?'

'We did,' Sam said. 'Darius Cassavetes has admitted multiple charges of attempted murder and the theft of the St Piran carving. The evidence is foolproof. He won't be squirming away from this.'

'Well done, Sam,' Loveday said. 'I'm so proud of you.'

'It was a marathon all right,' Sam agreed. 'But we got the right result in the end.'

'Are you still in the office?'

'I'm just about to leave.'

'Great, because guess what? Spiro has invited us for dinner on his yacht tonight. Tom and Maya and April Rose will be there too. And there's more.' He could tell she was grinning. 'He only wants us to stay the night in one of his plush staterooms.'

Sam was grinning too. 'Am I right in suspecting you might want us to accept this invitation?'

Loveday giggled. 'You have such a knack for getting to the heart of things, Inspector.'

It was his turn to laugh. 'Isn't that what detectives do?' he said.

THE END

Cover design by Craig Duncan
www.craigduncan.com

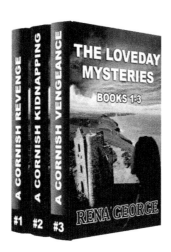

Inherit the Dream

Fire in the Blood

Where Moonbeams Dance

A Moment Like This

Printed in Great Britain
by Amazon

82960488R00163